BOUND

BOUND

Tethered Souls Series

J. H. Laing

NEW DEGREE PRESS

COPYRIGHT © 2021 J. H. LAING

BOUND

Tethered Souls Series

ISBN

978-1-63730-696-3   *Paperback*

978-1-63730-786-1   *Kindle Ebook*

979-8-88504-020-4   *Digital Ebook*

To Mom and Dad for your unconditional
love and for believing in me.

And to Grams and Gramps for being examples of
living your lives to the fullest, taking risks, and having
fun while bringing others along for the ride.

CONTENTS

CHAPTER 1

———

GABE

Her proximity sped up my bloodstone heart. As I stood on Amber's balcony listening closely for her movements, a spoon clanked as she stirred something providing a clue. The glass door she had propped open welcomed me into her bedroom. The white walls deepened her purple comforter. I kneeled at her bed and wrapped the disheveled sheets into my fists, pounding them against her mattress. *Puta madre.* If only Antonio and Holly had left me alone with her last night, this wouldn't have happened.

An antique clock sat ticking on her nightstand at ten o'clock in the morning. Standing up, I scanned her room for evidence of Marco other than the trail of his scent. A picture, a shirt, anything. My fingers drew a line across the refurbished paint of her dresser until it landed on a photo of her hugging a gray-haired woman on the beach. I picked it up and rubbed my thumb over the face of the woman. *Hm.*

Frozen in place listening to her slamming cabinets as she poured cereal into a bowl, a vibration that only an ant would sense from this distance caught my attention. A woman's voice came through clearly. *Must be on speaker.*

"It's all your fault," Amber said.

"My fault? No way. Keep your legs together, girl," Jennifer said.

I clenched my teeth. My soul poked my gut and whispered in my mind, *Get closer.* I blocked his command so I could concentrate.

"I just couldn't, Jenn. I mean. Damn, Gabe. He got me all worked up last night."

You've got to be kidding me.

You see, go to her! My soul demanded again.

"So whatcha gonna do about Marco?" Jennifer asked.

"Nothing. It is what it is. Just sex."

"Great sex."

"Yeah," Amber sighed.

She doesn't know great sex. My knuckles pushed her bedroom door open, and I hovered slightly above the ground in her direction to avoid startling her. Stopping before the kitchen entrance, I spread my palm against the cool blue wall.

"And Gabe?"

"There's nothing I can do. I … I … I need some water, hang on." Amber coughed—dry mouthed like me. A machine clicked on as water filled a glass.

"Amber? Are you alright?" Jennifer asked.

My eyes shut as her gulps echoed in my ears, then heavy breaths and a few more coughs.

"I'm fine. I just needed to drink. I've been so dehydrated."

"LA pollution mixed with desert-like heat doesn't help."

"No. I guess not. Better than our humid New York summers, am I right?"

"Definitely!" Jennifer said. "So, don't dodge the question. And Gabe?"

"Like I said. There's nothing I can do. He said he'd find me. What the hell does that even mean anyhow?

"It's a little creepy," Jennifer said.

"You think?" Amber scuffed her feet across the floor. "He's not to me. There's something about him. He feels so familiar."

I leaned against the wall listening to her describe what she felt in her soul.

"You've probably seen him at the studio. You know he works with Antonio, right?"

"I figured that much. Antonio and some hot woman stole him away from me last night to talk about business. Do you know what Gabe does exactly?"

"No. Probably a producer."

"I can't get him out of my mind, Jenn."

Good.

"He's the sexiest man I've ever encountered. I get ... well, you know. I need to see him." A chair creaked.

"Just say it, girl. You gotta get you some." They burst out laughing.

"I do. I can't deny it. Damn. I need to turn the air down."

Go to her now, my soul whispered again. *Catori knows we're here.*

I answered my soul, *Look, I know you're connecting with her soul. Are you not listening to Amber's conversation?* The wall in front of the kitchen held the thermostat. Her footsteps drew near. I bolted for Amber's bedroom before she could see me as she came out into the hallway. *What am I doing here?*

"So, I'll see you at work tomorrow, right?" Jennifer asked.

"Yes, of course. Where else would I be?"

"I don't know. Just be careful."

"You worry too much."

"Maybe. But I love you, girl."

"I love you, too. See you tomorrow."

They hung up, and I cracked the door open. She heightened my senses having left her lavender scent in the hallway. I swooped my tongue over my fangs as I walked back toward the kitchen.

She crunched on her cereal. "Ugh. I can't even eat this," she said. The chair scratched the tile.

My presence disrupted her appetite, which was not what I wanted to do.

The water tapped against the stainless steel and music started playing. She sang. *Great voice. She's full of surprises.*

With each reincarnation comes a new discovery. I recognized my privilege. Finding my soul mate over and over again across the centuries. How many more times can a soul be reincarnated? Surely there's a limit. Catori is one hell of a soul.

Finally, my soul huffed as I approached the kitchen entrance.

My mouth dropped as I watched Amber sway back and forth singing along, washing the dishes. She splashed her caramel arms. Her pink nighty so short her cheeks popped out ever so slightly every time she moved. *My God.* I put my hands in my pockets and leaned on the doorframe. Her curls bounced along. All I could think about at that moment was to take her on the kitchen table. And if she caught me staring, I'd make her forget about Marco. I shook my head. *Focus. Get out before you mess things up.*

"*What are you looking at?*" A husky voice on my left startled me. An apparition stood with his arms crossed and brows furrowed.

I just stared knowing that if I had replied, Amber would hear me.

"*Well?*" The apparition asked as he stepped closer attempting to intimidate me, which was useless since he couldn't touch me. Clearly, he had died very fit because he had rock hard arms and solid pecks peeking through his tight shirt. Along with Amber, he resembled the woman from the photo on the dresser.

Amber's phone rang, and she twisted around to pick it up. I shifted swiftly out of sight. Still eyeing the ghost lurking next to me.

"You see me, don't you?" The bald muscular figure moved closer standing in front of the kitchen doorframe while I placed my body like camouflage against the wall.

I nodded.

The music stopped. "Hi, Grams. How are you?"

Amber went quiet. On the other end of the line, a faint whisper spoke. She responded, "What? Sure. No problem. I can come help you sort that out next weekend. Alright?"

The ghost watched Amber like a protector. *A brother?*

In the opposite direction, a ting and then the sound of a soft thump caught my attention. *What the ...?* There was someone else in her bedroom. The figure and I locked eyes.

"I'm fine. Really. Of course, I miss her, Grams."

My eyes darted between her bedroom door and the kitchen frame.

"The truth is, I don't want to end up like her. I care too much about life to take mine like Mom did. So today, I'm not sad. I'm grateful to be alive."

Her words pierced my chest. I peeked in at Amber with her phone to her ear, circling her fingers on the tabletop.

"She's talking about my wife," the ghost whispered.

Another shuffling sound came from her bedroom.

The apparition shouted in the direction of shuffling, *"We're coming for you mother fucker!"* The ghost shook his hands in the air. *"What are you waiting for? It's another one like you,"* he said as he moved swiftly toward the bedroom, and I sped behind him barely tapping the laminate.

We found a man picking up the clock that he had knocked onto the floor. I locked the door behind me. The invader looked up. Recognizing the familiar bloodshot eyes and wrinkled skin, I knew he had been starved prior to coming here. With sarcasm in his smile, he exposed his fangs and stepped onto the bed rushing at me. My back hit the wall, and the building shook. The young vamp held his withered, tattooed arm to my neck. His nostrils flared as his attention shifted to the door. He needed blood and Amber smelled promising.

"Go to her!" I said to her father's ghost.

I head-butted the newly made vampire causing him to stumble back, barely comprehending what Amber said to her grandma. Maybe she was hanging up. I'm sure she heard the noise and felt the jolt. The vampire swung at me with his right and I ducked. Popping back up, I jabbed him in the nose followed by a swing into his ribs with my left. The bottom of my foot hit his steel abs, and he fell onto the bed. I picked him up by the collar and dragged him to the balcony. With him in a headlock, I flew us both up to the roof of the multistory building, slamming him down onto the asphalt face first and pressing my knee into the back of his neck. Lifting his arms up behind him, I asked, "Who sent you?"

He groaned.

"Who sent you?" I pulled up more, hearing a slight rip.

"Ahhhh. Fuck! Who do you think?"

"Vance?"

"Yes!"

"Why?"

"Let go, and I'll tell you."

"Why?" I pulled tighter just at the point of dislocation. A guttural groan reverberated out of his throat.

"He … he … told me to fol-low you."

In outrage, I yanked, and his arms popped out of their sockets. He fell limp, cried out, and fainted. I jumped up, pulled my phone out of my back pocket, and dialed. "Sal, we've got a problem. Send someone to the cabin. You'll be dropping off one of Vance's guys in less than an hour. Meet me on the roof of Amber's building. Bring the serum." I hung up and texted Sal my location.

I rolled the vampire over, face up, and patted him down. As I pulled out his cell phone, a text popped up from an unlisted caller.

Any updates? It read.

I shut the phone down and tucked it in my pocket. *I'll deal with this later.*

I couldn't leave Amber's room a mess. One thing left to do. Straddling the young vampire's body, I lifted his torso with his arms hanging limp. Grabbing his head in my hands, I twisted. Snap.

Moving swiftly, I leaned over the roof's edge to see if anyone was nearby. A woman walking her dog below might see me, but I took the chance and flew back down landing on Amber's balcony. *I'm glad she lives on a quiet street.*

Amber fumbled with the doorknob trying to unlock it. "Dammit," she said, "this paperclip isn't working."

Moving around her room quickly, I placed the clock back on the nightstand, and fixed the covers on her bed. I looked around for any other trace of the fight. Then I noticed a large crack on the wall next to the door. *Puta madre!* These threats from Vance won't stop. If he found out about her, she'd be dead again. *It's time to let her go.*

No! My soul demanded, *We've got it this time. You can keep her safe.*

I don't think I can. Vance has people following me. For how long now? It's been years, why now?

It doesn't matter. You must stay focused, my soul said.

It's for the best. I can't do this to her again. You heard what she said about living life.

My soul continued to argue from within. I locked my jaw to bare down on the pain he inflicted inside. And for good reason. As she jiggled a little more, taking in a deep breath, I unlocked the door.

She pushed it open with me behind it. Peeking her head into the room, she called out, "Hello."

I grabbed Amber from behind and covered her mouth. "Don't scream."

She squealed and wriggled around trying to get me to release her.

"It's me. Gabe. I'm not going to hurt you. I just need to talk to you. Okay?"

Amber nodded. Her heartbeat pulsed against my arm. Her warm breath hit my hand with every exhale.

My soul continued to fight within me.

"I'm going to release you so I can explain."

She nodded again.

"Please don't scream." I released my hand and turned her to face me. Our eyes met; her mouth parted in disbelief. My heart sank.

"Gabe! What the hell?" She shoved me, but I didn't move. Not because the force of her push was that weak, but because she didn't have the strength of a vampire.

"I came here to tell you something." I took a step closer, and she lifted her palm on my chest.

"How did you get in here? I'm ..." Her face scrunched up as she looked at the open door behind me.

I pressed my body up against hers placing my hands on her cheeks. "Listen. I have to ..."

She closed her eyes.

"Please look at me."

She drew her angry hazels up to meet my devastation.

"I'm in love with you."

"What? We just met. This is …"

"Amber." I drew her in. "I know you don't understand. But you also know I'm not here to hurt you."

Her breath slowed and she stared into my eyes as I held her face in my hands. Her eyes softened and her bottom leaned into the side of her dresser.

"I'm letting you go."

"Letting me go," she repeated.

"Yes. You won't remember me. You'll forget everything that happened at Antonio's last night between us."

"Forget," she whispered with tears streaming to meet my thumb at her lips.

Cold and steady, I spoke, "You don't know me. You never met me. You'll go back to your life before you met me. The other night at Antonio's mansion, you had a good time dancing."

"Dancing."

"Yes. And you ran into Marco. You remember?"

"Yes. I remember Marco."

"Good."

"And you brought Marco home."

"Yes."

My soul expanded his essence within me as if trying to press me apart to escape. His yelling muffled by my concentrated efforts.

"And the door jammed today because there was a small earthquake. And you worked it open."

"Earthquake."

"I need you to lock up after I leave. You'll always keep your windows and doors locked, from now on."

She nodded.

"Okay." I stroked her wet cheeks once more and kissed her thick lips goodbye. "I release you," I said letting go of her, and I flew back up to the roof.

Hovering over the temporarily dead vampire, I screamed into the smug sky.

Sal's short, stocky frame walked onto the rooftop from the stairwell. He paused, waiting for me to call him over.

Now we've got to get this clown to the cabin. "Vamonos," I said.

Sal grabbed the limp bastard.

"We can't let him go back to Vance to report in. I didn't want him trying anything on the ride over to the cabin."

Sal nodded.

"I'm going to stay close by for now. I can't risk another attack on her."

"Qué paso?" he asked.

"Vance's goons are following me. And I can't put her in danger."

"Qué estás diciendo? What?"

"I compelled her to forget me."

Sal lifted his hands in the air. "Pero porque?"

Placing my hand on my forehead, I squeezed. "I don't need a lecture. Just get this guy out of here. Apurate. Dale!"

Sal nodded.

"I'll be there soon."

"Cuidate," he said and lifted the man over his shoulder. He went back out the way he came.

This visit was just evidence that Vance knew I'd returned from my Los Angeles hiatus. But he couldn't have known about her. *Could he?* It's for the best. Better that she does not know I exist. I can protect her from a distance.

CHAPTER 2

GABE

Water pattered off the tiles and pellets tapped her skin as she heaved air in and out of her lungs in the shower. With no recollection of our meeting, she'd possibly attribute her suffering and loss to the anniversary of her mother's death. *It was for the best.*

My soul scolded me for making Catori wail in pain. I cradled my head between my knees listening to Amber from the balcony. I couldn't leave her yet. Not after what I'd done.

After the crying stopped, she went about her day as if nothing happened, so I left. Compelling her to forget me caused a butterfly effect. I'd now have to find Jennifer and Marco and compel them to forget seeing me with Amber at the party. This was a huge mess, but it was the right decision.

Amber's fierce confidence in how she walked and drew people in demonstrated the power of reincarnation. Catori grew stronger over the years, but she'd always thrived independently. Who was I, an immortal vampire, to take away the fourth life she'd been given, all for my own selfish desire for freedom? And Amber would have to lose her freedom for me to have my own. She'd have to choose death.

The back tire of my Audi slipped on the gravel as I sped around mountainous curves on Big Tujunga Canyon Road. I swerved, pulling it back onto the paved road. Not even the engine racing, or the wind blowing around me with the top down, could alleviate my soul's inner monologue. His threats dug into my gut like a jagged knife, twisting. We ached for our soul mate. I hit the steering wheel yelling out into the night.

A call came through from Holly but I ignored it. I was sure she'd just push me to return to Mexico. Dealing with border crossing issues were on Antonio and her this time.

Another few miles and I'd arrive at the cabin. I made countless attempts to concentrate on my pending duty of assisting the vampire being held there. We needed to help him fully transition before it was too late. But it was useless to think I could get her out of my mind. *Amber*.

I called on some of my vampires to keep watch across the city for any sign of danger. Vance wouldn't just send one of his minions to follow me. He'd likely have many. If Vance found out about Amber ... I shook my head ... he couldn't. She is the key to my freedom from Vance's control. He doesn't even need me anymore. Year after year, he consumes more power through possession biting, and I'm left to clean up his mess transitioning newbie vamps.

Pulling up to the cabin, I set the car in park and leaned against the headrest. No doubt, Sal would soon challenge my decision as well. I exhaled out of my mouth as if I even needed to breathe just as Sal swung open the front door.

"Apurate, Gabe!"

I jumped out of the car, landing on the porch in front of him. "Qué paso?"

"Ven. You'll have to see it for yourself."

Cali sat on the couch with solemn eyes like the deer's head above her as she watched us enter. Cali, my loyal vampire, took an oath to me after I had saved her from a vampire gang led by Eli, a soulless goon. He left her in the hands of vampire hunters. I saved her from the torture chamber they had concocted in their garage in the outskirts of Hemet. Although still connected to Eli, she served him only when he commanded it. Fortunately for me, that didn't happen often.

I grabbed her pudgy hand and pulled her to a standing position. She followed as Sal led me past the kitchen. Past the full vial of serum on the marble island. *That couldn't be good.* We walked to the back of the house and turned left, down to the holding cells. He went through security protocols, scanning his hand to unlock the steel door. Caught between the walls, another sliding door opened. When we entered the transformation cell, dust particles and a pair of silver shackles surrounded an empty seat in the middle of the room.

"Where is he?" My throat went dry as I asked the question I knew the answer to.

"We were too late," Sal said. "They starved him of blood. We just didn't have enough time to replenish him before his heart dried out."

"Qué cabrón," I mumbled. Vance's vampire didn't have a chance.

**

The glow of the fire pit highlighted Sal's face as we sat in silence under the starlit sky. We've made it our lives' mission to save as many newbie vampires from their irrevocable deaths as possible. And we both knew some of them weren't worth saving. And that truth came out when it was time for them to call their souls back home to them.

"You're making a mistake," Sal broke the silence. "And you know it."

I took a swig of my O negative. "I don't need a lecture."

"We have a plan. It's a good one."

"We don't know if it will work."

"It will work."

"Sal, you don't understand." I took another swig.

"No te entiendo, cabrón! You're one of the luckiest vampires I know. And you just give up! Over the centuries, you continue to find her in various bodies perfectly placed in your path each time. I haven't met anyone else who has had so many opportunities to reunite with a soul mate."

"It's better for her this way. I'm being selfish to constantly put her life at risk just because I want to be free."

"Maybe the universe is trying to tell you something different."

"Basta!" Standing up, I threw the bottle into the forest behind the house. "Enough. I've decided. We'll keep her safe this way."

My soul chimed in, *You're only keeping yourself safe this way. Besides, Sal's soul wants freedom, too.*

I crossed my arms staring into the dark forest with hints of moonlight dancing on the treetops. *Sal chose to stay bound to me. He knows I'd release him any time he'd like.*

I thought I was ready this time—prepared. Too many voices interrupted the solace of the forest. Cali spoke to one of our vampires in the city about the new direction with Amber. My soul nagged incessantly. And Sal ...

"Cual es el plan? Huh?" Sal stood up. "You'll leave Los Angeles? Relocate? Hide from her for the rest of her life?" He stepped toward me placing his hand on my shoulder.

"There's something drawing the two of you together. There's a reason you two are reintroduced over the years. And it's your obligation to see it through this time." Sal squeezed my shoulder and walked back into the house.

"Fuuuuuccccck!" I looked back at the house and then took off into the forest. Crunching twigs under the soles of my shoes until I took flight through an opening in the ponderosa pine. I couldn't go back now. She'd be safe from me. No more vampires lurking around her. She'd be safe.

CHAPTER 3

GABE

The grip I had on the steering wheel from my soul's relentless mourning of his mate caused a crack in the leather. Driving west on I-10, I headed to one of my favorite spots, Santa Monica. Before I left Los Angeles, my feet needed to shuffle through the sand as the crest of the waves swept over them one last time.

Inhaling the salty air as I drove up to Broadway to make a left, I stopped at a red light. Barricades blocked the road not allowing for anything but foot traffic. A runway set up in front of the department store and a large crowd of suits and gowns squeezed into the elegantly decorated showcase. I drove north a little further and pulled into a parking garage.

As I drove in, my soul flipped. *It's her. It's her. She's here.*

The cool evening air chilled my shirt where sweat had quickly accumulated. *It can't be.*

It is, my soul said. *I can hear her sorrow.*

Amber's? I asked my soul.

No, pendejo. Catori's.

She couldn't possibly be here. Clenching my jaw, I curved around the crowded parking lot searching for an empty space.

There was a spot open on the roof top. I pulled in next to a Volkswagen Beetle. Scanning across the top of cars in an effort to find her. *Nobody's here,* I growled at my soul. Meanwhile, my palms started sweating, and the cool ocean breeze did little to relieve my warm skin.

Escucha bien, my soul said.

I locked my car and began walking toward the elevator. A few voices chattered as the crowd heckled and clapped at the newest fashion statements, nothing more.

Come on, Gabe, my soul urged.

I can't help it if she's not talking.

My feet barely tapped each step as I darted down the dingy stairwell. Just as I stepped out into the first floor of the garage, the elevator doors opened, and Amber walked out. I paused, taking her in as if seeing her for the first time since the night of the party.

Hair up, hoops hanging low to meet her long neck, and a floral cocktail dress swaying as she strode past me. Her lashes lifted and head turned to me. Her smirk, like that of our first night together, was filled with assurance that she didn't need me. My body hunched forward and my hand swept through my hair.

"Hi," she said as she kept walking past me and out onto the street.

Go! My soul commanded. *Undo this mess, Gabe. Catori, we're here.* My soul cried out. *Tell Amber to stop. Please.*

I stood motionless as she vanished around the corner. I licked my dry lips with a parched tongue and took a deep breath. *What are the odds?* Taking a few swift strides alongside a couple, I reached the sidewalk and looked left. There Amber stood waiting to get into a club. Her ID hit the hand of the bouncer, but she looked over her shoulder and caught me staring from across the street. She smiled and turned back to the bouncer holding her ID in his hand.

"It's your lucky night. Sexy women are getting in free." He stepped to the side, handed her the card, and allowed her in as he watched her ass disappear through the doorway.

My fangs erupted skinning into my bottom lip.

Go to her, Gabe. It's inevitable. We're meant to be with them.

Covering my mouth, I wiped the blood dribbling down my chin, and walked past the club at my soul's objection. I headed west to Santa Monica beach toward the sunset. My original plan.

CHAPTER 4

AMBER

Neo soul vibrations warmed my chest. I tapped my fingers on the shiny cocktail table as I bopped my head to the rhythm that sparked envy mixed with admiration for her beautiful voice. Spotlights hovered directly above her as she glided across the stage, highlighting her shimmering ensemble and tightly wrapped hair lined with sequins. And the crowd was in sync with her reconcilable flow.

Monday night soul sessions at The Blue Vibe had kept me grounded for the few months since moving back to Los Angeles. They kept me connected to what I'd lost over the years. Dad. Mom. My voice. And today I'd felt an inexplicable loss. So many memories flooded my mind, taking me back to my early childhood before death and cancer. I couldn't comprehend this darker sense of loss. An unresolved sadness. Like purpose no longer existed.

I rubbed my neck. Was it the anniversary of my mother's death? My encounter with Marco the other night? Did he really get under my skin this deeply? Neither made sense. I was over both of them.

Marco had asked me to commit. But that's not what I wanted. No commitment. If I had to choose, he could possibly be one to settle down with at some point. He let me be, we had fun together, and he got that I needed space with a sprinkle of attention. And his fingers …

My wine glass—still half-full—touched my lips, and with a slow sip I didn't allow much in. A dark shadow loomed over the glass. I was no longer interested. I scanned the venue dressed in fiery red and sprinkled with various shades of skin. Couples held hands, charcuterie boards sat mostly bare, and candles flickered on the tables. The room melded together with the illuminating melody coming from the stage.

I brought the glass to my lips once more and inhaled. *I don't really love Marco. Do I?* I wiped my brow with a napkin. My encounter with him the other night felt empty. Raw. My attention swung back to the singer telling the crowd they'd be returning after a fifteen-minute break. My shoulders tensed, and I got the distinct feeling someone was watching me. I looked behind me to see a man in a gray suit at the bar. He raised his tumbler and cocked his head in invitation. *Here we go.* I shifted, picked up my phone, and checked the time. A quarter to ten. Time to head out since it seemed this guy would soon intrude on my contemplative evening.

Out of my peripheral vision, I watched him step up with a glass of wine in one hand and his tumbler in the other.

"Hi," he said.

I looked up from my phone. "Hey." The small hoop in his earlobe, his thinly trimmed mustache, and his bright smile would lure me in on any other night. Just not tonight.

"May I." He gestured to the empty stool and placed the wine glass on the table.

"Actually, I was just leaving. So, yes. You can have my table." I stood up and grabbed my purse and wrap off the back of the stool.

"Ah. I see how it is." He took a sip of his drink.

"What's that?"

"You're stuck up?"

"Enjoy the show." I took two steps away from him, but he grabbed my arm forcing me to stop. I looked down at his hand then back up into his face. "Let go. I'm not interested." I gritted my teeth at the impressions on my skin and yanked.

"Stuck up, bitch."

My heart raced as I walked away without looking back. I strode past the performers chatting with some of the guests in the audience. I faked a smile. "Nice set," I said as I caught the lead singer's eyes.

"You leavin' already?"

"Yeah. Early morning tomorrow. But you're great. Really great."

"Thank you." She smiled and turned back to her conversation.

"Later sexy," the bouncer said as I walked outside.

Usually that wouldn't bother me, but I had been poked, and the bear clawed from within eager for release. I covered my shoulders with cashmere to protect me from the cool ocean breeze. Santa Monica gave no solace as tourists, locals, and drunks flooded the street. Rock music thumped out of a bar from across the road as I turned into the parking garage.

A familiar prickly sensation ran up the hair on the back of my neck. A gnawing presence of death. *Oh spirits. Not tonight.* I tightened the wrap to my chest while looking around. If it wasn't the consistent sense of death taunting me, it would be the ever-present concern for safety that looms over Los

Angeles streets stopping me in my tracks to ask myself if I should turn around each time I visited a club alone. But I wouldn't let these fears stop me from living life or having a good time.

My boots carried me in quick, long strides toward the elevator where a couple walking hand in hand had just gotten in.

"Hold the elevator." I scurried in, peering out into the garage. A temporary relief settled my nerves as the couple fondled one another in the corner. I looked up and smirked at the security camera. They got off on the second floor. As the elevator doors closed, I pulled my keys out of my purse sticking the ridged edge of my apartment key between my fingers. The elevator doors slid open to the rooftop level.

My car sat amidst a barren lot consoled by a lonely SUV, a sweet convertible, and one Volkswagen Bug. My stride changed into a light skip. My head clouded, and my skin warmed despite the breeze.

"Hey!" a husky voice called out from behind the SUV parked across from my vehicle.

Clutching the wrap tighter, I kept walking as I pressed the unlock button for my CR-V.

"Hey. I'm talking to you."

The music from the fashion show block party pounded the air.

With my hand on the door, I froze. Taking a deep breath, I turned around as he took a few steps closer. He wore a beanie, black jacket, and blue jeans.

"Where do you think you're going?"

Shit, shit, shit. I rotated slowly keeping a grip around the door handle. "I don't want any trouble."

"Heh." He took a few more steps toward me and stopped in arm's distance.

The muzzle in line with my chest. His bloodshot eyes narrowed. His hand shook. *Unstable. Okay. Damn I wish I'd listened more to Grams when she was teaching me spells.*

"I'll give you my purse. I ... I have cash in my wallet."

"That's not what I want." He licked his scarred lips as he looked me up and down.

Fuck.

"Drop the wrap."

I swallowed, dry mouthed, not able to speak. I clutched tighter.

"Now!" he yelled.

Startled, I slipped the cashmere off my shoulders and into my hand.

"Turn around."

I bit down on my lips. "Look ... I'm sure ..."

"Shut up and turn around. Slowly."

Not breathing, I began to twirl. My knees buckled. *Think. Think.* As I faced the rooftop's edge, I watched the sky morph to angst. As I made the full circle and met his lustful eyes, a tall man in black stole my breath with his delicious eyes and full lips stepping up behind my uninvited guest. The same man who watched me walk into the club from across the street. He held his index finger up to his lips behind the gun wielding man.

The gunman followed my eyes.

The man in black blew into his face. "Boo!"

The creep startled, stepping back shaking the gun. A shot went off, and I dropped to my knees covering my head. I could barely make out what was happening and did a quick assessment. *Ears ringing, no pain. Not shot.* I watched as the man in black used swift motions to disarm the unstable one. My hero unloaded the gun and placed the bullets into his pocket. He then put the gun in the back of his pants. The uninvited guest stepped forward to punch my hero but caught a fist to the stomach and one to his mouth. The creep's tooth landed a foot away from my boots.

The creep stood up, a little off center, and looked back at me. The man in black grabbed him by the arms and put him in a headlock. He punched him twice in the stomach and then held him up to face me. The attacker hunched forward with blood dripping from his mouth as the man in black nodded, confirming all the pent-up rage inside of me. I jumped to my feet and charged, kneeing him twice in the balls.

"How about you turn around slowly, asshole?"

The attacker groaned.

The man in black pushed the guy away from me out into the center of the parking lot. The creep swayed before falling face first into the ground.

My hero walked over to me as I stared at the lifeless figure. "Is he …?"

"Dead?"

I nodded biting my bottom lip.

"No. Not yet," the man growled.

A presence of death had been following me throughout the night, so it was difficult to tell his current state.

My hero lifted my chin as he looked over my face and neck searching for injuries. "Are you okay?"

His sexy accent sang to me as I met his compassion. His dark eyes drew me in. "I … I'm fine." I clutched my wrap in my hand. *I should call the cops.*

"Let me." His delicate touch traced down my arm to pull the cashmere out of my grip. He covered my shoulders, not taking his chocolate eyes off of mine.

"Thank you." *Call the cops.*

He nodded and pulled me into him as if my heart were in his hands. I breathed his earthly scent in, and tears streamed as he stroked my back. *Focus. You don't know him.*

"I've got you," he said with his chin resting on the top of my head.

In this moment, my sullen mood lifted. What felt like loss a few hours ago now felt like home. I pulled back and wiped the tears from my eyes. "I can't ..."

"I'm glad you're okay." His thumb stroked my cheek. Familiar. Warm. He reeled me in with his hook. "You should get going." He leaned over and grabbed my purse lying on the ground along with the keys.

I should, I thought *as* I scanned the empty rooftop. "Were you following me?"

"No. I'm parked over there." He pointed to the convertible. "This was a coincidence." His eyes squinted looking as perplexed as I felt about his timely presence.

And a calm settled over me. A familiarity. My heart fluttered. Hand to my head, I asked, "How did you ..." I opened my arms to the man lying on the ground.

"I've had years of training." He handed me my things.

"Training in what?"

"A little bit of this, some of that."

"Shouldn't we call the cops?"

"No." The man looked down at the creep and back at me. "I'll take care of it from here."

"Are you a cop?" I narrowed my eyes on him.

"Something like that. Really. Don't worry. You've been through enough."

I knew I shouldn't leave. The right thing to do would be to call 911. But inside, I worried more that I might never see this dark-eyed hero again. *Get it together. Jump in the car and just peel out.* But I couldn't. I didn't want to move.

"It's late. You should …," the hero said.

"You feel, I mean look, so familiar."

"Do I?" He put his hand in his pocket.

"Have we met?"

"What? No. I don't believe so."

"Are you sure? There's something about you." I stepped forward and placed my hand on his cheek.

The man covered my hand with his. "I wish I could say we met in better circumstances. But, well, you see that's not the case." He smiled.

"Right." I lingered. He brought my hand down and let go. "Well, I guess I'll get going." I unlocked the car.

"Yep." He opened the driver's side for me. "No telling when he'll wake up."

I stepped into the vehicle and placed my things on the passenger side. He blocked my view of the man lying on the cement. I was torn. I knew the right thing to do would be to stay, but my gut told me otherwise. Grams always told me to trust my gut.

"What's your name, hero?"

He looked into my eyes. Butterflies fluttered in my stomach. His hand reached up and cupped the back of my neck. Pulling our foreheads together, he kept his eyes on me. "Gabe."

I pressed my forehead deeper, skull to skull. "I'm Amber."

"Mucho gusto," he whispered over my lips. He pulled back still rubbing his thumb along the hairline of my neck.

"I could stay," I said as I clutched his forearm. "Help you …"

"You should go." His eyes narrowed as if in pain, fighting to restrain himself. "Please. Go. It's for the best." He stepped back.

I noticed his fitted black V-neck hugging his chest as he shut my driver's side door. My hands gripped the steering wheel as I stared through the window at him.

He mouthed it once more, "Go." He stepped away from the vehicle.

I started the engine, buckled, and shifted the car in reverse. My heart leapt for more, but he clearly didn't want to take this conversation to greater depths. I released my foot off the brake and began to roll backward. Shifting into drive, he had already turned away from me, standing over the body with his hands in his pockets. *What's he gonna do?* I bit down on my lip. *I don't really want to know.* It's better that way.

CHAPTER 5

———

GABE

Antonio's newest studio warehouse was located just east of the LA Fashion District. As I walked in, the less than perfect construction set my teeth on edge. A faint whistle blew through a flap of metal on the roof. The vast open ceilings created a draft. I narrowed my eyes as I scanned the empty space around the back entrance. *No security?* That wouldn't do after Amber's attack last night.

A soft but high-pitched whistle blew through a tired ceiling. Purposeful dingy walls opened up into a lobby with a set for a kitchen scene to the right. I could hear Marco speaking to someone in one of the dressing rooms down the hall to my left. Straight ahead, the crew set up for today's filming in the larger sound stage at the front of the studio.

One thing became clear to me last night; with or without me, Amber could be harmed even if the perpetrator wasn't a vampire. We would be better together. Releasing Amber was a huge mistake. Our souls were destined to cross paths as each time before, and this time, Sal and I were ready. As much as I thought I could, I would never be able to resist her.

I wandered through the dusty unclaimed kitchen studio set. Empty espresso cupboards posed no threat. I pulled out every drawer. No knives. *That's good.* Pausing at the refrigerator, I honed in on her voice as I opened it.

Distinguishable like a harp, her voice came into focus. "Did someone turn on the heat? I feel like I'm having hot flashes," Amber said.

I chuckled. I love how our bodies reacted to one another over the years. It never got old regardless of the discomfort. A unique distinguishing quality that confirmed she was the one, every time.

Jennifer laughed. "You're too young for that, my friend. Maybe you just need to take better care of yourself. You know. Work out."

Jennifer. Just who I was looking for. I needed to talk to her and compel her to forget the night at the mansion. I couldn't let her confuse Amber.

"Damn, Jenn."

"You know I love you, girl. Now go on … make me look hot for this next scene."

Amber's voice echoed in my mind as if right in front of me. She mumbled something to herself about being dizzy again.

What are you waiting for? My soul questioned.

Relax. I'm going.

The dim lighting set the mood for more carnal pursuits. Left up to me, I'd find a dark corner and give her the chance to get closer so we could continue where we'd left off the night we met at Antonio's with her shallow breaths and heart rate escalating with every touch. But she wouldn't remember that anyhow.

Marco's voice grated on my nerves as he spoke his lines to his costar on the far end of the warehouse. Balling my hands into fists, I took a deep breath. Amber's voice soothed me as she told Jennifer good luck, and a door closed down at the end of the hall.

My soul pushed at my stomach as if he could nudge me along. I wiped the moisture on my forehead with the back of my hand. My heart raced mimicking hers. *I'll talk with her soon enough,* I told my soul.

I closed my eyes as I stood in the back lobby. A singeing heat outlined the brand on my chest. *He's here,* I announced to my soul. *Joder. Why didn't someone text me?*

I checked my phone. *No power. Dammit, Vance.* Commotion swirled about the studio as folks began asking each other why they suddenly had no cell signal. Gritting my teeth, I stood statue-like staring at the door to the back parking lot. Memories of all the deaths Catori had to endure haunted me. My brand seared my skin. Vance is angry. *A warning.* He hummed a familiar tune drawing me to him.

I squinted into the bright blue sky, a typical LA backdrop. My maker, dressed in a blazer, leaned up against his Aston Martin Valkyrie searching his phone. Over the years, he's kept up with the trends of the time. Clothing, cars, technology. Always determined to be part of the small percentage who had everything first, and a collector of historical relics. I became fascinated with that hobby. Being beckoned to help Vance clean up messes has mostly been a burden. But because of him, I found Lina—Catori's second soul reincarnation—in Paris debuting her paintings as one of the first females to be publicly recognized as an artist. I took one for my collection to remember her by.

"Vance."

"Ah, Gabe. What a coincidence to find you here." Vance's narrow eyes looked at me through the top of his sunglasses. His streaked, blond hair sat perfectly in place.

"Is it?"

"Not really, brother. Where else would you be, right?"

Brothers was far from what we were.

"I didn't know you were back," I said.

"Yes. Well. Likewise. I've got business to take care of along the border."

Does Holly know he's back? I've been too preoccupied to return her call from the other night.

Vance stood tall slipping his phone into his pocket. He stepped forward pulling me in for our typical greeting. I clenched my teeth while he superficially embraced me. "Who's caught your attention, brother?" He set his sunglasses on strands of hair splayed across the top of his head, peering at me with his sapphires.

I crossed my arms. "So, what do you need, Vance? You don't just stop by for small talk."

"True." He took a step forward placing both hands on my shoulders. "Antonio's crew is complicating matters for me. I'm here to ..." Vance's eyes shifted black. He sniffed the air drawing a circle with his nose. He snapped his neck in the direction of a man dressed in goth clothes walking by. Placing my hands atop of his shoulders squaring him to me, he snapped his face back meeting my eyes like daggers warning him to keep it together. In a low growl, Vance said, "I'm taking care of business, Gabe. So, where's Antonio?" His eyes faded back to blue.

"He's not here today, but I'll let him know you stopped by."

"Why are you always so protective of him?" He shoved my chest, jerking himself free from my hold. "He can't possibly meet your standards of integrity."

"Just stay away from him. If you need something, I'll take care of it."

My maker raised his eyebrow. "You'll take care of it?"

"Always."

He straightened his jacket, dropped his sunglasses back down, and ran his hands through his hair scrunching it into spikes. "By the way, I'm looking forward to meeting her."

"Who?"

He stepped closer breathing into my neck as he spoke. "Your soul mate, of course."

Placing my hand in my pocket and not taking my eyes off Vance, I said, "Can't meet someone who doesn't exist yet."

He stepped back and pressed a button lifting the wing of his Valkyrie scoffing under his breath, "We'll see." His grin tore through me like a knife slicing my chest in half. He definitely had people watching me. I was going to have to be more careful, which meant I'd have to make sure everyone was on full alert to launch my plan.

Vance got into his car. His engine roared and his tires spun as he pulled out of the parking lot.

A notification popped up alerting me that we all had cell service again. I texted Cali to meet me at the back entrance of the studio. She had been waiting on standby for my call at the front. She flew over the roof and landed in front of me, crushing the earth with the heels of her boots. I placed my finger to my lips, indicating to her that Vance was still in listening range.

She nodded.

I texted her to stay put and keep an eye on Amber. She winked her long lashes at me and squeezed my arm confirming her commitment to me.

I'm heading to Holly's after I chat with Marco for a minute. I texted.

Okay. I've got this. Cali texted.

Thank you.

I walked back into the studio and quickly identified Marco practicing his lines in his dressing room. *Time to compel the bastard.*

CHAPTER 6

———

AMBER

The crew had propped open the doors to eliminate a chemical scent caused by a lighting equipment malfunction. Fans were set across the studio blowing out the stench, surely giving everyone a free high for the day. Foul language and grunts hovered over us as the director stood on the ledge of the staircase waving his arms around at the crew. Goose pimples danced along my skin from the chill circulating in the air.

Our leading actress sat in the makeup chair in front of me as I applied a touch up on her lips. Bang. I jumped, jerking the lip liner away from her. Someone smacked a pole into a steel column behind us.

"You okay?" Zara asked.

"Yeah. Just startled me." To say the least. I was still on edge from the attack last night.

Zara's long lashes settled against her dark circles as she meditated to get into her zone for a scene where Jenn would confront her about indiscretions with Jenn's dangerous husband played by Marco.

While applying lipstick, I looked up just as Jenn past by holding a handful of grapes. *Odd. Usually, she fasts before her scenes.* She scurried toward the back bar propping herself on a stool. She twisted the cap off a water bottle and began gulping it down. Watching her drink reminded me of my dry mouth. I reached for my bottle only to grab air. I looked around. *Damn. I left it in Jenn's dressing room.*

Despite the cool air blowing about, I wiped beads of sweat with the back of my hand accumulating along my hairline. Wearing a tank top made the heat more tolerable, but my ankle boots stifled my toes. I turned to grab the liquid eyeliner off of the mobile makeup station, causing a crick in my neck. "Ah."

"What's wrong?" Zara's eyes popped open. "Did you mess up my makeup?"

"No. No. I'm good," I said as I rubbed my neck. Zara's one swollen eye carefully crafted by the key makeup artist on set drew my thoughts to actually being hit. If only the attacker who taunted me last night had gotten the chance to ... I shivered. *What an asshole.* I took a deep breath. "Close your eyes for me once more. I'm almost done," I said to her. Keeping a steady hand proved difficult today as I drew a black line along her eyelid. "Okay. Done."

"Great. Thanks, Amber." She looked at herself in the mirror. "Damn, I look ugly." She huffed and walked away.

I fanned my face while inhaling the fumes floating about the studio. *I got to get some air.* A man dressed in black, resembling Gabe, walked up stairs to visit with the director. My heart skipped a beat. I placed my hand on my stomach. Once the man turned to lean on the railing, disappointment set in realizing it was not Gabe. "I've got you," replayed in my mind.

I set the script back down that I was using to fan myself with, and a pack of eye shadow slid off the counter and onto the floor. "Ugh," I said as the plastic top popped off and the powder cracked. I squatted down to pick it up, trying to scoop up the brown dust that settled onto the cement floor. Feeling lightheaded, I grabbed hold of the makeup counter to push myself back up.

Kevin, a crew member, reached out his thick hand just as my legs weakened underneath me. "You alright?" Kevin asked.

"Yeah, thanks. It's the fumes."

"We can't have the most beautiful woman in the room pass out." He smiled as he squeezed my hand. "Let me get you a water."

"No, I'm fine." I smiled pulling my hand back and wiping my eyeshadow-stained fingertips along my jeans. "Really. Thank you though. I'm gonna get some air." I grabbed my bag and tossed it over my shoulder.

"Alright. Holler if you need me." He winked and walked away.

My jeans stuck uncomfortably to my thighs as I headed to the back of the warehouse to grab my water bottle.

I texted Grams, **Just confirming our yoga plans this weekend.** Grams loved taking me to spiritually engaging retreats.

She answered, **We're on, baby.**

I wrote back. **By the way, there's a presence in my apartment. Can you stop by in the next few days to take care of it? Speaking of spirits, there seems to be a lot of them lurking around me lately. A prickle up my skin caught my attention a few times at the studio this morning.**

Not looking where I was going, my knuckles slammed into a gray shirt with tight abs. "Ow." Drawing my eyes up, I recognized the man standing in front of me. Today in gray and not black.

"You should really watch where you're going." Gabe smiled down at me.

Shaking my hand out and squinting at him in disbelief. "Yeah. I guess so." He took my hand to caress it and a simmer of warmth flushed my cheeks. "What are you doing here?" I asked not able to break free of his desirable eyes.

"I was making my rounds."

"Your rounds? Because you work here?"

"Something like that."

"A man of mystery." Slipping my phone into my pocket, I took a step back. "So why haven't I seen you here before?"

"I just got back from a trip a few weeks ago." Gabe rubbed his neck.

"And. What is it you sort of do around here?"

He smiled. "I work with Antonio. I'm a producer."

"Huh. That's not what I expected you to say. After last night, security would have been my guess." I crossed my arms.

Gabe took a step closer, wiping a bead of sweat with his thumb off my temple. Looking up, only inches apart, I touched his hand to my cheek, sending an electric pulse down my neck. He leaned forward placing his forehead to mine.

"Gabe," I whispered. Not wanting this moment to end, I realized that he'd probably done something illegal last night. Stepping back, I took his chin. "What did you do last night? After I left?"

His face hardened. "Nothing you need to worry about. He won't be bothering anyone ever again."

My body shuttered as I swallowed a dry lump.

He rubbed my biceps sending a shallow breath to my gut distracting me of the fact he was dangerous. As much as I tried to conceal my concern for the danger, I didn't believe he'd hurt me. Ever. There was something about him. A magnetism. A solace. I shook my head. "You look troubled. And you shouldn't be."

"Why shouldn't I be?"

"Amber," Marco called out as he walked into the back lobby. "Hey. I need to be on set in five minutes."

I let go of Gabe and peeked around his body to find Marco's eyes firing lasers at Gabe's back as he stared at the two of us. From a distance, he looked about the height of Gabe, but he was about a few inches shorter. His black curls hung low around his eyes as he stood shirtless in his natural olive skin crossing his arms. Pecks flexing as they do when he was jealous.

I waved him along. "I'll be right with you."

"Don't take too long. Shit," Marco called out as he strutted like a peacock back to his dressing room.

I rolled my eyes.

"I see he hasn't changed much while I was gone," Gabe raised an eyebrow.

"You know him, too?"

"Yes. Unfortunately, all too well."

I tilted my head examining him. His confident, firm stance and narrowed eyes pulling me in. I adjusted my bag onto my shoulder. "Well, I've got to get back to work."

"Yeah. Okay. When can I see you again?" His eyes penetrated me, halting my breath and tensing my core.

"Well. You know where to find me now, don't you?"

He nodded, leaned forward, and placed his lips against my cheek. "Nos vemos."

I instinctively licked my lips. *He's dangerous. What was I thinking?* He pulled back with a grin that warned me that I may have found my match.

CHAPTER 7

GABE

For a vampire, walking into a tattoo parlor is like a kid walking into a candy store. The sweet smell of a sugar high mixed in with various shapes and colors sped up my heart. Vampires, unlike kids, have to shut down senses to hold back from taking free samples here and there. Coming to Holly's parlor centered in Santa Barbara was out of necessity, otherwise, I typically stay away.

Her tattoo joint drew in various tourists on vacation wanting to fulfill their lifelong dream of getting needle art on their asses, all clueless to the danger they were walking into. It was packed as usual but especially so for a Tuesday afternoon. Bodies splayed out in various directions on tables and chairs around the shop. Artists hovered, bent forward, and grooved the needles in and out of flesh. The red walls filled with local art displaying naked bodies with bold colors heating a viewer's eyes. The bamboo shelves showcased local jewelry and body piercing products.

A man with his motorcycle helmet on his knee sat on a velvet bench awaiting his turn. His lady friend, securely seated next to him, flipped her red curls while gawking at me. I looked away, focused on the voice that filtered from the back of the room.

Walking up to the counter, I watched Holly sporting a new boy cut as she whispered to one of her clients, "Would you like a private room?" The young man in a sleeveless shirt and dreads nodded and followed her sleek figure around the back wall of the shop. I shook my head knowing that he wasn't going home with a tattoo today.

"Can I help you?" A new assistant sat at the front counter with a ring in her nose and blue streaks in her hair.

"Yeah. I need to talk to your boss for a moment."

"Holly?"

"Yes." I smiled and sparked my charm reaching into the depths of her mind. "How about you walk me back there?"

The woman stood up with ease not taking her eyes off mine. "I can walk you back to her," she said.

"That would be great." I walked around the counter holding my breath as I passed each client. Excess arm skin flattened against the table as the woman closed her eyes as if meditating, a smooth bare bottom popped up as the needle penetrated her skin for the first time, and a man with a grizzly beard sat still, clenching his fist as an artist worked on a wolf's snout on top of his shoulder. Squirming bodies over crackling paper and yelps chimed in harmony.

"Right this way." She gestured showing me to a hallway lit only by candles and an emergency exit sign.

"I can find my way from here. You've been a great help. I release you." Our connection broke. The blue-haired girl nodded and walked away. With caution, I opened the door that headed down to the basement of the building that Holly had built many years ago. I tuned in to laughter and several groans. Holly, like Vance, had a way of sucking me into situations. It had been a while since my last syphoning.

"Gabriel," she whispered.

I hadn't even come into full view, nor had she, as I descended. But she already intended to draw me in.

"My name's not Gabriel," the man with the dreads said.

"No? Does it really matter?"

Smacking of flesh and wet tongues colliding awoke my desire for Amber. No one else here would suffice. A mix of flavors, shy, bold, sexy, average. None had the soul ... the connection I sought.

The room closed in with so many patrons being pleasured by Holly's vampire crew. Syphons attached to some.

"Oh. Gabriel."

"What the hell? Why do you keep calling me that?" The young man that Holly was riding over a chair didn't seem to be compelled. If he had, he wouldn't care what she called him.

Shit. I stopped in place, hiding in the shadows in between syphoning and grinding, eyeing the room. Most looked compelled. Engaged. Lost. But her guy. *What the hell are you doing, Holly?*

She bent over the locs guy's ear and whispered, "Think you can be a soldier for me?"

Goddammit.

"I'll be anything you want me to be. But, sure as hell not Gabriel." He hoisted Holly off the chair, and she let out a cackle as he slammed her up against the wall.

"Oh. Yeah," she called out. "Harder."

I froze. I could intervene. I should. I quieted my mind. My soul told me to get out.

"Oh shit. Ahhhhhh. Yeah." He thrusted one last time and rested his head on top of her shoulder.

I bolted over to the guy and grabbed him by his dread-locks out of her grasp. Holly dropped to the ground landing in a crouch.

"What the fuck?" the guy asked.

Pulling him around out of her reach, I dragged him up the stairs.

"Get the hell off me," he attempted to detach my hand from his hair, but he couldn't.

I threw him out into the hallway shoving him against the wall, rattling the painting of a disfigured dragon. His chest heaved up and down with his face turning pale as he caught sight of my fangs. *Now I've got your attention.* His eyes locked with mine.

"You went to a tattoo parlor today. You had a good time."

"Had a good time," he repeated.

"Funny story. You had to leave naked because you met a hot chick."

"Yeah. Hot."

"Just you and her. In the bathroom at the tattoo parlor. No one else there, and you can't remember the name of the place you went to."

"I can't remember."

"Go out the back. Get some clothes." I eased my arm off his chest and pulled out my wallet. "It's on me." I handed him a few hundred-dollar bills. And blinked my eyes. He looked around, and I pointed him in the direction of the door. He covered himself with his hands and ran out the exit. *Cabrón.* I turned around sensing Holly behind me.

She shoved me into the same spot I had held her spoiled soldier.

"Working hard as usual I see." My tone snide.

"Gabriel." Still fully naked, in heels, she pushed her breasts into my chest. "I'm truly disappointed in you."

"I'll take disappointed." I stood up off the wall, and she took one step back. "What the hell were you doing?"

"I'm a maker. I was ... helping him transition in a way he'd never forget." She looked me up and down.

Locking my jaw, I stared blankly at her.

"So, Amber's pretty." She stood with one hand on her hip.

Holly had met her at Antonio's party prior to me compelling Amber to forget. "She is."

"And is she …?"

"Vance is back in town, Holly."

She placed both hands on her hips, breasts perked up. "We're not ready yet. How do you know?"

"He stopped by Antonio's studio. I need bloodstone. And," I said as I placed my hand on her shoulder, "I need to know where your allegiance lies."

"I'm no one's bitch, Gabriel." She pushed my hand off. "Not yours anymore. And I won't ever align with Vance. Ever. You know what he did to my family."

I nodded.

She put her hand on my arm. "I'll help you. I'm always here for you, and I'll get you more bloodstone. But it seems rather odd that you need more since Sal just came by for some. What aren't you telling me?"

Standing motionless, I stared blankly at her. The truth was I needed a backup in case something went wrong,

She stepped closer, placing her hand over my heart. "I'm here for you. Whatever you need."

I took her hand in mine distancing her from my body. "For now, the bloodstone, and I'll be on my way."

She turned, disappearing down the stairs to the basement as I waited for her to get me what I hoped to use on Amber.

Holly called out, "You should've let me turn that guy if you want to protect her."

Possibly. I clenched my jaw. My soul mate was back, and a lot was at stake. And Holly always knew it was just a matter of time for me to meet Catori, Amber's soul, again.

CHAPTER 8

AMBER

The Escalade pulled around the driveway, idling in front of the illuminated mansion. Circular towers separated the east from the west side of Antonio's medieval style home. Even on a Wednesday night, Los Angeles elite lined the stairs seeking refuge in the mansion. While at work today, Jenn asked me to come out tonight, and I didn't refuse after having an intoxicating dream about Gabe telling me to go to Antonio's. I left that part out when I had agreed to join her.

As I opened my side of the door, a hand reached in to assist me. My red heel got caught between the cobblestones causing me to stumble forward into the driver's arms. "Thanks," I said giving him a smile.

"My pleasure, beautiful." His crow's feet crinkled behind his owl-like spectacles. "Watch your step ladies." He saluted, winking at me, and hopped back into the vehicle in order not to hold the line up.

I locked arms with Jenn as she slid her hand into Benjamin's. We walked up the path skipping the line and heading straight to the VIP entrance. The bouncer opened the red velvet stanchion allowing us through the extravagant ramp built like a drawbridge.

We hadn't even made it to coat check before a trickle of sweat dripped down the back of my neck. The vaulted ceiling in the marble foyer allowed for excellent air flow and still felt cool enough with the chilly mountainous air coming in from the front door. My temperature ran hotter than most people on any given day, but these overactive glands were becoming a concern. Waking up from night sweats lately had me wonder about hormones. I was too young for that.

Benjamin grabbed our wrist bags to check them in, and Jenn and I continued to the main lounge at the back of the mansion. The house rhythm drew us into the room, lifting our hands to the music and stepping with each beat.

"Hey. Did you hear me, Amber?" Jenn stopped at the bar still nodding her head to the music.

Fewer bodies crowded the lounge than last Saturday, making it easier to spot Gabe if he showed up. "No. Sorry. What did you say?"

Benjamin stepped up behind Jenn, already swaying into her body. "We're hittin' the dance floor! You comin'?"

I leaned on the bar, pressing my cleavage in the direction of the bartender. He smiled and held up his finger indicating I was next. "No. I need a drink first."

"All right. See ya," Jenn said. Benjamin lifted her hand over her head, twirling her around as they walked out of the lounge toward the ballroom in the west side of the house.

Scanning the space for Gabe, I noticed wooden panels on the walls holding up paintings of lustful gargoyles that I hadn't paid much attention to before. *Man, I'm thirsty.* The bartender served a couple of martinis to our mayor and his girlfriend. I wondered if the mayor's wife had a clue. I tapped the bar and huffed out air. Antonio had a strict policy on confidentiality. What happened in the mansion, stayed in the mansion. Anyone who had been invited here had to sign an NDA.

"Displeased?" The bartender said with a thick Boston accent.

"I don't have much of a poker face. Do I?"

"No. Hey. You're the one who downed a bottle of water in front of me last weekend."

"Yes. That was me." A foggy memory of the conversation with the balding bartender had me squint trying to recall why I had been so thirsty.

"What can I get ya?"

"Let's start with tequila. And …" I swallowed air into my parched mouth. "Water."

"You got it."

I sensed someone behind me. When I turned around, a woman stood with her arms crossed, staring at me inches from my face. My stomach dropped as I sensed death but clearly saw a woman in front of me. Alive.

"Hi there." I stood tall looking up into her eyes. "Give a girl some space, will ya?" The woman sported a boy cut style slicked to her skull. Distracted by her beautiful mocha skin that matched her translucent irises, she stepped forward and pressed my back into the bar. "What the hell?" *Definitely alive. Are my instincts waning?*

"You have pretty eyes."

You, too. "Thank you. But you could tell me that from over there." I motioned with my hands.

"I like this view." Her breath smelled like cinnamon. "Red is a good color on you." She commented on my strapless ensemble.

"Look. I appreciate the compliment, but I'm meeting someone here."

"I see. So, you don't remember me?"

"Should I?" She moved over to a stool next to me.

"Yes. I met you here last Saturday. Down by the cellar." She tilted her head as she spoke.

Cellar? "I'm sorry. That night's a little foggy. I don't remember meeting you." *And I don't remember a cellar.*

"Hmph," she said as the bartender placed the tequila in front of me. The woman grabbed it and swallowed the shot.

"I'll get you another," the bartender said.

I smiled.

"One for me, too." Marco slid his arms around my waist startling me.

I looked over my shoulder at him. My body tightened. "Uh. Hi." I looked left for the woman, but she was gone. Pushing off the bar and out of Marco's grip, I swiveled around scanning the room. She was nowhere to be seen, and the shot glass sat empty on the bar. *Strange.*

"Who are you looking for?" Marco asked.

I sat on a stool and grabbed a cocktail napkin dabbing my forehead.

"Here you go." The bartender placed the tequila in front of us and winked at me as he walked away.

"Jennifer told me you were coming out with her tonight," Marco said.

"She did, did she?" *Dammit Jenn.*

"I'm glad you're here. That we're both here."

"Uh-huh." I looked over my shoulder feeling as if someone were behind me again. Bodies began to fill the room, but no one was close enough to cause a radiating heat on my back like the woman with mesmerizing eyes. I lifted my glass, downing the shot. It burned along my scratchy throat. I dabbed my forehead again. This feverish ordeal was getting old and getting sick wasn't an option for me for the next couple of weeks. I couldn't lose the gig that Jenn had gotten me on her film.

"You didn't wait for me." Marco raised his glass.

"Nope." I shifted away from him leaning my back against the bar as I sat facing the crowd.

"Why you being so cold?" He crunched his face as he leaned over me. He wiped a bead of sweat from my hairline. "Am I making you hot?"

I looked up at him. "I'm sure it's the tequila."

"Hm." He grinned widely. "Let's go play pool. I saw Zara and Philip in there."

I looked around, still feeling as if eyes were searing into my skin.

"Well?"

"Sure. Why not?" As I stood up, my head spun causing me to clutch the bar and sit back down. Marco hadn't noticed as he ordered four more shots of tequila to be delivered to us in the pool room. I grabbed the water that sat unopened in front of me, stood up, and steadied myself. *What the hell's going on?*

CHAPTER 9

GABE

Murmurs and slurs bounced around my mind as I headed up the drawbridge entrance searching for Amber's voice. Frank, the bartender, spoke and Marco replied. And then I caught wind of her raspy voice. *Time to intervene.*

Brushing past the crowd in the foyer, I heard Amber agree to follow Marco to play pool. As I stepped into the lounge, I watched her steady herself on the bar and sit back down next to Marco.

We're having our effect on her again, my soul said.

I can see that.

Amber's strapless red dress clutched tightly around her caramel skin. She stood up and followed behind Marco with a water bottle in hand. My fangs popped out and in the dim light; no one would notice.

He moved through the crowd making space for her. She looked over her shoulder and then over toward the sliding glass door. I pushed a man out of the way.

"Watch it!" he said.

I apologized with my hand as I went by.

Before she walked into the pool room, I stepped in front of her. "Hey," I said. She fell into my arms. Our bodies colliding sent a jolt to my heart.

Amber brushed her hair behind her ear as she straightened her posture. "Hi." She looked up with a sinister smile.

"Am I interrupting?" I asked.

She looked past me as Marco kept going. "No."

He didn't seem to notice her no longer in tow. "Good."

"Did you just get here?" she asked.

Moving her curls off her shoulder, I nodded. Her hair draping her shoulders brought my eyes down to her breasts warmly secured. "I'd like to show you something. In the garden." I intertwined her long fingers in mine and pulled her in the direction of the sliding glass doors. As we reached the pergola deck overlooking the rose garden, I placed my hand on the small of her back allowing her to exit first. I turned to find Marco walking back into the lounge looking for Amber. I stretched my lips concealing my smug content as we locked eyes.

I cupped her hand as we walked off the deck. The mountain air cooled my heated skin. I looked down at Amber's feet. "You may want to take off your shoes." Just as I mentioned this, her heel got stuck in the grass. I grabbed her around the waist before she hit the ground. She looked up at me as I smiled, straightening her upright.

"Don't even say a word," she grumbled.

"No. Not saying a word."

"Alright," she chuckled. A waiter walked by with a tray and Amber stopped him to put her unopened water bottle on top. "Thank you," she said to him as she leaned over and took off her shoes placing them in her free hand. We took a few steps. "This lawn is soft like a golf course."

"Do you walk barefoot on golf courses often?" I raised my eyebrow.

"There was a time." She looked up at me and then back down at the path in front of her.

"These guys would probably agree with you." I waved in the direction of the lighting crew who always came to Antonio's parties for a putting playoff. "They're practicing for the PGA Tour."

"Ah. I see. Are they barefoot, too?"

I laughed. The three men stopped on the middle of the green to gawk at Amber's full figure. She smiled and waved at them, and they lifted their hands to acknowledge her. One man's eyes lingered a little too long for my liking. We kept walking toward the far end of the garden behind the roses and cypress trees. Her warm hand sat perfectly in mine. I turned my face away, scrunching it to keep my fangs in.

"How long have you known Antonio?"

Her question pulled my attention back to face her. "Many years."

"So, you've come out here often?" Amber asked. "You know, during Antonio's parties?" Her tone hinted at an interrogation.

"Yes." I cocked my head watching her size me up.

She doesn't trust you yet, my soul said.

No kidding, I responded.

We took a few more steps in silence. "I love Antonio's garden, especially this."

I led Amber into a labyrinth of bushes, low enough to see from one side of the enclosed maze to the other. This maze always brought back memories of the times I used to play with Antonio out here when he was a child. When he looked up to me like a father.

"Wow," Amber said. Her head reached just over the height of the bushes trimmed in such a way that there was little visibility between the leaves. "This is incredible."

I ducked down and disappeared behind a bush two rows away before Amber could notice.

"Gabe? Where'd you go?"

I listened as she took a few steps forward and then left. "Gabe?"

As Amber turned the corner, I popped up eight more rows away.

Her lips parted. "How did you?"

I ducked down again.

"Gabe!" Her feet shuffled along the grass following a zigzag path. Our eyes met as she turned the corner to sneak a peek. She jumped back. "Gabe! Jesus!" She stood bent over staring at the ground for a moment with her palm over her chest, but when she straightened up again, I was gone.

I watched her through a hole in the leaves as she frantically looked around, still holding her heart.

"Where are you?" She ducked back down, and her arm scraped against the bush. "Shit."

I caught a whiff of a small scratch seeping out tiny droplets of blood. *Like a raspberry truffle.* My eyes transitioned to black. I shook my head, willing them to shift back to brown. I took a few more steps and popped up at the same time as Amber. I was at the end of the labyrinth, and she was still in the middle.

"That's impossible," she muttered.

"The tequila's slowing you down," I smirked and ducked down once more regaining control of my hunger.

"Wait a minute. Were you watching me at the bar?"

"Of course. And so were many others," I called out unseen.

She sneered and ran hunched over as fast as she could to the end of the row she was on until her head hit a button on my shirt. "Ow, geez!" Amber squealed as she rubbed her forehead, "Where did you come from?" She stepped back looking up into my eyes. "How did you ...?"

I grabbed her arm to steady her. Speechless, she rested her hands on my chest to distance us more. The thumping of my heart sped up with the sound of her breaths. "How could you have gotten here so fast?" Amber persisted.

"I come out here all the time." I grinned again. She measured the distance with her eyes probably trying to make sense of my speed. I cut her thoughts off by grabbing her hand and leading her through the maze. "I've done this a thousand times." Her disgruntled face had me elaborate. "When Antonio and I were kids, that is." We reached the end of the labyrinth and entered the back of the garden, lined with concrete paths leading to fountains, benches, and an ivy-covered guest cottage off to the west. I led Amber to the bench close to the cottage's entrance. The fountain was off limits since that was one of Marco's favorite spots to bring women.

I sat down on the bench, and Amber sat on my lap.

"What?" she whispered as she looked at my puzzled, pleased grin. Her forwardness didn't surprise me after the first night she approached me at the mansion. And she wouldn't remember that since I had compelled her to forget that night.

Through my peripheral vision, I watched her sway in my direction as Frank handed me the drinks. A pleasurable jolt hit me as she brushed her forearm with mine while leaning on the bar next to me. I placed a glass in front of her. She looked up at me with her lips parted slightly as she took the other glass I offered.

"Thanks," she said. "I saw you over here by yourself and ... well. It's not good to drink alone."

"No. I guess not." I squared my body toward her, inhaling her sweet lavender scent. Her shimmering eyeshadow caught the light as she looked down at her glass, swirling it. She opened her stance and met my curiosity. Her heartbeat pounded alongside the techno music. I kept my eyes from dropping to her neck not wanting to break our connection. Our eyes locked, people chatted, music played, but I only heard her breathing and the thumping of her heart. I took her hand, flipped it up toward the ceiling revealing her wrist, and brushed my thumb over her veins. She shivered, not breaking eye contact. "I didn't need rescuing."

"Maybe I did."

I took a mental note of her open stance and smile. Shoulders relaxed. Not afraid.

She bit down on her lip. "And I prefer tequila."

I could feel our enrapturing souls—just like that night—and I knew she felt it as well, probably attributing it to the alcohol. The more time she and I spent together, the more trouble our souls were able to get into. Sighing, I wrapped my arms around her waist. In the moonlight, she was even more irresistible.

"Tell me something that not many people know about you," I said as she traced her thumbnail across my chin.

"Well." She tilted her head up exposing her neck. She brought her eyes back down to meet mine. "I can sense death."

My body tensed. "You sense death. Care to elaborate?"

"I know when spirits are present."

"Huh. And do you sense something now?"

"Definitely. All evening there's been a presence lurking around me."

I kissed her thumb as she passed it over my lips. I hadn't seen any spirits yet and none were speaking to me.

Is it us? My soul asked.

I don't know, I replied in my mind. "When did you learn of your gift?"

"Hm. The first time I really felt and acknowledged it was when I was six." With her lips in my ear, she whispered, "But that shouldn't scare a gangsta like you, right? I mean, you did take out a man with a gun for me."

I pulled back and looked into her hazels. "I think I can handle it."

"I feel like I've known you forever," Amber whispered. Her lips touched my cheek as her fingers filtered through my hair. "There's something ... I can't explain it ... your earthly scent, your alluring touch, and your eyes ... I can't resist." Her lips enveloped mine. I pulled her closer toward me, rubbing her back with my hand. Our tongues met, twisting and encircling one another. The intensity hardened me. My mouth strayed from her lips over to her taunting neck. She moaned. I drew my tongue back over to find her lips. Her hands grabbed my hair tightly. I wanted to carry her into the cottage and make—

Zzzzzzzzz. Pop! My arm jerked up, and my reflexes stopped the impending golf ball from hitting the back of Amber's head. She flinched and pulled away from our kiss. I showed her the ball. A ball that could have hurt her. The anger, the possibility of her injured, snapped my calm reserves. I squeezed the offending projectile and cracked the golf ball open.

Amber gasped. "What the—" She jumped up.

I shrugged throwing the limp ball over Antonio's stone wall. Amber persisted, "How did you?"

I heard the guys coming. The trio fumbled in the bushes in a drunken stupor for their lost ball. "Amber, please." I reached for her hand, but she refused, still eyeing me. "Sit."

I grabbed her by the hand and pulled her onto my lap. My lips found hers, and she surrendered.

"Hey guys, I think it's over here," Jorge, one of the lighting crew shouted out.

"No way it could've gone that far. If it did, I owe you twenty bucks," Kevin replied, "And, yeah, Manny's got it for you."

"Screw you. I'm not frontin' you any more money," Manny said.

"Oh. Hey, shhhh. There's a couple of love birds," Jorge said as they strode around the corner.

"Ah. Beautiful, Amber," Kevin said. The one who lingered.

"Ahem." Manny cleared his throat. "Pardon me."

He'd gotten Amber's attention as she pulled away from the kiss.

"Have you seen our balls … I mean, ball?" Manny bowed and nearly fell over.

"No. We haven't." I put on my joker's grin.

"You don't have to be such a jerk," Manny slurred.

Amber slid off my lap as I stood up, pushing her behind me. "We don't have what you're looking for."

Manny stumbled forward, while Kevin lost his grip on Manny's arm. Jorge stood cross-armed watching everything unfold. "So, you're a tough guy, huh?" Manny looked past me at Amber. "You like assholes like this, sexy? I can be an asshole."

"If I were you, I'd walk away," I said.

Manny came at me with his arm cocked back and swung. I caught his fist and tugged him into me, forcing eye contact. He grunted.

"Shit," Kevin and Jorge muttered.

Amber gasped.

I held my hand up warning his friends not to take a step closer.

"Get off me man, you're breaking my hand."

"I don't like how you spoke to my friend."

"Ahhhh," Manny hollered as I squeezed more. He tried to move but couldn't as I drew him into compulsion.

"You'll apologize."

He spoke looking into my eyes, "I'm sorry."

"That's a great start but how about looking at her." I faced him to Amber.

"I'm sorry."

Amber gave a slight head nod holding her bottom lip.

I twisted him back around to face me. "Alright. Go home, sober up, and never speak to anyone like that again. You understand?"

"Yeah. Got it."

"Bien. Now go on and get yourself to bed." I brushed his shoulders and blinked releasing my control."

Manny held his fist as he walked backward keeping his eyes on me. A perplexed look came across his face. He looked at Amber and then down and faced his friends. "Let's go." Kevin put his arm on Manny's back and Manny shrugged it off. "I'm fine. I just need to sober up."

"You need to get to a hospital. I heard bones cracking," Jorge said.

Manny muttered something under his breath, and they disappeared back the way they came down a side path.

Not turning around, I felt Amber's warmth move away from me. I twisted to face her. Still tugging her bottom lip as her hazels judged me. I stepped closer to her, "Are you okay?"

"Who are you, Gabe?" She threw her hands up. "What are you?"

I reached out to her, but she resisted and paced. "Amber, relax." I stood still watching her wrecking ball fury.

She began counting on her fingers. "You move swiftly through the maze in less than seconds. You catch golf balls in midair and crush them. You are insanely strong. What else do I need to know?" She finally turned and stood still to meet my gaze.

With my hand in my pocket, I took a step closer. "Amber, I …"

She stepped back.

"Don't be afraid."

"Afraid? I'm not afraid of you!" She paused. "Should I be?"

"No. No, of course not. I'm just different from most men." I took another step toward her. "You feel it. You know it."

"What do I know, Gabe? Tell me." She crossed her arms.

Taking enough steps forward to pull her into me, she remained stonelike, not embracing me as I'd hoped she would. I rubbed her bare arms. "What do you feel?" Our hearts beat in sync. My thumbs circled her smooth skin.

She looked away, and I tugged her gently to answer. Her lashes lifted. "Engulfed. So many things really." Her chest rose as she inhaled.

I wrapped my arms around her as she lay her head on my chest, perfectly fitting in my caress.

We were so enthralled in each other's warmth as Antonio approached. "Gabe. Amber," he said.

Always perfect timing.

Amber stepped away from me.

"Would either one of you know anything about Manny?"

"He's drunk." I crossed my arms.

"I see." Antonio looked at Amber.

"So, Amber, how will you be getting home this evening? Jennifer and Benjamin have just left," he stated looking at me, "leaving you without a ride home."

"I'll take her," I blurted out.

Antonio's eyes were telling me otherwise.

"No. Actually, I think I'll take a ride from one of your drivers if that's all right with you, Antonio." She looked directly at me.

"Of course," he answered.

"I can drive you home, Amber."

Antonio inched closer and patted my back, "I think it's best if one of my driver's takes her home. They've had a slow night."

"Great." Her shoulders softened as she leaned forward hugging her arms.

Walking back up toward the house on the West lawn, Antonio and Amber chatted about work-related things and all I could think about was how I could get her to say yes to allowing me to drive her so that Marco wouldn't swoop in and drag her away. We stopped at the coat check to grab Amber's handbag.

We reached the valet curb on the side of the house. "Good to catch up, Antonio. Thanks for walking us out," I said as smoothly as I could without trying to give up the fact that I'd be hanging out a little longer than he'd expect.

"I'll call you tomorrow about some work details," he said.

"Sure." I shook his hand and pulled him in for a hug.

"Amber, it's always a pleasure." He leaned over and kissed her cheek. Then he turned away and spoke to a valet. "Hey Colin, please pull a car around for Amber, and take her home for me."

"Sure thing," Colin answered.

Antonio walked back up the drawbridge. As some of the last few guests to leave the mansion, I hadn't realized the time, 3:30 a.m. His knack for sensing my hunger was also quite irritating. I turned to Amber. "I'm not going to let someone else drive you home."

"Not let someone?"

"That's right. Come on." I held my hand out for her.

She stood still, hip out, eyeing me.

"Well?"

She looked around and back at me. "Where'd you park?"

"I have a spot in Antonio's garage."

"Of course, you do."

I smiled as she placed her hand in mine.

"I'll go with you on one condition."

"What's that?"

"You tell me something you haven't told anyone."

I grinned not fully committing to her request, yet.

CHAPTER 10

———

GABE

Tires screeched as valets circled cars up the ramps in the underground garage hidden on the side of Antonio's home. Amber followed me to my Audi, and I opened the door for her to get in. When I got into the driver's seat, she looked over at me, and shook her head in her hand causing her lavender scent to circulate. Her heartbeat sped up. I stopped breathing.

"Where to?" I asked even though I already knew.

"Do you know the Trivis Apartments?"

"Yes." An intensity built up inside me as Amber's soul connected with mine. But my blood thirst hunger also grew alongside the desire to consume her. I cracked my window, and an awkward silence increased the tension.

Amber looked over at me as I shifted gears. "Who are you, really?"

I pulled her hand to my lips.

"You're driving me crazy!" She yanked her hand away. "Just answer me. What makes you so special? Fast? Strong?" She stopped breathing for a moment. "Are you on steroids?"

"Steroids?" I laughed.

"Why are you laughing? It all makes sense."

"No, no. I'm not." I looked at her.

"Watch the road!"

"I am." I continued to look in her direction. "Bueno, I'm not on steroids, but yes, I am *special* as you say."

"So, tell me about the training you've had. You know. The one that allows you to knock men out and crush hands."

I huffed, gripping the steering wheel.

"Well?"

"Over the years, I've been in quite a few fights. I've fought alongside some dangerous …" A hunger pang sent a signal to my fangs, so I turned my head away from her. My voice deepened, "Folks."

"I've seen things, Gabe. I … I know that supernatural exists. I just …"

Amber leaned against the passenger door revealing more of her cleavage. *Focus.*

"Well, you're going to think I'm crazy," she said.

"I highly doubt that." I grinned, but her face remained serious. I wasn't sure either one of us was ready for the vampires exist conversation.

"My Grams is a psychic medium."

Phew. I grabbed Amber's hand and nodded. "Yes. Supernatural does exist."

She placed her hand on mine staring at me. "You can tell me. I've been through a lot. I've seen Grams possessed before." Her intensifying pulse echoed deep in my ears. "So, I can probably handle whatever it is you want to tell me. Military operative. Gang member." Her thumb brushed my cheek. "Bring it on, Gabe."

"Look. I want to tell you more about me, but this isn't how I want to share my past with you."

"Well crushing a golf ball in front of me and disarming a man doesn't give you the luxury of taking your time to find the perfect place to explain yourself to me. We're past that." Huffing, she shifted her body away and faced the door. "I don't have patience for games."

"Look. We just met. I can't give all my secrets out on our first date." I grabbed her hand.

"This isn't even a date. Uh." Amber rolled the window down. She grabbed her stomach.

Sweat built along my brow, and I copied her by rolling my window down all the way. Our souls' yearnings started to interfere with our own bonding. The air pouring in stifled our conversation. My craving for Amber intensified. As my soul told Catori that he needed to feel her, Amber squeezed her knees together. *Mmm.*

She rubbed her face and looked over at me. Her eyes attentive to my mouth. I smiled showing her my pointed teeth. She needed a little more time to process, and I needed more time to gain her trust.

"Hey." I brushed her cheek. "We're here."

"You can park over there."

She guided me to a guest spot that Marco had frequented. As I pulled into the space, I felt a strangling sense of jealousy. "I'll walk you up."

"It's not necessary." She gathered her things and opened the door.

I jumped out of the car and slammed the door shut. Tempted to run around and lift her up against the car, I restrained myself, taking small steps toward her. She closed the door and walked past me in the direction of the elevator. A bubble of fury ballooned inside because she didn't invite me up. My hunger brought my attention to her heartbeat, her breath, her neck. The elevator door opened and we stepped in. As the doors closed, Amber grabbed my hand. *Shit.* Her smooth skin and inviting gesture warned me. By the time we reached the eighth floor, I felt confused. Unfocused.

"What's wrong?" She asked as we walked down the hallway.

"Oh. Nothing. I'm just getting hungry." I patted my belly.

"Oh. I have some food inside if you want to come in."

"No," I blurted out, and she stopped walking. "I mean. No, thanks." I smiled and we proceeded.

When we reached her door, the thumping of her heart sped up my own. I sensed her desires. She unlocked the door, but I stopped her before she opened it. I wouldn't be able to resist entering with her.

Amber turned to face me. "You should come inside. You know." She placed her hands on my chest. "Since you insisted on walking me up."

"I had a wonderful night with you, but it's better if I go."

She didn't pull away, but moved in closer. My fangs shook within my gums, warning me that they needed a release.

"Are you sure?" She rubbed her fingers through my hair.

Damn, she's got me. Stroking her face, I leaned forward to kiss her goodnight. Her hand slipped around my waist. My kiss intensified as my lips found their way along her chin to her earlobe. I heard her gasp lightly as my tongue found a helpless vein on her neck.

"Last chance, Gabe. Are you coming inside?" She broke my concentration with her succulent suggestion.

I pushed back and put my hands through my hair. I smiled while gritting my teeth. "No. Not tonight." She attempted to touch my lips, but I turned away. My restraint weakened. My fangs popped out. I jogged toward the stairwell. "I've gotta go. I'll call you."

"Gabe!" she called out. "What the hell?"

I made it down the stairs and fled on foot. I didn't know where I was heading, but I knew I was on my way to feed. It didn't take me long to find a stray cat in the street. It's one of those things that I didn't like to do, but I left myself unprepared tonight. Better it than her.

CHAPTER 11

——

AMBER

I awoke to cold damp sheets with my covers at the edge of my bed. My nightgown clung to me as I rolled over to check the time on my phone.

Eleven. I've got to be at the studio by 2 p.m.

I rolled onto my back, and I stretched my arms and legs in opposite directions as I clutched my phone in my hand.

Why am I sweating so much? I sat up.

As usual, I read the notifications on my phone, and my stomach swirled and growled. Typical of how I feel after drinking, except for the heart palpitations. But I didn't drink that much last night. I came across a headline in the Thursday edition of the *LA Times*, "Blood Donors Wanted."

Apparently, Los Angeles was running out of blood more rapidly than other California cities. They equated it to the large amounts of violent crimes in and around the area lately. The numbers climbed weekly. Not surprising after the encounter I had in the parking garage the other night. *Ugh. Gabe. Who the hell are you?*

My phone buzzed, and I swiped to answer. "Good morning, Jenn."

"Hey. Am I interrupting?"

"Interrupting?" I yawned.

"Well, I noticed you walk out to the courtyard with Gabe."

"Yeah. I ran into him, and we took a walk in the garden. Wait, how do you know him?"

"He hangs out at the studio with Antonio. He's been gone for a while though. Felt like almost a year. Did I wake you?"

"No."

"So, Gabe, huh?"

"I guess. I don't really know." I stood up, walked over to the window, and stared at the cloudy sky.

"Marco was pretty pissed. He left early," Jenn said. "Gabe seems dark. Don't you get creeped out by him?"

"Why would you say that?" Flashbacks of the various encounters I had with him, raced through my mind, including him running away from me last night.

"He just gives me a bad vibe. He's hot. But …"

Even if she were right, the feelings I have when I'm with him are inexplicable. "I can't explain it, Jenn. He's intoxicating. I can't stop thinking about him."

"When did you meet exactly?"

A hazy fog fell across my mind as if there was something I was forgetting. Can I even tell her about the night I was held at gunpoint? I just left a man on the ground. Possibly dead, now. "We met at The Blue Vibe." *Technically.*

"Well, I don't get it."

"Anyhow. Is there something you needed? I've got to get ready for work."

"Just watch out for him."

I sighed and walked into the bathroom twirling my curls as I watched my smile fade in the mirror. *How dare she.*

"Have you spoken to your grandma about him?"

"No. Not yet."

"Maybe you should."

"Maybe." Her probing made me think about his strength in the garden.

"I wouldn't wait. You should call her today."

"Yes, Mom." She pissed me off. So pushy and judgmental. I wouldn't dare tell her about Gabe watching me or the golf ball. She would just throw it back in my face. Maybe she was right. "Look, I've gotta go. We have work today."

"Alright."

"Bye." I hung up before waiting for her to respond.

Gabe admitted to watching me at the bar. Somewhat stalker-like, I guess. I've experienced creepier things with Grams's work. It's going to take a lot more to concern me than a desire to watch me from across the room, not to mention his insane speed and strength.

* *

A well-needed shower cooled me off after the call with Jenn. I pulled a blouse over my head, tucking it into my jeans. Picking up my phone, I noticed a missed call from Grams. *Damn.* Pressing play, I listened.

"Hi, baby. It's me. Look. When you get a chance, give me a call. I had a dream. Well. You know how my dreams go. Anyhow, I saw a shadow over you. Following you. Be careful and call me immediately when you get this, so I know you're alright. Bye."

Stuffing a few extra toners in my bag and a new mascara, I was ready for work. I called Grams while heating water in the teapot. She picked up on the first ring.

"So, you are alive."

"Yes. I am. So, tell me more about this dream."

"I had it last night. It was dark; you were walking. Then there was a shadow. It looked like a man, but it was too dark to tell. You were clutching something. Then running. And the shadow moved in closer. You ran but the shadow was faster. You were frightened. And then …"

I pulled the teapot off the stove before it whistled. "Then what, Grams?"

"You were gone."

"Gone?" I poured the water into my favorite mug with the saying *Carpe Diem*. "What do you mean? Dead?"

"I'm not sure, baby. Is there anything you aren't telling me?"

Should I tell her? I sat down at the kitchen table and dunked the teabag a few times and let it settle. "I met a guy."

"I see."

"He's mysterious. A bit elusive. I feel safe with him though."

"And when did you meet him?"

"We met on Monday." I took a sip of tea. "He doesn't answer me directly. He says he wants to tell me more about himself, but when I ask, he avoids the topic."

"You need to be careful. Take precautions. I know you, Amber. You like to take risks and live carefree. But I'm telling you, tune into your gut. You hear me?"

"Yes, ma'am."

"Do you still have the crystals I gave you?"

"Yes." *Somewhere in my closet.*

"I want you to use the amethyst today. Put it to your third eye and meditate. Repeat the phrase, 'I trust my intuition.'"

"I will." I rolled my eyes.

"Promise me, baby."

"I will. I promise."

"You keep me posted on everything you and your new friend do from here on out."

"Everything?"

"You know what I mean. But yes! Everything."

I chuckled. "Grams. I'm really not afraid of him. He's actually protective."

"Possessive or protective?"

"I don't know. I don't think he's possessive. He left me at my door last night. No explanation, just told me he'd call me later and took off running. I was pushing him for answers." *And other things.*

"I trust you. If you need me, I'm here. I'm glad we'll be together this weekend. Maybe I can read your aura."

"Sure."

"Alright, I gotta go. I've got a customer."

"Okay. Love you, Grams."

"Love you, too."

I hung up and took another sip of my tea. *A shadow.* I should've probably told her about the man with the gun. But if she had it last night, the timing's off. *God damn it's so freaking hot in here.* A call to maintenance was happening now. I poured my tea into a to-go mug and grabbed my bag. I shuddered as I felt a spirit's presence in my living room. *As if I needed more creeps in my life.*

I'd be working with Marco today. No doubt he'd be pissed.

I locked the door behind me. I felt like I was walking the hall of shame after Gabe had run away from me last night. *Maybe he's married.* I stepped into the elevator, pulled out my lip gloss, and spread it on my lips. No man was going to keep me obsessing today. He's either in or he's out. I blew a kiss to myself in the elevator doors' reflection. But despite my internal pep talk, I still hoped I'd run into him again.

CHAPTER 12

AMBER

Having impressed the key makeup artist in the early weeks of working on set with Jenn provided me with the perks of working with lead actors. But it also had its downsides. My first actor to make pretty today happened to be Marco. I was used to sucking up my personal pride for career advancement. And working with Marco helped me build character having to face him in his dressing room after walking off with Gabe last night. I knew I'd hear about.

An image of Gabe standing rows away from me in the labyrinth with a smug face popped into my mind as I placed my knuckles parallel to Marco's dressing room door, hovering. My heart raced as my thoughts wandered to our kiss on the bench. The AC needed to be cranked up higher or sweat would burn my eyes. *A little bronzer here, a touch of eye enhancers there, and I'm out.*

After one big breath, I knocked on the steel door of Marco's dressing room. A shadow caught my eye at the other end of the dimly lit hallway, and I squinted into the vacant space. Nobody was there. Grams's call had me a little on edge as well as the lingering sense of death that seemed to be haunting the studio lately.

Marco's assistant startled me as he yanked open the door. He was on the phone and waved me in as he stepped out. I rubbed the back of my neck. Marco sat in his chair mumbling his lines. The mood in the room matched the dimly lit hallway as he narrowed his eyes to look up at me through the mirror.

"Hey," I said, and placed my bag on the stool to the side of him.

He wore gym shorts and no shirt. His curls hung low over his eyes as he looked back down at the script. Stifling air mixed with a hint of awkwardness, I waited for him to acknowledge me. He didn't so I plopped down on the leather couch. I searched my phone as he continued to ignore me. *No calls or texts from Gabe either.*

Instead of asking me to get started, he threw his paper down on the counter. He pinned me to the couch with his eyes and asked, "So, how was your night?"

"Fine, thanks." I stood up, placed my phone in my back pocket, and wiped my hands down the sides of my jeans. "Are you ready?"

Marco stood up, abs flexing. His bare feet slapped the linoleum as he walked over to me. His face inches from mine. "Did you sleep with him?"

"What? That's none of your business." I took a step back, but the couch trapped me in place.

"Did you?"

I stared blankly at him.

Marco grabbed my arms squeezing, with a light shake. "Don't lie to me."

"Get your hands off me!"

He looked at his grip on my biceps, let go, and stepped back. Running his hands through his hair, he turned around walking toward the door. He hit the wall with the back of his fist.

My shoulders jerked up. I grabbed my bag and walked to the door. "I'll get someone else to do your makeup."

Marco blocked the door frame with his body. "No. Please. I'm sorry."

"Move!"

"I'm sorry, Amber." He placed his hand on my wrist, and I yanked it away.

He put his hands up. "I'm sorry. Really. Please stay."

My breathing accelerated. My mouth yearned for water like a desert cactus. I stepped back. *Not this again. Shit.* Off balance, I leaned into the door to steady myself.

He looked at me and then at the ground.

His assistant knocked. "Marco?"

"Everything's fine," he said while looking at me, "we're fine."

"I heard a—"

"We're fine." He looked at me nodding to get me to agree with him.

Pushing off the door, I walked back over to the counter. "Fine." I placed my bag back on the stool. My stomach churned as if on a roller-coaster ride.

"I've been thinking of you a lot, Amber." Marco slid back up onto his chair.

"Is that so?"

"It is."

"So, boy meets girl in the gym scene today, huh?"

"Don't change the subject."

"This is one sexy scene," I said. "That won't be a problem for you though."

As I turned around, I watched his brows furrow through the mirror. I placed a headband over his curls, moving them out of his face. He closed his eyes for a moment as if relaxed by my touch. I took a cleanser to his skin and in doing so, my hip joined his thigh.

"Where did you go last night? I thought we were having a nice time." Marco's eyes remained closed, but his teeth clenched.

I applied concealer while biting my bottom lip. Thoughts of Gabe and our kiss made it impossible for me to concentrate.

"Well?" Marco asked again.

"I've got less than fifteen minutes to make you a star. Please, let's talk about this later." I reached for the eyeliner. Marco's hand grabbed my elbow, stopping me from turning back to the makeup counter. As I faced him again, his eyes demanded an answer.

"I'm not having this discussion with you."

"I miss you." He attempted to draw me in with his lustful eyes.

I grabbed the liner. "Look up."

Marco complied. "I'd like to know when you're going to take me up on my offer."

"I'm not looking for a relationship." I turned for the eyebrow pencil. My heart palpitated harder now.

"I need more, Amber. A little over a week ago you showed me more than friendship."

With the pencil in hand, I stepped forward again, but Marco refused to look away from me. Someone knocked. His eyes pleaded with me not to answer, but I walked over to the door and opened it. Gabe stood tall with a hand in his pocket. His dark eyes met my hazels.

Breathless, I whispered, "Hey."

"Someone told me you were in here, so I knocked. Am I interrupting?"

"What do you think?" Marco huffed and stood up flashing his pecks.

Locking eyes with me, Gabe asked, "Can I speak with you for a moment after you finish up?"

"Sure." I looked back at Marco still standing firm, staring Gabe down. "I'll be out in another ten minutes."

"Okay. I'll wait here." He pointed to the hallway.

"Okay." I nodded and closed the door.

Marco remained standing. "What's he doing here?"

"I don't know. I'm as surprised as you are."

"Dripping."

"You're disgusting." I pushed him back toward his seat. Marco hesitantly sat down. "Let's finish up here."

Still brooding, I continued to color in his brows.

My mind wandered as Marco finally closed his eyes. I couldn't wait to speak with Gabe. Like with my first crush, I obsessed over him. My hero's magnetism, calm assurance, and warmth drew me in completely.

I finished with Marco and started packing my bag. He stood up and grabbed his water bottle. Watching him through the mirror, he had blocked the door, arms crossed and standing in open stance. I threw my bag over my shoulder and walked straight into him, pushing past him to grab the doorknob.

Marco shifted. "You'll give in to me soon enough."

Ignoring him, I walked out.

CHAPTER 13

GABE

The warehouse echoed with rolling wheels and slapping cables along the cement. I heard the film crew drag gym equipment across the floor and adjust props. Someone dropped a weight from one of the bench press machines. It rolled. Waiting for Amber in this desolate hallway made me cringe while Marco forced his desperation over her. Every instinct I had to break down the door and carry her out of there had me thirsty for blood. The slow glide of my fangs pricked at my lower lip. My dry mouth kicked in, muscles tensed, eyes turned black, and nose snarled. My nails tore through the drywall behind me as I leaned against it. Visions crept in of Marco's final gasps for life as I drained him. Amber had things under control though. She bolted out of the dressing room, and the door slammed behind her.

"Actors." She huffed.

"Hmm." I reached down for her hand and cupped it. So fragile and smooth. I tugged her away from Marco's dressing room. She followed me through a lounge and into an empty set of an interrogation room. We stopped in front of the table, and I sat down on the edge to level our eyes. "I'm sure you don't have much time."

Amber looked down at her cell. "Yeah. I have another actor to get to, but I have a few minutes."

"I'm sorry about last night," I said shaking my head. My thoughts collided with our souls reminiscing—forced memories of the love triangle that existed between Catori and her fiancé when we first met at the mission. My soul questioned Catori about Amber's loyalty to me.

Amber's eyes dropped toward the floor. "Sorry for what, Gabe?"

I pulled her chin up. "I would've liked to stay over. I wasn't feeling well." Amber tried to look down again, but I cupped her face and her body moved in closer between my thighs. A longing in her eyes softened my voice. "The reason I stopped by today was to ask you to go with me to visit Mission San Gabriel. Would you like to go there with me tomorrow?"

"Interesting choice." She raised an eyebrow. "A real date, huh? That depends."

"On what?" I pulled her close to me.

She placed her arms around my neck. "On how much you plan on opening up."

"I see. So, you're giving me an ultimatum, Amber." My forehead rested on hers. "Is that right?"

"Yes." She brushed her thumb across my lips. I fought the urge to devour her.

"The place I'm taking you to is very special to me." I pulled her wrist to my mouth and pressed my lips over the delicate veins and was rewarded by her shiver. "I want to show you a little piece of my history." With her hand in mine, our lips hovered. "So will you join me tomorrow?"

"Yes."

"Good. Then, how about 2 p.m.?"

"Okay."

"Let's meet there. I'll be driving back into town."

"Where exactly will you be driving from?"

"Always so curious." I pecked her on the lips.

"Again, with your evasive answers." Amber tried to pull away, but I held her in place. She turned her head, and my kiss landed on the corner of her mouth. She sighed.

"I have business to attend to in Santa Ynez."

"What kind of business?"

"I'm going to check in on my vineyard," I whispered in her ear. "Is that okay with you?"

Her heartbeat sped up. "I suppose," she sighed out. "A vineyard, huh?" She met my eyes. "See, was that so hard?"

Had she only remembered that we'd shared a glass of one of my finest reds on the night we met at Antonio's. I hated keeping things from her. I stood up towering over her. "I'll see you tomorrow." Pulling her in for a hug, I rested my chin upon the top of her head. She reciprocated as if melding into one another.

Amber nodded as her phone buzzed. She picked up. "I'm on my way."

"Give me your phone." Her quizzical face said no. "I need to give you my number." She unlocked it, handed it to me, and I typed in my contact information. "Here."

"Thanks. I'll see you tomorrow." Her full lips gripped mine creating a fire within only she could put out. The teeth she showed me as she took steps backing away confirmed she knew her effect on me. On anyone for that matter. *Mi cielo.* She walked away with a sway of confidence.

Before leaving, I climbed the stairs up to Antonio's office. We had a deal. I kept him informed on who I wanted to be with when it involved his business, and he watched over me to ensure I didn't fall back into bad habits. Antonio was on the phone when I walked in.

Not long ago, I would take people down to his cellar to syphon their blood. This used to be an approved method by Antonio's father.

"What are you doing?" Ten-year-old Antonio asked.

Caught with an IV tube in hand. One end attached to a slender pale arm. The other end in my mouth. I turned and the tube fell out, spraying blood everywhere as it fell to the side of the table.

"Antonio."

His eyes wide, and mouth opened. "No." He took a step back.

"Antonio. It's … it's fine, really." I fumbled for a cloth.

"No. No. No." He shook his head and took a few more steps back.

I yanked the tube from my compelled partner. Grabbing a cloth, I put it on her arm. "Hold this tight."

She nodded.

"Antonio." I took a step closer to him. "Campion."

"Alejate de mi. No me toques." Antonio began to run back up the stairs.

I stopped in front of him halfway up, cutting him off.

"Campion. Por favor."

"Ahhhhh. Papi! Pa …" I wrapped my arms around him, covering his mouth, holding him tight.

"Antonio, ya! Callate!" I held him tight against me. His breathing quickened and heart pounded. "Listen," I softened my tone as I spoke, "this is normal for vampires. I'm a vampire. She's not getting hurt. I don't hurt people. Okay. Do you hear me? I won't hurt you. Do you understand?"

He remained still.

"*Antonio. I need to feed.*" I took a deep breath. "*I'm going to let you go. And, when I do, I want you to go straight to your room. Do you hear me? Forget about this.*"

He nodded his head.

"*We can talk tomorrow.*" I lifted one finger from his mouth at a time before letting him go and stepping out of his way.

He ran up the stairs and twisted around with stormy eyes. Sniffling, he said, "Stay away from me!" And he ran out of the cellar.

Antonio hung up his call and stood up. "Gabe, qué tal?"

I stepped forward and greeted him with a half hug. "I'm here to talk with you about, Amber."

"I see." He gestured for me to have a seat.

"I'm pursuing her."

"Claro que sí, hombre."

"We need protection. She needs protection."

"Understood," Antonio said.

"And discretion."

"Claro."

"Vance is back."

Antonio's eyebrows furrowed. "Cabrón." Antonio grabbed a pack of cigarettes out of his drawer. He lit one up with a shaking hand.

"He's been looking for you. He's concerned about business," I said.

"How do you know? Have you spoken to him?"

"Yes. He stopped by the studio the other day when you weren't here."

"Joder." Antonio stood up and began pacing.

"Have you been cutting corners, Antonio?"

"No. I've had a change in leadership. Said they're having troubles smuggling in the blood from Mexico."

"Let me know if I can help. I have Cali monitoring Vance and the studio."

"Okay, good." Antonio stood looking out the window. He turned back to face me. "Thanks."

"Stay alert," I said.

Antonio nodded.

I stood up. "You know the drill." We bumped fists, and I walked out.

CHAPTER 14

———

AMBER

Tree-lined streets and tall buildings hovered over me as my yoga mat swung under arm. The trees cast long shadows warning me the specter in Grams's dream could appear anywhere. Yoga cleared my head this morning but also brought my attention to the swirling in my stomach every time I thought about Gabe. *Could he be my shadow figure? Should I cancel today's date?*

Turning the corner, I stopped short nearly walking into a leather jacket with legs standing in a line. My favorite cafe never ceased to serve multitudes of people per day. Suits texted on their phones, dog parents snuggled miniature poodles and terriers, and kids sat in strollers watching the traffic zoom by.

As we took micro steps forward, a man walked up behind me flashing a bright white smile, swinging his keys on his finger. His blond hair stood stiffly atop his head and his height measured that of Gabe's. *Hm.* The man's chiseled features caught my attention for a moment, but he was no comparison to Gabe.

I texted him. **I'm looking forward to seeing you this afternoon.**

Me, too. Ya pronto. Gabe wrote back.

I texted Grams. **Hey. I've got a date this afternoon. I'll call you afterward. Unless you have any new visions to share?**

No response, so I dropped my phone back into my mini backpack.

"You can step forward," the man behind me sung. The hair on the back of my neck stood up along with goosebumps down my arms.

"Oh." I looked up and saw about a two-foot gap between me and the leather jacket. "Thanks." I moved forward.

His pale face fell over my shoulder and close to my ear. "You smell good."

I turned around, and he pulled back looking down at me. He lifted his sunglasses over his blond hair, and his dazzling blue eyes pierced through me. I shifted holding my backpack tighter with my mat glued to my bare ribcage. "Are you seriously flirting with me with that line?"

He smiled. "You just have a scent." He leaned closer taking in another drastic sniff. He whispered, "One that I find ... appealing."

"If you like me like this, I can't imagine how I'd smell to you after a shower."

"Is that an invitation?"

His voice sat deep in the pit of my stomach. Safety lingered further away. "No. I'm taken." I faced forward toward the leather jacket as shadows clumsily scurried through my mind. My muscles tensed and my heart sped up. *Hurry up folks. I need to get the hell out of here.*

"Taken. That just sounds like he has a claim over you," he spoke into my ponytail. "Like you're his possession. Does he claim you?"

Twisting back to face him, I rolled my eyes. "Sure."

"That's too bad. I was about to ask you out."

Shaking my head, we finally made it into the cafe. My phone vibrated. *Thank God a distraction.* I pulled it out.

Grams answered back. **Sounds good, baby. Where are you going?**

Mission San Gabriel.

That's an interesting choice, she texted.

No, not really, I answered back.

Alright. Well, you know what to do. You feel danger present, you just get the hell out of there.

Yep.

Grams's last comment about bolting seemed like the right thing to do at this very moment. Breathing in the roasted coffee beans and freshly baked breads, my stomach growled. We inched closer to the cashier.

"Hungry?" the blond's voice spoke into my ear again.

"Jesus. You again?"

"Yes. But certainly not Jesus."

"Right." I reached the counter.

I ordered a chai latte and a lemon poppyseed muffin, and then the blond cut in. "I'll take a black coffee."

"Excuse me? No. He's not with me."

"No, I insist."

A bloom of pink spread over the barista's face. "Name for the order?" The barista left her eyes on the blond.

"Am ... Amy."

"That'll be $9.89."

"Great." The blond pulled out cash.

"No, really." I put my hand out to block him as I slid my card into the chip reader.

"Now that was rude," he mumbled.

I walked away from the man and stood at the end of the bar to wait for my order with teeth clenched. *Hurry up.*

The man moved next to me. Just staring.

"Amy. Black coffee," a teen sporting a local band T-shirt said as he placed the drink down along with the muffin. I looked over at the blond and nudged my head indicating for him to pick it up. My eyes told him to get lost.

The man grabbed his coffee. He lifted it up to me. "Thank you."

I kept narrow eyes on him.

"I guess I'll see you around, Amy." He walked away placing the sunglasses back over his eyes. He stepped onto the sidewalk and took a sip of his coffee while looking up in the direction of the building across the street.

Distracted by his odd behavior, as if he were waiting for me to come out, I didn't hear them call Amy again. I grabbed my tea and sat down at a table just as a couple left.

The man's demeanor reminded me of Gabe in some ways. But it was not a peaceful feeling in my gut. He took one last sip of his coffee and threw it away. He looked back in the direction of the cafe, and I dropped my eyes pretending to text. When I looked back up, he jumped into a Valkyrie parked right in front of the cafe. He took off, and as he did, a sigh of relief blew through my lips. Usually I'm flattered by flirtation, but I seem to be attracting all sorts of unique people these past few days. *Maybe I do have a scent.*

Just as I placed the tea to my lips, the familiar boy cut-haired woman from the mansion walked in with a man on her arm.

Hm. I tried not to stare, but I couldn't look away. Her red ensemble resembled that of a woman just finishing a music video shoot, and her wide smile on her diamond-shaped face perplexed me as I recalled how serious she was the other night.

Her cold demeanor softened as many turned to admire her. Not that I blamed them. She was gorgeous. I got up, picked up my things, and left my treats on the table. Not looking in their direction, I exited the cafe jumping into an allergy triggering taxi that had just pulled in where the Valkyrie had parked. Even though I lived a few blocks away, I wasn't leaving anything to chance for a shadow figure to follow me home.

CHAPTER 15

———

AMBER

Before pulling into the parking lot of Mission San Gabriel, I waited at a red light admiring the church's simple elegance standing erect with aged walls in the midst of our modern city. Having only been to the mission once as a child, I remembered tales of an ambush gone wrong and lives brutally lost.

As the earth settles around you, you will find peace, popped into my mind. A horn startled me, alerting me that the light had changed. The phrase that so naturally crept into my mind confused me. Maybe I had read it somewhere before.

I drove into the parking lot, spotting Gabe standing at the front entrance. He stood with one hand in his pocket—his stance. Our eyes met for a brief moment sending a thump to my chest as I pulled around past him. He smiled, and I looked away with flushed cheeks and moist palms. *Damn! Even from a distance …*

As I circled my CR-V into a vacant spot, I put it in park. My hand, on the center of my stomach, rose with my breath as I closed my eyes. His welcoming grin jacked up my heart rate.

You will find peace. The phrase echoed internally. My eyes popped open, staring into the back window of another parked car. The classical music playing on the radio no longer soothed me. I shut off the engine, looked in the mirror, grabbed my things, anxious to get out and run over to him. As I placed my hand on the door, Gabe tapped on my window.

"Shit." I grabbed the steering wheel.

He laughed pulling the car door open.

"Not funny, Gabe."

He reached out his hand for mine. "What? I thought it was amusing."

When our hands touched, it sent a jolt into my core. I stepped out of the car, and he leaned forward kissing my cheek. His earthy fresh scent drew my attention to the confining black V-neck. My hand held his smooth face as he pulled away. Nausea swept through me, and my skin heated under the SoCal sun. I closed my eyes and swallowed a sudden dry mouth. He grabbed my hand speeding up my heart again as he pulled me out of the way to close the door. His smile told me he knew the effect he had on me. I locked the car and tucked my keys in my pocket.

"You look beautiful," he said, eyeing me as we walked hand in hand toward the entrance of the mission. I wore jean shorts and an off-the-shoulder flowered blouse.

"Thank you." I walked around the gift shop admiring the various books, artifacts, and photos for sale.

"I got our tickets before you arrived."

"Great." His hand slid around my abs, and I sucked in a breath just as I picked up a book about the Gabrielino-Tongva tribe. The rush he gave me made our attraction undeniable.

"Are you ready to see a piece of my history?" he asked.

I swiped my thumb along the glossy cover and placed the book back on the rack. Turning to face him, a deep emotional pull drew me into him, and I nodded.

He enlaced our hands and walked me out of the shop. The garden welcomed us with citrus trees, vines on trellises, and succulents everywhere.

We stopped in front of the gate of the cemetery. He stood and placed his hand in his pocket, holding on to an iron bar with the other. "This place is very special to me." A tear welled up in his eye.

I crossed my arms feeling a shiver rush through me. My hand landed on Gabe's shoulder as if on autopilot, drawn to comfort him—to touch him. "Are you okay?" My hand slid down his back as he pulled me into him. Death walked about us, and his hug comforted me from acknowledging its presence. The phrase haunted me again, *As the earth settles around you, you will find peace.* Immediately agitated, a sensation of guilt swarmed me.

He distracted me as he spoke over my head, "I'm fine. I'm just taking this all in."

"The cemetery?"

"Yes, the cemetery, you, everything."

I pulled back looking up into his defined cheekbones. "Do you have family buried in there?"

"Yes."

"Can we go in?"

"I'd rather not, beautiful. Not today." I lowered my head because I wanted to know everything about him and his family. I needed to know more.

Gabe's fingers slid in between mine as he pulled us in the direction of the old chapel. He looked back with a furrowed brow. *Did he feel the spirits, too?*

Gabe's touch evoked comfort. Our silence felt like home. The stroll through the garden took us on a path of cacti and statues of angels and saints. As I admired the adobe ceiling and rows of chapel seats, he admired me. Aging wood and sage drifted from the pew. Folks entering gestured the symbol of the cross. We walked in without the reverence but with just as much respect.

The narrow build of the chapel drew patrons' eyes up to the green wood and ornate gold trims at the front of the church. Gabe pulled me into a pew in the middle of the chapel. Wooden beams hung over our heads as we walked. We sat down among mostly vacant space. Some tourists walked up to the altar admiring the ornate carvings surrounded by shades of green and gold. I wrapped my arm under his, leaning my head on his shoulder. He intertwined our fingers, a natural fit.

"You've been patient. And curious, for good reason," he whispered. "I ... My ancestors helped start this mission. The people of this land were not given a choice. They had to convert to Catholicism or face the consequences. Many didn't want to lose their lives, so they surrendered. And I am deeply humbled when I visit this place. I know that many suffered. But at the same time, I feel a sense of peace here. I feel closer to the earth, to my ancestors, to the people of this land. They speak to me. I can hear their cries, their prayers, their joy."

I squeezed Gabe's hand, listening to him describe what he felt in this transformative space. There was something powerful here. Something calling out to me. A familiarity that penetrated my soul. I moved over, slightly twisting to face him and released his grip. "It's not your fault." My hand landed on his thigh, and he looked at it and then into my eyes. "You can't change the past."

"Hm." Gabe dropped his head as if praying. "I wish that were true."

"That you can't change the past?"

"No. That it wasn't my fault."

"You seem to be carrying the weight of the world on your shoulders here. And what you're saying doesn't make sense." His mesmerizing eyes met mine again, and he lifted his lips into a half smile. I brushed the back of my hand along his cheek. As if startled by someone, he turned his head in the direction of the empty pew next to us. He stared for a few seconds.

"What?" I felt a presence. I wondered if he did, too.

"Nothing." His scowl smoothed out as he looked back at me.

"So, this doesn't really explain to me your strength, speed, and animal magnetism." I crossed my legs and placed my chin on my hand. "You know. How you got me so ..." I grabbed his hand and placed it on my heart. "Enamored over you."

Gabe's chest rose and fell as if mimicking my own breaths. He drew his eyes from our hands to my lips and then met my hazels. He pulled me onto his lap in one smooth movement making me gasp.

"We should probably go." His searing lips landed on my shoulder, my skin desiring more.

"We should." Not aware of any other tourists in the chapel, I felt encased in an invisible bubble. All I could hear was the sound of my breaths and feel the pulsing of my heart in my earlobes. "What are you doing to me, hero?" I ran my fingers through his hair.

Gabe's soft lips pulled mine between his. He lingered as he let go. Then he kissed me again with more solicitation. I opened my eyes and caught a mother with her son staring as she dragged him to the back of the chapel. I pulled away from Gabe's enticement. "I'm really thirsty all of a sudden. How about we get something to drink?" I tried to stand up, but Gabe held me in place. His eyes pinning me to his.

"I want you to come over for dinner tonight," he said.

"Dinner? Tonight?"

"Yes."

"At your house?"

"Yes."

I shifted trying to break free. A rush of nausea swept over me. Grams's words to trust my gut swept through my mind.

"Are you okay?"

"I'm sorry. I don't know what's wrong with me. I've been getting these dizzy spells and a little bit of nausea lately." Going to his house took my thoughts toward passionate encounters. Trusting my gut is what I was doing. I've never felt this way about anyone before.

"Huh. So that's your way of turning me down?" He stood up, and I fell off his lap and onto the back of the pew in front of us.

"No. I really haven't been feeling well." I brushed my thumb over his lips. "I'd love to come over tonight. I just don't know if I should."

"You definitely shouldn't." Gabe kissed my thumb. "But you will."

"I will?"

"Definitely."

"You're so cocky."

"I prefer confident."

"So, if I come over tonight, what other skills will you reveal?" I stood up with my hands on my hips forcing him back.

"If you come over tonight, I'm going to show you my library."

"Your library? Is that what they're calling it these days?" I laughed out loud causing an echo in the chapel.

Gabe chuckled. He looked up toward the altar behind me and smiled pointing at me while shaking his head to the people staring at us. "I have a collection that I want to share with you. And if you're lucky, I might reveal other skills." He raised his eyebrows twice.

"Alright. So, what time do you want me there?" My hand brushed my stomach trying to calm the butterflies.

"You get there whenever you get there. I'll be waiting."

We walked out of the chapel and back out of the mission's gift shop. His light touch on the small of my back guided me to my car. I turned to say good-bye, but he spoke first.

"Amber, I feel something very powerful around you, and I think you feel it, too. You feel it. In your soul." He took my hand and placed it on his chest. Our eyes softened into each other. "I want you to come over tonight with an open mind. Can you do that for me?" His hands brushed strands of curls behind my ears. *An open mind?* Thoughts of tombs with freshly wrapped mummies popped into my head. His thumbs traced my earlobes, bringing me back to focus on him. "Will you?"

I nodded.

He drew his thumbs down my neck to meet my collar bone.

"Hmmm." I pulled him into me and kissed him. He pressed me into the car, devouring me. My body awoke at his command. I wrapped my arms around him, digging my nails under his shoulder blades. He let go, turned away, and placed a hand on the back of his neck.

"What's wrong?" I asked.

Taking in a deep breath, he answered, "I'm fine." He turned back to face me. "Let's pick this up later." A familiar fret on his face softened. "Sound good?" He nudged my cheek with his nose.

I stared at him while pulling the keys out of my pocket. "Yeah. Sure." I stepped into the CR-V, and he closed the door for me. *He's so odd sometimes.* Starting the engine, I rolled down the window.

"I'll text you my address." He placed his hand on the roof of the car and leaned in to steal one last kiss. "Nos vemos, corazón."

He watched as I pulled away.

CHAPTER 16

———

AMBER

Each time Gabe and I came together and then parted ways was like riding a roller coaster. *I do feel it in my soul.* Gabe took off rather quickly just like the night he left me. Although he kissed me good-bye, I knew he was hiding something from me. A lack of trust simmered up within. But we weren't in a relationship. He didn't owe me an explanation. I pulled onto Mission Road and, at the light, I called Grams before driving off. The loud ringing through the car's stereo system caused me to jump. I adjusted the volume.

"Baby girl, you alright?"

"Hi. Yes. I'm fine. I just finished part one of my date." Idling at an intersection, I checked my hair and makeup in the rearview mirror. *At least I still looked good. Can't be why he ran away again.*

"Part one?"

The acceleration on the gas secured my body against the driver's seat as the light turned green. "He wants me to come over for dinner tonight."

"I see. Hang on a second, baby." Grams's voice and background rumblings muffled. I could still hear her state, "One more round for me, too. Uh-huh, sugar." Laughter emerged from Grams and a commotion behind her. The clock taunted me that I'd be right in the middle of rush hour traffic any minute.

Grams got back to our conversation. "So, you were saying something about Gabriel."

"It's Gabe, Grams." The competition with the noise in the background elevated my voice when speaking to her.

"Well, I like Gabriel."

"I want to go. I just wondered if you've had anymore visions?"

"No, baby. Nothing more. That doesn't mean you let your guard down, now."

"I know." I slammed on my brakes as a car pulled out in front of me. *Asshole.*

"You're not seeking my approval then."

"No, not really. I don't know. There's something about him. I can't explain it. I feel a connection. It's stronger than any other connection I've ever felt with anyone."

"Baby, that's called love."

"I'm not sure. I mean, I just met him a few days ago." My shoulders tensed.

"What's really on your mind?"

"I don't fully trust him."

"Of course not. Trust needs to be earned."

"Yeah. I suppose you're right." A lull of silence fell on Grams's end, minus the clanking of plates and glasses. She had a point about trust. With most people, I don't normally open up. I've always been more careful about who I let into my life beyond a one-night stand. "Maybe I should hold off on going over there tonight." No one answered as if she had placed her phone down. "Grams, are you listening to me?"

"Amber, you called me in the middle of my happy hour. I picked up, didn't I?"

I sighed.

"Look. If you feel frightened by this man, or that he's not worth your investment, then you best not go to his place tonight. On the other hand, if you're afraid of falling in love, you shouldn't let this opportunity pass you by. But you didn't really call me for advice, did you?"

"There's something supernatural about him. I'm not sure what." I ran a red light.

"I see. So, what are you sensing?" I had finally caught her attention.

"I don't know. It sounds crazy, but there's a darkness." *Dare I say shadow.* "And he's incredibly strong."

"You know that whatever you sense is truth. Remember that."

"Yeah, I know."

"I'm not telling you not to go, but I am gonna tell you to pull out that book of spells I gave you. You hear me? You turn it to page thirty-six. You read that spell before you go. Got it?"

"Page thirty-six. Got it."

"Are you still coming down for our yoga retreat tomorrow?"

"Yes. Definitely." I cut off a jeep not allowing me over just in time to get into the left turn lane.

"Good, then make sure you come over right away, as soon as you leave his home. Don't go back to your apartment. I want you to come straight to me. Got it?"

"Yes, Ma'am."

"You say that spell and then you keep your phone on. You hear me?"

"Yes."

"And text me his address."

"Alright," I said with an edge in my voice as the jeep honked, alerting me to the green light.

"Okay. Now, I'm gonna hang up, and you go on and enjoy your evening. Love you, baby."

"Love you, too."

Grams's insight always gave me a serene warmth that layered me like a cozy blanket. Refusing Gabe's invitation to visit his home was not an option. I bit down on my lip. I needed to know the truth about him. Gabe's strength and speed kept my mind searching for answers. *No normal human can crush a golf ball. Maybe it wasn't a golf ball.* I pulled into the garage of my apartment complex, scurried out of my car, and looked at my phone, *4:30 p.m.* A new text came in from Gabe. *His address.* I clicked on the link and my map app opened. *He lives near a state park. Oh boy.* I would be driving deep into the Santa Monica Mountains tonight. The voice in the back of my head warned me of cabins and axes. I pushed it aside knowing that other folks lived in the mountains, too. *Completely normal.* And I will be getting answers, or he won't be getting much of me.

* *

My Honda CR-V shifted into a deep purr as it climbed the mountain up to Gabe's. The sunset began around eight o'clock, providing me with just enough light to see the curvy road bordered by rock and pine. As I drove down his desolate street, nausea lingered again. *Ugh.* I let out a deep breath. *What's wrong with me. Am I pregnant? That would be something. Hey, Gabe, I know we just met, but I'm carrying Marco's baby. You don't mind fathering his child, do you?* I laughed aloud and then shook my head. I contemplated turning back, but I couldn't. I had no idea what the hell was going on, as if there were some magnetic force between Gabe and me, and I knew deep inside that I was supposed to be with him tonight.

I pulled into the driveway and found a large iron gate with a young, balding man sitting in the ivy-covered booth waving me through. *Definitely wealthy and guarded.* The gates welcomed me, opening wide. I held up my hand to say thank you and pulled through.

The strawberry moon enhanced Gabe's dry land. Sculptures of bodies intertwined lined the driveway with elegant illumination highlighting the intimacy of each. He certainly didn't hold back his interest in the human body.

Reaching a roundabout, I parked my car and admired the Spanish architecture of his mansion. Cameras along the exterior of his home tucked in between ivy-vined walls. This was not something I noticed on Antonio's mansion but surely, they existed. Before getting out of the car, I stopped to text Grams my location as she had requested. I popped a Tums into my mouth and chewed quickly. Leaning my head back, I took a deep breath, and swallowed the partially eaten Tums. The rearview mirror still facing my direction from the drive away from the Mission allowed me to check my teeth before exiting the car.

The front door opened as I slipped my phone into my purse and locked my car. A man in a suit stood in the doorway as the large frame engulfed him. *Bodyguard, or a gangster?* Who was this guy and why would he be opening Gabe's door?

I counted twenty stairs before my heel reached the last step. "Hi."

"Good evening, Señorita," the man said in a thick accent like Gabe's.

He moved aside to allow me in. The door's closing caused a cool draft on my shoulders. I found myself in a marble foyer with exquisite paintings showcased as if in a gallery. Bold Mexican pottery scattered about the walls. I gaped at the size, the elegance, and the length of the home from the large double doors to the back of the dimly lit mansion.

"May I take your things?"

"Oh. No, thank you. I'd like to hold on to my purse for now," I said as it hung down by my side.

"Certainly."

"My name is …"

"Ms. Amber."

"Yes, Amber. And you are?" I held out my hand, but he bowed slightly holding his folded hands on his stomach.

"My name is Sal."

I put my hand down and clutched my purse in front of me. "Nice to meet you, Sal. You look so familiar to me. Have we met?"

He stood erect. "No, Ms. Amber. I don't believe so." His face still. No expression.

"Amber. I see you've met my partner in crime." Gabe bounced lightly down the illustrious staircase curved along the gallery wall. He was dressed in black to match his features, his chest and forearms exposed in a button-down shirt. My heart beat faster as he got closer. His smile gave me butterflies and when his lips touched my cheek, I quivered. My fingers skimmed over his chest and circled lower. I breathed him in. Gabe's eyes locked on mine as he pulled back and my hand resisted the withdrawal.

"Señor, les ofresco un cocktail?"

For a moment I had forgotten Sal was still standing there.

"Sí, Sal. Amber, how about a margarita?"

Distracted by the tattoo of a vine trailing his defined forearm as he opened his arms to the suggestion, "Mmm," came out.

Gabe tracked my eyes and grinned.

I caught myself tugging at my bottom lip and blushed. "Uh … Yes, please. On the rocks."

Sal left the room, and I stood there feeling like an eager teenager waiting for the parent to leave so she could make out with her boyfriend.

Gabe stepped closer. I subtly licked my lips.

"Can I take this for you?" He pointed to my purse that I tightly clutched.

The intensity of our attraction caused me to fumble my words. "Oh. Yeah. I mean no. No, thank you. Sal asked the same, but I …"

"No worries. If you need to run out screaming, it would be best to have your purse in hand." Gabe winked.

"Right." I smiled and softened my shoulders as I realized how ridiculously uncomfortable I must look.

"I had Sal prepare you something to eat, but first, I want to show you my library." His hand clasped mine, sending jolts of electricity up my arm. "Follow me."

In his grip, we glided across the floor, and I sensed I would follow him anywhere even if it meant a life of crime.

CHAPTER 17

AMBER

Off to the right of Gabe's front door, we entered a library with massive floor-to-ceiling shelves. Books were neatly organized, and notorious first editions undoubtedly sat somewhere in the midst of his collection. My mouth parted at the height of the ceiling, with slanted wooden beams highlighting the elegance of this space. Likened to the size of a ballroom, the side wall in front of us supported a reading nook on the second level surrounded by more books. A glossy cherry wood railing secured the nook leading one to a side staircase in the back of the room.

The library was decorated with collections of oil paintings, busts, and sculptures. Encased artifacts were strategically placed around the center of the room. Pottery, books, and tools glistened with gentle lighting, and weapons—including a harpoon—hung on the walls.

"This is incredible!" His home mirrored a museum, from the sculptures along the driveway, the beautiful art hanging in the foyer, and now this.

"I've had lots of time on my hands." Gabe looked over at me taunting me with his evasive dialogue. "You know, to collect that is." He took a step closer placing our bodies an inch apart from one another.

"I see." My temperature rose despite the cool air required to maintain this exquisite room. Was it the excitement of the world that Gabe slowly pulled me into or our fierce attraction? Still unclear, but I liked it. My nausea had subsided slightly.

He slid his fingers gently under the handles of my purse, pulling it out of my hands. He placed it on a bench in the center of the room where we stood. Running with my purse in hand didn't seem like much of an option anymore.

Rubbing my hands along my dress, I said, "You were saying something about eating before …" I hugged my arms ignoring the tingles of death nearby. *Not tonight spirits.*

"You look beautiful," he said, distracting me.

I may have gone a little over the top with a shorter-than-usual strapless dress.

He hugged me while caressing my back, dropping his head down until his mouth hovered over my ear. The heat from my chest traveled between my legs. His earthen scent hypnotized me as my lips hovered over his chest. Bringing my face up to meet his, his tongue entered my mouth with determination. Circling and enveloping my lips unleashing desire from every part of my body. He tightened his arms around my waist. The weight of my stance lightened as if I were lifting off the ground.

"Eh-hem." Sal interrupted our kiss.

Gabe took a step back as Sal walked over to us with drinks in hand. I turned away to look down at one of the books encased next to us.

"Sus bebidas, Señor." Sal handed them to Gabe and then whispered something in his ear.

I kept my head down straining to hear what Sal was saying while admiring a delicate copy of Aztec mythology.

"Un momento, por favor," Gabe responded slightly irritated. "We'll be in the dining hall in a moment."

Sal left the room once more. Gabe turned and handed me a drink.

"I feel like your father just walked in on us."

"Well. He did." Gabe raised his glass and we clanked them together.

"He's not really your …"

He smiled. "Sal used to be a priest."

"Oh. Really?" I raised an eyebrow.

"Don't let him fool you though. He's no saint." Gabe shook his head. "Sal and I are very close. More like brothers." He took a sip of his drink and tightened his lips. "Brothers who don't always agree."

I nodded. "Well, I'm an only child so I don't know what that's like. Do you have siblings, Gabe?"

"I had five. You know. Big Catholic family."

"Had?"

"They're deceased." He watched me as he took another sip. "I'm sorry."

"No importa." He waved his hand. "Don't worry about it."

"I really love this library you've created. And this book …" My nails tapped the glass. "It's beautiful. How did you come across all of these artifacts?"

"Traveling is a hobby, so I just collect as I go from country to country."

I walked away from Gabe and brushed my fingertips over each case I passed. One set toward the back of the room called me to it. As I peered into the dimly lit case, I saw a large family tree. At the top, it stated *Vampire Legend*. Alone at the highest point stood a Neanderthal with a staff slightly hunched forward and fangs with blood dripping from them. A chill shivered up my spine. Gabe's hand brushed my arm, and I jumped spilling some of my drink on the glass.

"Sorry, I startled you," Gabe said handing me a handkerchief.

"No, no. It's my fault." I wiped my hand and then the glass case.

"Don't worry about that. We'll clean it later. That's why they're encased." Gabe grabbed my drink and set both of ours on a table beside us.

I rubbed my sticky hands together as he returned to me just staring. The heat in his eyes gave me goosebumps. I brushed my arms, and he took me by surprise as he pinned me to the case with the family tree. My palms landed on his chest as he slid his hand up the back of my neck. My hands reached around his waist. The angular edge of the glass pressed into my back. He let out a low groan of desire and devoured my lips once more. He distracted my question-filled mind as he slowed his tongue, exploring my mouth. As he pulled back, my bottom lip remained between his.

The vampire legend above us taunted me. His words from our discussion the other day popped into my mind, *Supernatural does exist.* Not wanting this moment ruined by my thoughts, I pushed his hips managing to distance us just enough for me to take few steps forward walking him around the case. I pushed him up against the wall, my hands flat against his chest. A pleased grin swept across his face.

"I think you promised me a meal." I opened another button on his shirt, kissed his chest, then looked back up at his dark eyes. "I'm getting hungry."

"A mi también." Gabe grabbed my waist and flipped us, pinning me to the wall. I gasped at how swiftly he moved our positions. His forearm pressed into the wooden panels beside my head while his other hand warmed my hip. His eyes penetrated me, and my heart raced. "We've got a long night ahead of us. Let's get you something to eat." His lips met mine pulling me into an alluring fog unable to focus on anything else but his electrifying intensity. My nails dug into his chest. His thumb brushed my stomach, and a moan escaped me. He released me, stepped back, and grabbed my hand.

Tease. "Damn," I whispered. The chemistry between us sparked even with the light squeeze of my hand. He walked us toward the center of the room, and I planted myself as I noticed a painting on the wall of a woman being lured into darkness. Yanking my arm back from his, I remembered why I came tonight. He turned and faced me as I crossed my arms. "There you go with your charms again. I thought you were going to explain things to me tonight." I looked over at the case and then back at him. "I need an honest explanation, Gabe."

"Certainly. I will tell you everything. But let's discuss this over a meal."

"Discuss what? I mean, you are … well, what are you?" I stepped forward and cupped his face. "I mean? I don't know what I mean?" I looked over at the family tree again. Letting go of him, I looked up and around. There were mystical beings in various corners of the room. The artwork on the wall showed men and women embraced in various positions, drinking from one another. My palms began to sweat and my heart raced. Gabe stepped closer, and I took a step back.

He watched me as my finger tugged my bottom lip.

"What?" I asked.

"Nothing. I can't look at you?" He smirked while leaning his arm on the glass case next to us, sheltering a fragile piece of pottery as I stepped back another two steps.

He was thoroughly enjoying making me uncomfortable. I looked down at my hands. Then, I looked back at him. "So?"

"I'm gifted." He smiled.

"Gifted? Huh." I crossed my arms.

"I am." Gabe slid closer, moving to the edge of the case. "I have talents that not everyone has."

"Like speed."

"That's one."

"Name the others."

"I can fly."

"You can fly a plane?

"No. I can fly."

I stepped back another few feet. *Flying, really?* "Gabe, you do realize how ridiculous …"

As I said this, Gabe lifted slowly into the air, flying over to the far back corner of the room, hanging on to the spiral staircase that would lead a bookworm to an enchanted reading nook.

"*Wha—*" I covered my mouth.

He flew up landing in the reading nook on the library's second floor in less than a second. I lifted my head back, watching him stare down at me. The grip of his hands wrapped around the thick wooden railing allowed him to push himself up into a handstand.

"Gabe. Stop fuckin' around." He pushed himself up and down demonstrating balance and strength like a gymnast on a pommel horse. I stepped back looking for a string or something securing him.

He shifted into a seated position on the rail. Sitting casually for a moment and smiling down at me, not settling, he flew over toward the front of the library. His flight took him to the wings of a stone gargoyle statue.

"I fly." He did a back flip pausing in midair, hovering—watching me as if I were his prey.

I gasped, eyeing the library's exit and looking back up at him.

He descended slowly toward me, landing feet first in front of me. I stepped around the case, putting it between us. He walked one step at a time, following me as I walked in the other direction. My eyes darted to my purse and then the exit toward the foyer. "Gabe. You're …"

"I'm not going to hurt you."

I measured the distance between us. By the time my eyes met his, he was in front of me grabbing me into him.

"What else do you want to know?" His whispering lips tickled my ear, my breath constricted and body woozy.

I must have been drugged.

"What else?" His lips were still on my neck.

I was paralyzed in his arms—in his warmth. *Warmth? Shouldn't he be cold?* It became clear to me what he was. I parted my lips, but nothing came out. He lifted my chin to meet his eyes. He looked like the same Gabe I was falling for. But this was different. He couldn't be.

"Amber, I told you no secrets."

"I think I should go," I whispered still clinging to his arms. Dizzy.

He rubbed my nose with his. "No."

"Gabe, I … I should go." I tried to push away but he held me too tight to move.

"I'll fly low."

"Wait. What?" I used all my force to try and wiggle free, but he pinned me to his chest. "Gabe!"

Our lift into the air seemed effortless. He slid us across the room, remaining four feet from the ground. I buried my head into his chest and whispered, "This can't be happening."

We landed near a bench at the front end of the library. "Look at me."

I looked up as my feet touched the ground.

"I'm going to release you, but you need to promise me that you won't run. Promise me."

I didn't acknowledge.

"Amber, promise me." He used his nose to nudge me to look at him again. "This is really important. What I'm about to show you."

Unable to take in a full breath, I nodded.

Gabe released me slowly, still holding me by his side. "Read this." He pointed to the floor. A mosaic tile read *Our Souls United*.

I drew my eyes up the wall. A painting of two lovers intertwined hung above the tile, with her feeding from his neck and him from her wrist. I looked back into his eyes as he held me; my body grew heavy. I shook. I couldn't catch my breath. A darkness, as if my eyes closed, surrounded me as I heard, "Amber, Amber ..." in the distance.

CHAPTER 18

—

AMBER

My droopy eyelids opened to a dim room. Windows the length of the wall were draped with elegant gold curtains. Now in a cozy den, with little decor aside from table lamps, I lay stiffly with my feet propped up on pillows. I shifted my arm, and it brushed the cold leather couch. A wood fire burned behind Gabe who held my hand while sitting on the floor next to me. Sal muttered to him in Spanish while pouring a drink from a bar in the corner of the room. Gabe answered in short phrases. His angst-filled eyes turned to meet mine as I squeezed his hand.

"Are you alright?"

"I think so." I attempted to sit up, but was too dizzy to.

"Just relax a moment," Gabe said.

"How long have I been out?" I touched my head and squinted my eyes from a headache.

"Only a few minutes."

"I had the weirdest dream. I dreamt that you and I were flying. And ..."

"It wasn't a dream, Amber," Gabe said.

Sal crossed his arms and looked at Gabe with disapproval. He took another sip of his drink, sucking his teeth in as he swallowed.

"I'm not going to lie to her, Sal."

"No te pido que mientas. Solo pienso que ..." Sal said.

"Basta! Amber will make her own decisions. I will not force her ..."

Sal walked out of the room. Gabe got up and sat down on a leather armchair adjacent to the couch.

As I tried to make sense of what I had thought was a dream, I swung my legs over the edge of the cushion and sat up pulling a pillow onto my lap. *If it wasn't a dream ...* "What are you? Are you a ...?" I tugged on my bottom lip.

Gabe stared at me, bringing temple fingertips to his lips. "Finish your question."

The truth bubbled up from the pit of my stomach. As he sat there so still, I couldn't help but feel lured to him. I needed to touch him. Explore him. "Are you a vampire?"

"Yes." He propped his head on his fist.

"You don't look like a vampire."

"No?" He cracked a smile. "And what does a vampire look like exactly?"

"You should be pale, cold. And you don't have fangs."

Gabe leaned forward resting his elbows on his knees. "I do." He opened his mouth as sharp fangs grew, just missing his bottom lip. Then he looked away toward the fireplace, retracting them swiftly.

As I rushed over to him, the pillow fell to the ground. "Show me again." I placed my hands on the arms of the chair.

He looked up at me.

"Show me!"

His fangs popped out again. I grabbed his jaw as I straddled him. Gabe hissed trying to turn his head, but I pulled his chin back to me. His black eyes spoke danger. I tried to jump off him, but he grabbed my wrists holding me down. Lips to fangs met.

"Amber. I'm a vampire. A real vampire. I'm not going to hurt you." He retracted his fangs like a measuring tape snapping back and loosened his grip.

I pushed off him, angling for the door that Sal exited through.

"Let's go eat. You need something to eat."

Still not looking at him, I said, "I should go."

"Maybe, but you won't."

I turned around, and he was inches from my face. I put my hands on my hips. "I won't?"

"No. You won't. You'll stay here and have dinner with me. And ..." He grabbed my purse off the floor. "If after dinner you're not satisfied with my answers, you may leave." He held my purse out in front of him. "Fair?"

I looked away and back at him, grabbing my purse. "For now."

CHAPTER 19

GABE

Like her shadow, I walked behind Amber through the kitchen, passing Sal who was leaning behind the island. She glanced at him and stopped, causing me to halt at her unexpected pause and nearly bump into her. She turned and walked over to the refrigerator and opened the doors. Bottles of blood disguised as IPAs lined most of the shelving. Apples, salads, and eggs for Amber found homes to the left and various other snacks sat tucked away in the dairy and meat drawers. Sal had over-prepared for her visit, reassuring me that he understood she might be an extended house guest. Snapping the refrigerator closed, Amber walked through the double swinging doors that led into the dining room.

Don't let her leave, my soul commanded.

I know what I need to do, I responded in my mind. I wouldn't let her leave. Not yet. She had to know why I brought her here tonight.

Amber sat down at the place setting with a plate of salmon, quinoa, and asparagus. I stood behind assisting her with her chair as she scooted in. She grabbed a glass of water in front of her and drank a few gulps. I longed to ensure her safety and well-being before anything else.

I circled around to the chair at the head of the table to her left. "I'm sure you're hungry. Please." I gestured to her as I sat. Amber's hand shook as she set the glass down. Nervous or hungry? I made sure to control my movements so as not to startle her.

Placing the napkin on her lap, she asked, "Is that human blood in your fridge?"

"Yes. I mostly utilize my connections through blood banks to obtain it."

"Mostly?"

"I hunt animals on occasion."

Amber's eyes followed my goblet as I took a sip. "Is that ... blood?"

I nodded, setting the goblet back down. She looked at her plate and over at my empty place mat. "So, you don't hunt humans?"

"No."

"Have you?"

Cringing, I answered. "Yes, earlier in my vampire life."

She closed her eyes, inhaled deeply, and picked up her fork. "I don't anymore."

Amber swung her fork around as she asked, "How old are you, Gabe?"

My eyes followed the object carefully, not fully convinced she didn't have other plans for that fork.

"Thirty-five."

"Thirty-five? That's just ..."

"The age I was when I was turned."

She dug the side of her fork into the salmon and looked back up at me. "So, you're fast and you can fly. Obviously strong. A protector." Her eyelashes lifted to me as she placed a piece of the fish into her mouth.

Every gesture seemed like a sexual innuendo with her. She's so different from the soul I first met long ago. Evolved. I leaned forward. "And I have excellent stamina."

She blushed.

I took another few sips of blood to tame my desire for her. "What else?" She asked.

"I have heightened senses. Like, I can hear conversations more than a mile away if I choose to. And I can sense danger." I eyed Amber as she shifted, placing another bite of salmon into her mouth. "I'm glad you're eating."

"Are you forcing me to desire you?"

"What? No! Of course not."

"Are you able to control people?"

I took another drink and sucked my teeth pulling my lips in. Her eyes locked on mine. "Yes. I can. I can compel people and make them think or do what I want them to." I leaned in placing my elbows on the table.

"Have you tried …?" Amber put her fork down. "Have you compelled me?"

I looked down and then up.

"I can't believe this." Amber stood up forcing the chair back with her legs. "When?"

I jumped up, angling my body to block the exit. "Amber, I …" I stepped closer but she blocked me with her arms out. "I asked you if you felt scared around me the first night we met." I omitted the point about compelling her to forget about me and go on about her life without me. She wouldn't even remember our flaming first encounter at Antonio's.

With her hand on her hip, she asked, "What did I say?"

"You said yes, but not out of fear. It was because I was drawing you in too fast. That's how I knew … how I confirmed …"

Amber crossed her arms. "Confirmed what, Gabe?"

"That you were the one." I looked at her and tapped the dining room table gently. "My, soul mate."

"Soul mate?"

"Yes. Most women are frightened by me. Attracted to me, but frightened. You, in all your forms, have never been afraid." She reached over the table for the glass of water and finished it off. "Amber, please sit. Eat."

"Don't tell me what to do!"

"I didn't. I simply asked you to sit and eat." I sat back down at the table.

Amber walked around to the back of her chair and put her hands on the top stretching out like a cat, cleavage distracting me. "We are soul mates, you say. How can that be? I thought vampires didn't have souls." She stood back up firmly gripping the chair.

"Most people think that. Vampires have souls … at least most of us do. We are not dead as most people imagine." I motioned for her to sit back down, "Please."

Amber walked around the chair and sat back down slowly. "How's that possible?"

"We die, but becoming a vampire is a rebirth. We are an immortal form aided by bloodstone. It keeps us human-like with an added benefit of never aging." I watched her biting her bottom lip. I readjusted myself to resist my desire for her. My soul knew very clearly what would be happening tonight if she stayed. He made sure I knew what he needed, with various details of what Amber's soul and he were conversing about. His needs came first tonight.

"Bloodstone?"

"Yes. It's part of the transitioning process. It's injected into our hearts."

Amber placed her elbows on the table. "Am I here tonight because ..."

"I'm not going to hurt you." I reached for her hand across the table. "Por favor."

She slowly placed it in mine, not making full eye contact. "Why am I here?"

"Because I'm in love with you."

Amber looked up at me.

"Because we are soul mates. The same way you know it. You feel it, too."

Amber rubbed her stomach with her free hand. "I'm feeling a lot of things. The presence of death for one thing. Which now makes sense since you are technically dead."

I raised an eyebrow. *If my soul's intact, how could she sense death around me?*

"And even if it were true—that I'm your soul mate— now what?"

"That's up to you. I will not force you to unite with me."

"You won't force me to what? What the hell does that even mean? You're going to turn me into a vampire?"

Brushing her hand, I thought carefully on how to phrase the answer. "You will always have a choice in this. We can unite our souls tonight if you choose to stay. And at some point, to completely unite, you would need to be a vampire. But that wouldn't ... couldn't happen tonight."

Amber yanked her hand from mine. "I need a drink." She looked around frantically. "Can you? I mean." She fanned herself with her hands.

"Sal, trae otra bebida a Amber."

"Just the tequila," she said.

Sal poked his head out from the kitchen, "Por supuesto."

"Amber." I put both hands out asking for hers again. She shook her head, still fanning her face. I crossed my arms in front of me. "If we unite tonight, our souls will be at peace. We'd be promised to one another, in a sense. Like an engagement."

"Engaged?" She raised her eyebrow.

"If you choose to fully unite with me, it would be like a marriage bond. Fully connected. Until death do us part."

Amber stood up again, and I jumped up. She walked toward the kitchen meeting Sal halfway, grabbed the shot glass, and downed it. Placing the glass on the table, she picked up her purse and pushed past me, walking out into the hallway.

I hunched forward slightly as my soul punched me hard twice. *You're screwing this up,* he said.

I followed her, trying to give her space by remaining in the frame of the dining room. She stopped in the foyer and looked at the front door, then at the library. Her eyes peered at me from over her shoulder. I kept my hands in my pockets and my face cool. *Please don't leave.* She walked back into the library, and I glided across the floor awaiting her next move in the entrance of my sanctuary.

Amber scanned the room again and moved toward a bench near the mosaic I had shown her at the front of the room. "You're so warm. I just didn't expect. I considered gangster, secret operative, but not a vampire."

"Bloodstone helps with my warmth. Hollywood has done a great job convoluting the reality. Well, we vampires have had something to do with that over time." I inched closer to her keeping a distance.

"Is that why you're a producer?"

"I have a cover in Hollywood. It's easier to blend in."

"Can you read minds?"

"No."

"I have so many questions." She shifted her body to face me while taking a seat.

My stroll felt like heavy weights had been tied to my feet as I controlled my impulse to run to her and instead sat down next to her. "I have answers."

In silence, Amber looked down and then brought her lashes back up to meet my gaze. She rubbed her stomach. "I have a peace inside. I know that I'm supposed to be here with you tonight. But I'm not ready to be a vampire."

I kissed the back of her hand and then placed it in my palm fiddling with her fingers. "Tonight's about our souls. If you stay, only our souls unite."

Squeezing my hand. "I don't know exactly what that means, Gabe. But I know I want to stay and find out."

"Is that the drink talking?" I brushed her nose.

"No. I am thinking clearly. My heart hasn't stopped racing since I got here. Since I met you …"

Pulling her onto my lap, I stroked her face. Meeting her soft lips, I hovered. "Are you sure you're ready for this?"

She nodded. "I don't know why, but I trust you."

Her words sent a rush of warmth into my chest. "Okay." I kissed her lightly on the lips. "Then we'll start tonight."

"And if I choose not to fully unite with you?"

"We can be together for as long as you live."

"As long as I live?"

"Yes."

"So, you don't turn me into a vampire?"

"No."

"And after I die?"

"I continue to live." Amber's mouth rested on my neck as I stroked her back. The vagueness of the conversation hinted at me—nudged me. She deserved to know more. Like how she was in danger, and I was dependent on her for my own freedom. But I didn't want to ruin the moment. *I can't lose you, again.*

My soul urged me to snap out of it. *You will lose her if you say something now.*

"This is a lot to take in." Amber pulled out of our hug and held my face. "I don't even know your full name."

I laughed. "No. I guess you don't, do you? It's Gabriel Manuel Acosta Chapulin."

"Nice to meet you, Gabriel. I'm Amber Cecile Jones."

Inside I cringed at her calling me Gabriel. We'll work on that but not tonight. "Mucho gusto." I pulled her forehead to mine while looking into her eyes. And if she did have the power to compel, I was certain this spell she had me under could command me to do anything, including staking my own heart. I'd do anything for her. Anything to protect her.

"So uniting, huh?"

"Yes. Sal set up a quiet picnic for us out back. We need to give them space to …" I whispered over her mouth, "breathe."

Her body tensed as her luscious mouth curled into a wide grin pulling my lips to hers. I tightened my arm around her waist, enjoying the hints of tequila and salmon on her tongue. She had no idea how much restraint I had to use around her tonight. I pulled back from her kiss and stood up holding on to her as we embraced each other. My hand rubbing her back, I looked into her hazels. "Lista?"

She nodded.

Ándale, my soul insisted before she could change her mind.

CHAPTER 20

GABE

The turquoise cross, warmed from the heat of my pocket, was what was left of the rosary that my soul mate gave to me shortly before her first death. Placing it over my lips, I closed my eyes remembering the sunset sky painted behind her on the evening she gave it to me.

Catori found me in the vineyard. Her eyes darted around the field. Most of the men were off hunting, and the women gathered for evening prayers and education.

"Es para ti." She allowed the rosary's cross to fall down the side of her palm while she held it out to me, still looking behind her. "Tómalo."

Reaching out to take it, our hands brushed together causing her to jolt her head back in my direction. Her dark brown eyes drew a line down the wooden beads as they fell in between my fingers, the turquoise cross still warm from her clasp. She met my eyes and then looked down with a coy smile.

"Gracias, Catori. Es hermoso." I took a step closer squishing the mud beneath my boot. "Como tú."

Catori brought her eyes back up as I stood in silence over her. My heartbeat thumped like it would break through my chest. She took a step back, and I took another step forward.

"Me voy."

"No." My boots brought me inches from her forehead as she bowed it to the earth. "Mírame."

She met my heat as I bent forward placing my lips directly over hers, breathing in her sagebrush scent.

"Estoy comprometida." Alerting me to what I already knew. She was promised to another man in her tribe, and I knew she wasn't in love with him.

"Sí," I whispered over her mouth.

Catori couldn't look away. I placed my mouth on top of her lips, pecking gently at first until her bottom lip took hold of mine. Our eyes closed. My fingers held her head underneath her braids exploring her mouth with every tilt.

Startled by a bell in the distance, she pulled back, touched her fingers to her lips, looked at me, and ran back to the village.

A vibration from a text jolted me back to the present moment. *Amber. Another chance.*

The text from Holly read, **He's still at his office. He hasn't mentioned you or your soul mate.**

Good. Thanks for taking the shift tonight. I replied.

Holly, a reliable ally, watched Vance while Sal helped me out at home.

The bathroom door creaked open. Amber's heels clanked across the marble floor inching toward me as I waited in the conservatory at the back of the house. Like a groom on his wedding day, my soul paced back and forth, which felt more like gas bubbles. I slipped the cross and phone back into my pocket, rotating to face her. "Ready?"

She nodded.

With our hands intertwined, she wrapped her arm around mine pulling me close to her supple breasts. We walked out of the sunroom and onto the patio. The waterfall pummeled into the center of the pool, temporarily drowning out her nervous breaths while splashing droplets onto the cement as we passed by. The pool's lights created a shadow effect along the bottom of it. Pausing at the edge of the stone deck overlooking vacant acres of land that followed out into the darkness of the forest, I gave her room to absorb the depth of my backyard and the privacy of this arid state land. We leaned on to the rocks and our hips met with comfort. A sign that she really did feel our souls drawing together.

"We're going there." I pointed to the far right of the yard. The faint glow of the tiki torches bordered the fence separating my lot from the mountains in the distance.

Squinting, she said, "It's quite far from the house."

"It is." My lips rested on her shoulder. "Do you want a ride over?"

Amber tilted her head up. "A ride?"

Scooping her into my arms, I grinned. "Hold on tight."

"Gabe, I'm not …" I leaped over the stone edge.

"Oh. My. Goooodddd," Amber squealed as I continued running toward the shimmer of light.

Taking long steady strides, with Amber resting her head on my shoulder as if we stood still, we flew past oak trees. Sage brush shifted as my leg hit its edge leaving a scented trail behind. We reached the location that Sal had prepared for us. Having lost her heels along the way, I lowered her bare feet onto the artificial grass covering the barren earth. The gardeners created a mini oasis here to shield our bodies from stones, dirt, and scattered twigs.

She turned 360 degrees taking in the beauty of the spot that Sal had prepared for us. Twinkling lights lined the iron gates. A blanket spread upon the grass held a tray with a bottle of chilled champagne and two glasses. A picnic basket sat in one corner with a red scarf wrapped around the handles. The ivy-covered statue of Aphrodite stood tall enough to reach the height of the iron gates near the edge of the fence accented with a red light glistening off her curves.

Amber lifted her eyes toward our celestial sky. Crouching down next to the tray, I popped the cork, startling her as liquid flowed down the bottle and onto my hand. She turned to me with cat-like eyes, legs slightly open consoling her bare arms. She kneeled down in front of me crawling over to my side as if ready to pounce.

I poured her a glass and extended it out to her. She grabbed my forearm spilling more champagne as the bubbles teased the rim. "Easy there." I laughed while placing the bottle down. Her eyes narrowed. Sitting back on her heels, she stroked my hand as she removed the glass to set it down. Inching closer, she brought the liquid to her mouth and glided her tongue along the bubbly.

It had begun.

My soul pressed up against my insides as if against a window he could not break through to reach Amber's soul. My fiery cat released me holding her stomach as if cramping. Standing up, I held out my hand to steady her. Amber's heavy breaths indicated that our souls already began foreplay. Leading her to the fence, I carefully leaned her into the bars.

"It's cold," she winced.

"Not for long." I grabbed a rod with each hand, positioning her in between.

Amber's delicate fingers held my face. Licking her top lip, she pulled her body off the gate and wrapped her hands around my neck.

Shaking my head. "No! Grab the gate." My body trembled. I needed to concentrate. Remain in control. I clenched the iron bars tighter.

Amber's eyes met mine. Groaning, she released her grip from around my neck and wrapped her fingers around the iron poles. Her body undulated under me as I kept my distance, not wanting to crush her. She tried to pull me closer wrapping her arm around my waist.

I released a growl. My fangs slid down instinctively admiring her full figure popping out as her dress moved down her chest. *Fuck.* Gripping the bars tighter, she continued to rub her body near me and then back up against the bars. Her head rolled opening up her inviting neck. Turning away from her, I fixated on the tiki torch next to us. *Concentrate.*

"Uh, uh, ohhhhhhhh," her body jerked. Her hand yanked the front of my shirt. Buttons flew off. I refused to meet her release, breathing into my exposed chest.

She embraced me warmly caressing my back. The bars bent under my grip. My soul deeply embedded hers. She continued to undulate and moan. I groaned. Amber in turn moaned louder. Giving in, I locked eyes with hers as my waist thrust into hers pinning her against the gate. She moaned louder, dropping her head against my chest. She tossed her head to the side introducing me to her neck again.

Bending my head back toward the open sky, I roared, "Argggggghhhhhhhh," popping an iron bar from the gate, continuing to pin her with my waist, clenching the bars with one wobbling in hand. Her breath slowed, and my grip loosened. She let go of me, propping herself up with clenched hands on the fence. I stabbed the broken bar into the earth allowing my hand to cup her face.

Her hazel eyes softened and her shoulders hunched forward. My thumb brushed over her lips, and I turned her face away from me exposing her neck. *Focus.* I longed for a taste. To turn her. Her breath slowed as she let go of the bars and wrapped her arms around my back.

My grip loosened, tempted by her flesh. I couldn't let go, not yet. I couldn't lose control.

Amber rubbed my back commanding my muscles to relax. Weakening, my body slid to the ground, pulling her down with me. She embraced me as I wrapped my arms around her petite figure and took in each of her breaths.

It was done. We were united. Partially.

CHAPTER 21

AMBER

Silence under the starlit sky, embraced by Gabe, and united. A peace inside sat like a calm lake, widespread and eager for someone to penetrate the surface. I brushed my hand over his abs as he remained still, flexing only when my nails teased his skin. He unwrapped my hair allowing it to fall to the side. Wiggling loose, I propped myself up on his chest as he looked down his nose at me. *One … two …* I counted to thirty waiting for him to take a breath. When he finally did, with my ear to his chest, I heard a faint tapping sound as if on glass.

"How am I, doc?" he said.

"Well, I can barely hear your heartbeat. It's a rather abnormal tick actually. It's best if we get you to a hospital."

Gabe's eyes popped open. "I don't do hospitals."

"Really? Well, that's too bad because I have a really cute nurse's costume at home. We could …"

He sat up forcing me to my knees. "Now that I think about it, I could use a thorough examination by a beautiful nurse like you."

"I'm sure you could."

He pulled me on top of him; my dress hiked up as I adjusted my legs over his waist. "What do you want to examine next?"

I hovered over his mouth, brushing my lips against his. "Show me your fangs again."

"Ahhhh, the fangs." He rolled his head back. "Those are not to play with."

"But they're so sexy."

"Are they?"

"Very." My lips captured his bottom lip.

"Maybe another time," Gabe flipped me onto my back. My heart sped up as he circled his tongue around my neck, teasing. I closed my eyes in anticipation of his fangs piercing my flesh. The night sky hovered over us. His lips pressed against my skin shot twinges of desire through my core.

"Mmm, I ..." Reaching my hand in between his legs, he pulled back. "I want you to bite me." I brushed my thumb along his zipper.

"I can't bite you." He grabbed my hand pinning it to the grass.

Looking over at his large hand holding mine to the earth, I whispered, "You can."

"No. I can't." He kissed my chin.

"Why not?"

"Do you want me to turn you?"

His eyes pleaded for me to say yes. I parted my lips wanting to give him the answer he'd like to hear, but no words came out. I sighed. "Can't you just drink from me?"

Gabe kissed my nose. "No. Not without consequences. Turn vamp and I will."

"I want to know what it feels like. What happens if you bite me?"

Gabe released my hand to brush my forehead. "You'd go mad. You'd be desperate for me and go mad. If that happened, I would either have to turn you or let you die."

I knew in the depths of my soul that we were meant to be together. A quake shook through me as he had pinned me to the gate. No other man, or immortal, had ever made me feel what he made me feel. My body yearned for him to complete the transition. I wasn't about to tell Gabe that yet. My mind needed to take a moment to grasp all that just happened.

"Are you still with me?" Gabe's eyes softened and he sucked his lips inward.

A cloud passed over the moon. A heaviness trapped me beneath him. A sudden sensation of suffering. I tightened my eyes. "Yes. I'm with you. No biting." Inside, a tearing sensation divided my attention between his warm embrace and his body trapping me in place. Attempting to push through this roller coaster of emotions, I asked, "Should I be worried about them coming out during a kiss?"

"No. It can happen, but I'm careful. I've had lots of practice."

I raised my eyebrow. *Practice.*

"That's not what I meant. I meant that I can control when they come out."

I tried to push Gabe off, but he didn't budge. Huffing, "So how much practice have you had? With me ... my soul? Other women?" I clenched my fist bringing it to my forehead. The thought of him with another woman, even if she had my soul, contracted all my muscles. An irrational thought of a woman with long braids riding him—and one of a woman with a plump backside pressed into his groin, and another with his head buried between two dark-skinned legs—trampled into my mind. Hunting down these women and breaking their necks with my bare hands swept through my head with ease.

"Amber, it doesn't matter. Does it? How much practice have you had?" He rolled off me and onto his back. A sudden relief lifted my shoulders off the ground as I sat up clasping my arms around my knees, turning my head toward the blackness just beyond the gate.

Fair question. Changing the subject, I asked, "How many times have we met, Gabe?"

"This is the fourth time. I met you, Catori, in 1773."

"That's a long time ago." His age felt distant in the presence of his young frame. "Tell me more about her."

"Amber, it's best if I don't tell you much about your past."

"Why not? I can handle it."

"Yes, I have no doubt you can handle it. It's just …" He sat up next to me. "I don't want to tell you about Catori because I want to get to know you, Amber. I can tell you everything about my past and her and the other reincarnations of her … you. But I don't want to. Not yet. With every reincarnation, a soul grows. You are definitely not the same person you were back then, but you will always have certain natural qualities that remain."

Admiring him, I got distracted by his full lips while trying to make sense of what he said. I put my hands to my face and closed my eyes as his fingers slid up my arm. He rubbed my back sending heat into my chest, calming and warming me inside. Ever since I met him, my temperature had remained hot. I straightened my legs, reached for my toes, and sat back up to face him. "Gabe, what was this uniting all about anyhow? I know that it's one step closer to turning …"

He wrapped his arm around me and whispered in my ear, "You're mine, Amber." Inciting a passion at the sound of his claim. His breath taunted me as he left his nose in the crevice of my ear, nuzzling it. My body quivered. I turned to face him, and his eyes hooked mine. He climbed on top, cupping my head as he lay me back down onto the earth. His cocky smile watched my eyes as he positioned his body in between my legs, forcing them to spread. "You promised me."

Breathless. "Promised what?"

"That you want me and only me." He brushed his mouth against my lips as my hands reached around his shoulder blades. "Can you handle that, Amber? Being mine?"

My head swirled. The question seemed so simple, but I really didn't know how to answer. My body and soul betrayed my mind. His words hit me as if he had tricked me into submission. But I didn't submit. I couldn't.

Gabe's breath on my chest distracted me. "I want to know you. Every part of you." His hand moved up my thigh.

"I want to know you, too." Now my mouth betrayed me. Resisting him was impossible. He was home. His thumb found the seam of my satin and tugged gently. Like teetering on the edge of a roller coaster's highest peak, I held my breath for what was next.

His head jerked to the house.

Sensing his distress, my hand skimmed along his shoulder. "Gabe?"

"We've got to go."

"What? Now?"

"Now, Amber. Let's go."

I pushed myself into a seated position. Gabe had his cell in hand. "Sal, we have company! Yep." Gabe hung up.

"What's going on?"

Gabe pulled me up. "There's no time for me to explain." The rush of the swift motion of him sweeping me over his shoulder didn't compare to the speed he used to run us back into the house. I felt woozy from hanging upside down.

As he leaped into the air landing on the balcony of the second floor, my stomach moved to the back of my throat. Even though I should have felt like a rag doll being tossed around, his grip secured me so that my body barely moved.

As he sat me down on a bed, I said, "Gabe, what's going on?" I clutched my forehead trying to make the room stop spinning, and the brightly lit room didn't help.

"You have to trust me right now. You're in danger."

"What?"

"Listen, I'm going to protect you."

Sal knocked on the door and then entered holding what looked like incense, a spray bottle, and stones.

"Do you have it?" Gabe asked.

"Yes, here." Sal passed Gabe a necklace.

"Keep this on you. Don't take it off!" Gabe commanded as he fastened a thick purple amethyst stone hanging from a leather band around my neck.

I nodded, recognizing angst in his eyes.

Sal rushed about spritzing. Gabe lit a candle on the dresser.

"Romantic," I whispered under my breath.

Gabe looked at me scowling. "I wish it were." He walked back over to me grabbing my waist. "Listen. Everything will be fine, but you must do *exactly* what I say. Promise?"

I agreed.

"A man … vampire is coming, and I will try to keep him out of the house. No matter what, you stay locked in this room. Got it?"

"Okay."

He grabbed my chin. "Don't blow that out." He pointed to the candle. "This is serious, Amber. If he finds out about you …" Gabe brushed his hands through his hair. "He can't find out about you yet."

I stood silently watching his commanding certainty and concern over me. "This is your room. You'll have everything you need in here. And Sal brought your purse. It's over there. He pointed to a comfy armchair next to the entrance of the bedroom.

My bedroom?

"No phone calls please. He can hear conversations just like I can. Don't even mumble until we give you the okay. There's a mini-fridge in the corner as well."

"How long do you think you'll be gone?" I eyed the fridge.

"I don't know. When this is over, I'll come for you."

I nodded and crossed my arms as Gabe kissed my forehead.

He grabbed Sal and pushed him out of the room. He turned once more, "Lock behind me."

I scurried to the door, pushed Gabe out, and did as he said. I walked over to the candle burning on the dresser and breathed in the familiar citrus and green tea scent. With disheveled hair and a stone not matching my dress, I silently asked myself, *What have I gotten myself into?*

CHAPTER 22

GABE

I flew down to the foyer and rushed out the door with keys in my hand. Recognizing the sound of a Ferrari revving up in the driveway, I positioned myself next to my Audi pretending I was getting in. I scanned the area. Sal must've moved Amber's car to the garage. I opened the door to step in as he pulled up alongside me, always flashing a new toy as if overcompensating.

Vance stepped out of his car. Despite his bright shirt, his inner darkness matched that of the night. "Going somewhere, brother?" He closed the door.

"What brings you here?" I stepped away from my vehicle as he approached me for a friendly gestured greeting.

"Oh. You know. A little of this, a little of her." He eyed me suspiciously.

I sniffed and realized I'd forgotten to change my clothing with Amber's scent.

"You smell fresh." His nose twitched, and he looked at the house.

"I learned from the best."

"Ain't that the truth." He brushed his knuckles across his chest as if he were a master with women. He was only a master at using his bite to seduce them. "Aren't you going to invite me in?" Vance continued staring at the house.

"I was just heading out."

He tilted his head squinting at me, "How about a glass of O-negative first?"

I squeezed the keys in my hand knowing I had no choice. If I refused to let him in, he'd know something was up. "Can't promise O but yeah, come on in."

He patted my back as we walked toward the front door. Sal awaited us to ensure he was in position if things got out of hand.

"Sal. It's been a long time."

"Yes, Master Vance."

"This guy always cracked me up," Vance said slapping the back of his hand on Sal's shoulder. "Master Vance."

Sal stiffened, closing the door behind us.

"Would you mind getting us some beverages?" I asked Sal.

"Certainly." Sal walked to the kitchen.

Vance strutted for the library, and I followed closely behind him. "So, how's our collection? Oh wow." He took in a deep breath as he entered. "Same as always, remarkable!"

I watched him carefully trying to trace the scent of Amber back to the house. I grabbed one of my newest acquisitions to distract him, the quill from the Lewis and Clark expedition.

"Brother." He tenderly handled the relic. "Lewis and Clark?"

"Yep."

"Incredible. I've been searching for this one for years. Why didn't you tell me sooner?"

"I just received it last week." This was an honest statement, but I was never going to call and tell him about it.

"I knew I left my collection in good hands." He put his hand on my shoulder as I raised my eyebrow at him.

Sal walked in with two goblets of blood on a tray. I reached for my favorite goblet and handed Vance the other. Sal winked at me. *Ahhhh. So, he'd spelled Vance's drink.* This would keep him from tracking Amber.

"To quills," I raised my glass.

"To quills," Vance raised his and chugged down the blood. I followed suit. We both handed our goblets back to Sal, and he exited the room.

"How long will you be in town for this time?"

"I don't know. A day, three, a month. One never can tell."

"Huh. You know we don't need your oversight here. We've got things under control."

"That doesn't seem to be the case, and you know it. Antonio and Holly have all kinds of problems they aren't dealing with."

"If you'd just give them space to handle the business, you wouldn't have these problems."

"You should respect your elders," Vance stood tall and then took a step back into a fighting stance.

"You're finally admitting you're old," I smirked. It was childish. Vance blew a gasket at any mention of his age. A human trait he'd never learned to quell. But distracting him meant he wouldn't go looking for Amber.

The tell-tale tick in his jaw gave me enough warning. But his reflexes were faster than my reaction.

"Argh," Vance charged at me, flying us into the spiral staircase that led to the reading nook, and then flew me into the floor. The staircase fell over onto the floor, nearly crushing us as we rolled out of the way.

I scrambled to my feet, balled my fists, and charged back at him, flying him out of the library and crashing him into the mirror at the entrance of the foyer. Shards of glass scattered all over the floor. I only hoped that Amber would stay locked in her room.

Securing my arm against his throat, "You will not bring destruction into my home."

Vance pushed me off him, and I landed on the first step of the staircase in the foyer. We walked toward one another, meeting each other in the middle of the room.

He smirked, "I was just messing around. You're on edge, brother." He squinted at me, and then looked toward the second floor.

Sal stood near the dining room waiting for me to give him a signal.

I straightened up. "You know how serious I am about the library. You gave it to me for a reason." I walked back into it making note of the damage.

"Send me the bill," Vance scoffed while patting my back.

I looked over my shoulder, gritted my teeth. "Get. Out."

He backed away slowly. "Well. It was lovely, brother. I'll see you around." He walked toward the front door.

I followed him out to make sure he left. I stood with my arms by my side, ready as I watched his mischievous glide back to his obnoxious green car. As much as I hated him, there was always a gnawing reminder inside that we were connected. And that would be difficult to explain to Amber. She's already been exposed to too much tonight. *The story of Vance and Gabe can wait a bit longer.*

As he shifted into a slow crawl around the circular driveway, he looked up at my home. When Vance's curiosity was piqued, it always meant trouble. And no doubt, he wouldn't back down easily.

CHAPTER 23

———

GABE

From the second floor in the foyer, I assessed the damage from my tussle with Vance. The mirror, now scattered about the floor in hundreds of pieces, lay like a memento of how often he created chaos in the midst of monumental moments of history in my drawn-out vampire lifetime.

His theatrics go as far back as the time he found Holly and me in the bell tower at the Centennial celebration of July 4, 1876. That was Holly's first introduction to my maker. He managed to ruffle her feathers in a matter of minutes. Even back then, my soul became frantic in his presence, especially since he had killed our soul mate, Lina, once again only thirteen years prior.

With every Vance encounter, my soul created an edge within me that forced illogical responses to his provoking behaviors, like those of one being instigated by an older brother as if it were the last straw each time. This time it was different though. A power deep within stirred like no other. Because I knew this time would be different with Amber. Vance wasn't going to take her from us again. But the dread hung over us at the possibility that he could.

After knocking with no answer, I placed my hand on the doorknob and twisted the lock open with my mind, finding Amber tucked under the covers asleep. The soft light of the candle glow flickered in the mirror. Sal's magic worked. I left it burning to be on the safe side despite no longer feeling Vance nearby. Undressing to my briefs, I slid into the bed next to her nestling my body against her warm, smooth skin. She had found one of the nightgowns I had bought for her—short like the one I saw her wearing as she danced in her kitchen. I moved my hand along her thigh and around her waist, pulling her to me.

She grabbed my hand and muttered, "Everything alright?"

I whispered in her ear, "Fine. Get some rest." My heart pounded hard with her ass pressed into me. It would be painfully challenging to resist starting where we left off so not to disturb her. It was already near three o'clock in the morning. Instead of thinking about our souls uniting earlier, I allowed my thoughts to drift to the night Amber and I actually met for the first time at Antonio's mansion a week ago. It had been close to a century since our souls' last encounter.

"So, you were watching me?" She twisted just enough for me to open my frame towering over her as she looked up at me standing next to the bar.

The crowded lounge buzzed with conversation, techno music, and shakers as Frank mixed cocktails. I sipped my wine and pulled the glass down slowly while her hazels drew me in more. "I was."

"Why?" she asked.

"Why not?"

She smiled. "Should I be worried about this?" She lifted her glass.

"Worried?" I realized she wondered whether or not I dropped a roofie of some sort into her drink. I lowered my

*voice leaning into her ear, "Amber, I wouldn't need a drug if I
wanted to seduce you."*

*Her painted pink lips opened slightly as she caught her
breath. Her sweet scent permeated our space as her skin glistened. She swayed. Our bodies lost a sense of coordination
when we neared each other over the centuries.*

*"Do you want to sit down?" I pulled a barstool out and
offered it to her.*

*She leaned her hands on the stool emphasizing her voluptu-
ous figure, snuggly fit into her black halter top dress. "Actually,
I'm gonna hit the dance floor." She circled herself around the
stool. "Well. It's been fun."*

*My natural inclination was to pull her into me, but I
stepped back and rubbed my hand through my hair.* Damn.

She took a step closer and cupped my cheek. "See you around."

*My hand covered hers and her body quivered as I held
her in place for a moment taking in her beauty. I brought her
fingertips to my lips. "See you."*

*Amber took slow, calculated steps back from me while
withdrawing her hand. As she walked toward the ballroom,
she sat the glass of wine I gave her on an empty cocktail table
along the way.*

Go to her, *my soul commanded.*

*Amber wiped her hand on the back of her neck, and then
drew it down the side of her dress. I watched her until she was
completely out of view.* Let's give her a minute. She won't last
long on the dance floor tonight.

* *

Amber snuck out of bed at sunrise not realizing that I hadn't
slept all night. Vampires don't need sleep. I watched her sway
into the bathroom. A few minutes later, the shower turned

on. I threw the covers off, dropped my briefs, and followed her. Her silhouette teased me through the steamed glass.

She sang "Ave Maria," a church hymn from my past, as she lathered her arms.

Is Catori trying to tell us something? I said to my soul.

No answer.

Now you're short for words? I pulled my briefs back up and lay down on the bed. The water turned off, and a few minutes later, she walked out wrapped in a towel with her lavender bra straps showing.

She caught me staring. "Good morning," I said.

"Morning." She looked away tightening the grip on the towel as she walked to the closet.

So hard to resist her. I stood up, followed her, and watched as she pulled up a pair of black leggings over her matching lavender lace. Her breasts perfectly secured in the bra. "Where are you running off to?"

Amber jumped as she reached for a blouse off the hanger. "You startled me, Gabe. Are you always so quiet?"

"No." I moved closer to her and wrapped my arms around her. "I like to make noise in other circumstances."

She blushed and looked down.

I pulled her chin up. "You have a beautiful voice."

"Thank you." Her breasts pressed into my chest, distracting me. "Wait. Did you come into the bathroom while I was in the shower?"

"I did."

Her lips pecked my chest.

My nose brushed her temple, forcing her eyes to meet mine. "So, I'll ask you again." I hovered my lips over hers. "Where are you going?"

"I've got a date with Grams."

I moved my mouth to her ear. "The psychic medium?"

Amber's heart raced. "Yes."

"What if I said no?"

"Gabe, please." She pushed me away, placing her hand on her hip.

I lifted her in my arms, and she gasped as I ran her to the bed and crawled on top of her, pinning her arms over her head.

She attempted to move her hands, but she couldn't. "I really must go. Besides, I take it I'm safe, right?"

"For now." I brushed my free hand over her abs.

"Oh, Gabe." She arched her back. "I really have to go."

"Maybe I can change your mind." My lips brushed over her bra.

"It's hard enough for me to leave you here this morning, especially because you owe me an explanation about what happened last night."

Amber searched my face, and I released her. She watched me as I bent over to pick up my sweats and slid them on. I walked into the closet and grabbed her blouse passing it to her. Plopping down next to her, I sighed. "You're right. I owe you an explanation." I grabbed her hand as she bent her leg on the bed, twisting toward me.

"Who was he?"

"Vance Hastings. He's a very old vampire and is extremely powerful."

"So, he just shows up randomly from time to time?"

"Yes."

She stood up to collect her things, and looked at her cell. "Gabe, I as always, have lots of questions, and it seems like not enough time. You were quite intense last night. Candles, spells, oils, the necklace." Amber reached for her neck and realized she wasn't wearing it. She walked into the bathroom to retrieve it. As she came back out, she held it up. "I assume I need to wear this today as well."

"Yes."

"Were you cloaking my presence?"

"Yes, and more. I don't want him to know how special you are to me yet." She clasped the necklace in place. I stood up and took her hands in mine. "I won't let him hurt you."

"I don't even understand why he'd want to hurt me. Besides, I was untouchable last night."

I raised an eyebrow at her.

"I said a protection spell prior to coming over."

"Did you now?" *So full of surprises. Shit. How will I know what worked then?* "I need you to come back to me tonight." I brushed her cheek with my thumb. "Will you do that?"

Amber nodded again as she passed her fingers over the brand on my chest—two swords in the shape of a V. I grabbed her purse and handed it to her. As we walked down the stairs, she looked down at the cracked mirror splayed about like a crime scene.

At the bottom step, she stopped and turned to me. "What happened?"

"Complications." I half smiled.

Grabbing my hand, she pulled me close. "How did I not hear anything last night?"

"Sal had a special concoction for you. In the candle. To calm you and help you sleep."

"You didn't trust me?"

"No. No, it's not that."

"It's exactly that." She yanked her hand from mine and stepped briskly to the door. Just as she cracked it open, I slammed it shut and entrapped her body between my arms. Her cheek pressed against the door, her back pressed into my chest, as my mouth hovered over her ear. Her lips quivered holding back tears.

I whispered, "You have to trust me." I kissed her cheek, and she closed her eyes. "I know what I'm doing with Vance. Vampires don't play by the rules. I can't lose you." I snuggled my face into her neck and wrapped an arm around her waist. "You're my world. My home."

Amber turned to face me leaning her back on the door. "What if he'd come upstairs, and I was knocked out? How would I have defended myself?" A tear dropped down her cheek.

"Well, apparently you took care of that with your spell, right?" As she rolled her eyes, I knew my sarcasm was unwelcome. A heaviness sat upon my chest. And at the same time, her own precautions against me demonstrated her wisdom even though it trampled on my pride. "I'm sorry." I wiped her tear away and embraced her face in my hands. "There wasn't enough time to explain. And I know it was wrong not to include you in on the plan."

"To drug me."

"I didn't drug you. It was ..." *Well, you got me there.* I guess it was like drugging her. She put her head down, and I stepped back.

"I've gotta go."

I nodded.

Amber turned and opened the door. Sal had pulled her car around. He must have eavesdropped on our conversation. When we reached her car, Amber turned to face me. "I shouldn't be gone long." Rage still rolled across her face as she faked a smile.

"Okay." I pulled her close. "Forgive me." I gently placed my lips on hers, slowly tugging. Our mouths connected and our tongues slowed to meet one another with intention. She softened, melting into me more. The craving for her essence overwhelmed me. My fangs slid into place. My tongue continued down her neck and over to her ear, tracing a line to her chin. We took light breaths in between each lingering kiss. Jolts of ecstasy shivered down my body. When I pulled back, Amber's eyes opened slowly.

"You sure know how to make it hard for a girl to stay mad," Amber said. I smiled, nodding. She got into her car and drove away. As I watched her, the heaviness grew worse as if a thousand men had piled on top of me pressing me into the earth. I wondered if she'd return. If not, I'd have to seek her out tonight. For her safety and my own selfish desires.

CHAPTER 24

———

AMBER

The early morning drive from the mountains to Grams's house in Carlsbad was intense. What should have taken two hours, took three and a half. Not only did I have to deal with the stress of weekend commuters, but also the sunken heart gnawing at me to return to him. I assumed the uniting ceremony had solidified some sort of bond between us.

A festering anxiety sat within my chest at the thought of us being bound together. "You promised me," lingered in my thoughts. Committed. That's what we were. I rolled down my window.

"You have to trust me." The words he had spoken clouded my mind, causing me to swerve from hitting a parked car in Grams's neighborhood. The early morning calm of her street embraced me as I passed neighbors walking their dogs. Each home decorated with a coastal vibe and different color siding.

Shaking my head lightly, attempting to settle my thoughts, more rushed in: A dedicated room in his home with a closet full of clothing that fit me perfectly. Pressed against an iron gate while drawn into Gabe's desire. A powerful vampire that wants to hurt me. Spells and amethyst. My fingers tugged at the stone hanging around my neck. Protection masked in candlelight. *Super messed up.* I don't like feeling out of control. And this roller coaster has me gripping the bar, back pressed against the seat with unsettled anticipation. But when I am with him, I am home.

Not being able to call Jennifer about this one left me feeling disconnected from my life before being lured into a world of vampires. And I hadn't been truthful to Gabe about coming back to his home tonight. I parked my car along the street in front of her house. *You got this.* Walking up to her door, I considered how I would break it to her. *Hey Grams. I met my soul mate. Oh, by the way, he's also a vampire.* Closing my eyes tight, I knocked with an exhale. Shifting, I gently caressed the stone around my neck, uncertain whether I was consoling it or it was consoling me.

Grams yelled out, "I'm coming," and the door swung open. "Good morning, baby." She kissed my cheek and pulled me in by the hand.

"Morning, Grams." The door slammed behind me.

"Let's get you to the back. Come on, now."

"It was a long ride, can I …"

"No. Come on, now." She continued tugging me along, and I nearly lost my shoe in the hallway. Hanging beads separated the workroom from the hall, and she parted the strings as we walked through them. Sage simmered in a pot and a table was set with candles. She guided me to lie down on my back in between them.

"Grams?"

"Shh. I need you to be still. I feel a powerful spirit in your presence. Rage, passion, anxiety, desperation."

This presence she mentioned wasn't one that I felt. It was how I felt.

I lay still trying not to knock a candle onto the ground. She lifted my blouse slightly. I winced as she placed a cold stone on my stomach. She laid another on my forehead. She pulled off my shoes and laid stones on my ankles. I wanted to speak but knew better. She had done this to me a few times over the years. This time, I needed to make sure I wasn't losing my mind. I needed to surrender to her completely.

Grams began to sprinkle lilac powder into the air above me forcing me to close my eyes. When I opened them back up, her palm hovered over my face. She stood for a moment and moved slowly down to the center of my chest and paused. She moved further down and paused over my pelvis. Finally, she ended at my feet. She stepped back and around toward the center of my body. She began chanting, waving her hands in the air. She shook. Her head rolled back, and then she fell forward onto my stomach, panting.

"Grams!" I tried to sit up but couldn't move. "Grams."

She didn't move.

"Grams, speak to me."

"Thank you for helping me find Gabe." My head locked in place. I followed her with my eyes as she hung her head over my face. Her hand brushed my cheek. "He's still so handsome. So much the same as when I'd known him long ago."

"Catori?"

"Yes." My muscles contracted, but I was still unable to move.

"I have so many questions. Gabe says I'm in danger."

Grams's body moved over to the side and put her hand on mine. "You are in danger."

"What can I do about it?"

"There's not much you can do but become a vampire and fully unite with Gabe this time."

"I'm not sure I'm ready for that." Grams let go of my hand and walked away, closer to the sage burning on the table. My eyes strained to follow her.

"We need to help Gabe. It's the only way. His only way out."

"I still don't understand. Out of what?"

"He wants to be free. You are the only one who can help free him." She walked back over to me standing at the tip of my head looking down. She placed her hands on my cheeks. A warmth rushed through my body. "I want to thank you for allowing me to unite with his soul."

"What was that about anyhow?"

"It allows for a new union in this life. It's a vow. It helps … ahhh." Her head rolled forward and her shoulders hunched over. "Ahh. Amber, your grandmother can't hold … ahh."

"Catori. Don't leave yet. I have so many questions." My heart pounded. "What does it help with?"

With Grams's head dangling over me and chin tucked into her chest, she squealed as if trying to hold on longer, "Watch out for Gabe's maker. And don't trust—"

"His maker?"

"Yes, ahhhhhh." Grams dropped to the ground.

"Catori? Grams?" Pins and needles along my skin released the paralyzed grip the table had on me. I pushed up and slid off, careful not to knock the candles over. The stones clanked against her hardwood floor. I dropped to her side.

"Baby, I'm alright. I just need to lie here a moment."

"Grams."

"I'm alright."

I hugged her and then ran to the kitchen to grab a water. When I came back, she had propped herself up straight.

"Baby, you've got some history with this reincarnated soul. Aren't you the lucky one?"

I handed her the water. "I don't know, am I?"

"Yes." She took a sip, hands shaking. "Yes, I'll say."

"What do you remember?"

"Bits and pieces. There's some uncertainty. Reservation or warning. I'm not quite sure. I had glimpses into your soul's past lives. You were an artisan, a dancer, and painter. You were a pioneer for female artists making it all the way to Paris in the 1800s. It was incredible. Gabe is a constant for this one. And, ooh-wee is he sexy, baby girl."

"That he is." I laughed with relief that her humor was in tack.

"He's dangerous for you though." Her tone dropped.

"Grams, he's a …"

"Vampire. Yes. I know. And you've died each time at his maker's hand."

The gravity of her words felt as if someone reached in, grabbed my heart, and squeezed. I sat crisscross next to her. "Each time?" *What are my chances this time?* "What am I going to do? Catori wants me to let him turn me."

She grabbed my hand. "Amber, I don't want to lose you. I've already suffered so much loss. But this decision is yours."

I closed my eyes wishing she had just told me what to do. Her hand squeezed mine.

"Have you ever met a vampire?" I asked.

"Yes, I have. At least I think so. Only once. When I first started my practice. I remember a man coming in. Could've been Native American or Mexican. It was hard to tell. I remember his humble eyes. He asked me if I had any blood-stone. And, at that time, I didn't have many stones. When I said no, his humility turned into disappointment masked by anger. He showed me some sharp teeth, while growling on about how I should always carry bloodstone and stormed out. From that point on, I have carried it. No one has asked since."

"Grams, that's what makes vampires whole, so to speak. It completes their transition."

"Well, well. Look who's learned something overnight," Grams said.

I smiled and gently slapped her knee.

"I've got some investigating to do before you wander off. Good thing you'll be with me all weekend," Grams's tone turned to a threat.

I scrunched my face remembering Gabe's request for me to return. But a yoga retreat with Grams is just what I needed at this time. I could just text him.

"Drink," I insisted as beads of sweat fell from her temple.

She took a sip. "Now help an old lady up."

I smiled, grabbed her arm, and helped her to her feet.

"And, Amber. Don't call him while I'm gone either." She walked through the hanging beads and into her living room. I followed.

"Why can't I call him? Can I text—"

"Give me your phone." She dug into my purse that sat on her velvety golden chair.

"Grams!" I grabbed the purse out of her hands and placed it on the coffee table. "I'll find it."

I pulled out my cell and a text from Gabe popped up. **How's your aura? Miss you. Come back soon.**

I bit down on my lip. "How about one text just to …"

"Give me that girl." She walked up behind me. "You can't be so available."

I placed it in her palm. "If I had a man who looked like that waiting for me, well … mmm. Is it getting hot in here?" She started fanning her face. "Don't worry, you'll get it back."

Shit.

CHAPTER 25

AMBER

Turning into the parking garage, I placed my hand upon my belly as the butterflies fluttered. Most of the parking spots sat empty on a Monday morning. Many of my neighbors had already left for work.

The retreat was a tech-free event. Each time I had reached for my phone due to feeling ghostly vibrations on my ass, I rolled my eyes at the fact that I had become so addicted to it. By night, I submitted to the lack of technology. Grams and I sat quietly poolside under the moonlight when she brought up her research into vampires. Her community didn't share anything more than having heard a rumor about them living among us. She told me she knew some of them were lying.

Being with Grams gave me a sense of normalcy; it brought me back to how life was before I met Gabe. Yet there was an internal strain not allowing me to put Gabe out of my head. Most likely Catori's influence, now that I knew she was inside of me. And that just flipped my world upside down. Learning that a soul with previous lives was influencing me in some oddly specific way. And grappling with identity took on a whole new meaning.

When Grams handed me the phone this morning on my way out, I had five voicemails and numerous texts. But nothing from him past noon on Saturday. Seemed odd. Was he mad at me or just giving me space? Being lured into his world, although exciting, took me off the sidelines and into a game I had no experience in. I just wasn't ready to call him yet. A flicker of doubt crossed my mind as I wondered if I should have driven straight to his house instead of coming home to get ready for work. The phone hostage situation over the weekend promised to create tension between Gabe and me. And now that I knew about his maker, I couldn't stop looking over my shoulder.

Desire hummed through my body as I approached my apartment door. I'd always gotten this way when Gabe was nearby. I looked over my shoulder but saw no one. *Strange.*

Grams warned me to take caution. She also confirmed that soul mates cannot be denied each other. It's an unbreakable bond.

You're mine. You promised me. Shallow breaths took over as I inserted the key and looked behind me again. No one there. I turned back toward the door, unlocked, and entered peering into the hall as I closed the door and locked it quickly. Pressing my forehead into the door, visions of Gabe's lips, neck, chest, forearms flashed through my mind like a flip book. *Maybe I should call him.*

Dry air, like inhaling the scent of roasted coffee, made breathing harder, and warmth overwhelmed me. *That damn air conditioner.* I wiped my brow, and I acknowledged my rapid pulse and the heat building up between my legs. *Jesus.* The thermostat on the wall read a comfortable seventy-two like usual. "It can't be seventy-two in here." I threw my purse down on the couch and looked at myself in the mirrored walls lining the living room. "Ugh!" I tossed my curls. *Definitely need to change quickly before work.* I walked toward the hallway to my bedroom.

"I missed you."

Startled, I swung around holding my heart to face Gabe standing beside the sliding glass door of the balcony. "Geez, Gabe! You scared the hell out of me. How did you …?"

He sped toward me pulling me into his arms. "You scared the hell out of me, Amber. When you didn't text or call back, I thought …" He leaned his forehead against mine. "I thought he'd found you."

"Who? Your maker?"

Gabe pulled back searching my hazels. "How do you know about my maker?"

"Catori told me."

Gabe stepped back, sat on the arm of the couch, and stared at me. "Catori told you? You can hear her?"

"No. Grams … I mean. Catori jumped into Grams and spoke to me."

"What did she say?"

"She said you were handsome." I reached my hand and brushed his face. "She also said that I need to watch out for your maker."

He sighed. "She's right, Amber." He pulled me to him wrapping his arms around my waist. "When I didn't hear from you, I thought Vance got to you, so I went over to your grandma's house. When I saw you were safe, I had Sal keep tabs on you just in case."

I stepped back from him placing my hands on my hips. "First off, how do you know where Grams lives anyhow? And second, Sal was watching me?"

"Sal was watching out for *him*." He stepped into my personal space, and I took more steps back, holding my arms out as if I could ward him off.

My eyes focused on his angular jaw that I longed to nibble on. *Focus.* "And Grams?"

He placed his hands around my wrists, brushing his thumb along my veins, causing me to melt a little more inside despite my fury. "I followed you."

"You don't trust me?" I yanked my arms, but he held me in place.

"I don't trust Vance."

"Your maker?"

"Yes."

I looked up at his furrowed brows. *He's worried.*

"I do trust you. But I will never trust Vance."

Stepping closer to him, he released my wrists allowing me to wrap my arms around him. I rubbed his back. "I'm sorry I scared you. Grams took my phone."

"I like her style," he said.

Speaking into his chest, "Treating me like a prisoner?"

"No. Protective."

"Overprotective." I let go of him. "Having someone spy on me does cross a line, Gabe. I'm not sure what's worse." *Will I ever have privacy again?*

"I won't compromise your safety." The doorbell rang, and he walked toward the door.

"This *is* my home," I sped up to cross him off, "I'll answer the door."

Standing behind me as I looked through the peephole, he said, "It's for me. I'm expecting a delivery."

A delivery? I opened the door. "Hello."

"Heh. Yeah, I've got a delivery for Ms. Jones." A bulky man dressed in uniform rested his hand on a dolly. I looked over my shoulder smirking that the delivery was for me even though I hadn't ordered anything.

"Thanks, but I didn't …"

"Come on in." Gabe opened the door gesturing for the man to come in. "The kitchen's right through here." The man followed.

He knows where my kitchen is. How long had he been here prior to my arrival? We followed the delivery man and he set the boxes on the floor next to the fridge.

"Thanks," Gabe said.

"Sign here." The man's hand shook as he handed Gabe the pen.

"Here you go." Gabe handed it back.

"Have a good day, sir," the man said not looking up at us as he dragged his cart out of the kitchen while Gabe followed him to the door.

What exactly did he have delivered? I grabbed a knife and opened the box. Gabe walked in as I lifted a bag of blood into my hands. "Just curious about what you're bringing into my home." I raised my eyebrow at him.

He grabbed my waist pulling me into him. "I need sustenance," he whispered over my mouth. I quivered, feeling my knees buckle. I placed my free hand on his arms to steady myself. "Sangre." He smiled, lifting his eyebrows twice.

"Right." Heat filled my cheeks. I backed off leaning myself up against the countertop. He unloaded the blood into the refrigerator. When the box was empty, I handed him the one still in my hand.

"Now I see why your Grams is overprotective. You live like a bachelorette."

I laughed, "I know. It's terrible, huh?"

"Unacceptable. But leaves me plenty of space for my stash," he said half smiling. "I'll have Sal go shopping."

"It's not necessary, really."

"It's absolutely necessary."

"I'm not home much."

Gabe continued to empty the boxes ignoring my comment.

"It would've been nice if you'd discussed this with me first." I crossed my arms.

He stacked the empty boxes on the kitchen table. "Perhaps. But I need to ensure your safety, and this is one way."

My safety? From him? I hadn't really considered him hurting me.

"Do you have a key for me?"

"A key? Seems like you don't really have a need for a key."

"For Sal. I want to tuck it someplace safe for him."

I walked over to him and grabbed his hand. "I have an extra, but it really isn't …"

He pinned me against his chest while looking down at me. "Nonnegotiable, Amber."

"Are you always this stubborn?"

Smiling, he nodded.

I sighed. "It's in that drawer next to the fridge."

"Thank you." He kissed me on the forehead. Pulling back, he drew me in with his dark eyes. "Aren't you going to be late for work?"

"Probably. How do you know? Did you check up on my work schedule, too?"

"Whether you like it or not, I'm going to watch over you like a hawk. Your life's at risk and he's not going to …"

"Kill me this time?" I pushed away from him moving toward the cabinet. I pulled out a glass, filling it with water. A chair scratched against the tile as Gabe took a seat at the table. Turning to face him, his chin sat on his palm as he watched me.

"So, you know more than I thought you would by now."

"Yeah. So, stop keeping me in the dark. Just tell me the truth. If we're supposed to be partners, treat me like a partner."

He nodded knocking his knuckles on the table. "You're right. I will be straight with you. We're a team." He stood up.

"Look, I've got to get dressed for work. You can wait for me or not." Placing my glass down on the table, I walked past him, but he grabbed my arm gently pulling me into him. His mouth landed on my neck. Electricity shot through me.

"I'll wait," he whispered.

His mouth tickled causing me to squirm. "Alright." I wiggled free and walked to my room.

I found a purple blouse to match the amethyst necklace, pulled up my jeans, and fixed my hair into a ponytail. The thought of Gabe having been in my apartment without me made me think of Jenn's warning. A vampire boyfriend has complicated my need for independence and privacy. As I slid into my sandals, I paused and scanned the room. A large crack behind my door on the wall caught my attention. *I don't remember that.*

Sighing, I grabbed my makeup bag, and met Gabe in the living room. He stood looking out of the floor to ceiling windows lining the wall. I tossed my bag on the couch next to my purse.

"I thought I had a nice view," Gabe said.

"It's pretty remarkable, isn't it?" I slid my hands around his steel-like abs and leaned my head against his back. *So tight.*

He stroked my hands. "I'm so lucky to have found you again."

I let go of him and huffed. "I'm going to be late."

He turned to face me, "What? What did I say?"

"It's just. You don't know me, Gabe. What if I can't live up to your standards? I'm not Catori."

"I know." He pulled my chin up to look at him. "You're *not* Catori. I know that." He kissed me softly. "I don't expect you to be."

"It's a lot to take in." A tear welled up in my eye.

"I know."

He held me as I shook my head wiping tears with so much to process. *Vampires, soul mates, someone wants to hurt me.*

"It's a lot. But I need you to trust me today," he said as he squeezed my arms softly. "I'm going to the studio with you. Vance will most likely show up there."

"What am I supposed to do if he does?"

"Wearing the necklace is a great start." His fingers brushed it gently. "Sal's been to the studio and Antonio's aware of the situation. You just can't engage with me today. Promise not to speak to me, look at me, or talk about me at all if Vance is around. He can hear every conversation just like I can."

I tugged my lip. *How am I supposed to restrain myself around Gabe?* "Should we drive separately?"

"No. I'm driving you there. I'll know if he's there when we arrive, and if he is, I have a backup plan."

"Seems risky."

"If Vance is still around by the end of your workday, just catch a ride home with Jennifer." He hugged me tightly. "Vance is dangerous, and I will protect you … us."

His bloodstone heart pattered like rain tapping on glass with my ear pressed against his chest. Catori told me about him needing my help. Relinquishing control was not my strong suit. Neither was accepting help.

I squeezed him tighter. "I'll do what you say." *And now I trust.*

CHAPTER 26

GABE

Amber sprayed me with the concoction that Sal had created for covering scents when we arrived at the studio. I lingered in the car for thirty minutes before going in. Antonio stood next to the director while set designers fluffed pillows and straightened coffee tables for the apartment décor. Camera operators slid into position. Pulling Antonio in with a bro-hug, he muttered under his breath to me, "Mierda, cabrón," and put his hand through his hair as if he were calculating the consequences of having Vance visit. The filming was coming to an end this week. He didn't need any drama outside of his regular Hollywood bullshit.

Amber worked on Zara's makeup behind the set at a makeshift station. One of the perks of being a vampire—compelling. The key makeup artist had no choice but to assign Amber to the external final touches station today. I'm sure she wondered why she wasn't working with Marco. I searched the studio for a place to sit. Barstools lined a counter in the back of the room behind Amber. A few director's chairs had been scattered around the studio. Standing near the doorway seemed like the best place to be until Vance arrived.

Before settling into position, I walked behind Amber testing her to see if she'd react. She stood straight up and looked at me as Zara rambled on about how nervous she was regarding this upcoming scene. I narrowed my eyes at her defiance, and she dropped her eyes back down fixating on Zara's eyebrows. On the way over to the studio, Amber had described to me that today's filming would be some of the more intense scenes—a timely discovery of Marco's character's infidelity.

Jennifer walked over and took a seat next to Zara waiting for her turn. I admired Amber's ability to engage with her clients. She had actors laughing in their chairs and also had a talent for making everyone look their parts. Zara's purple eye resembled that of a black eye I'd received once from Catori's fiancé. He'd caught on to my scandalous attraction to her and confronted me in the vineyard one morning.

I hissed through my teeth as my brand heated, distracting me from the memory. Vance's singing along to a popular punk band came into focus. He'd be here soon.

I texted Amber, **He's on his way.**

She pulled her phone out of her back pocket, read my text with no emotion, and slid it back in place. She wiped her hands along her jeans.

Vance arrived in his 1970s sunglasses and open-collar button-down shirt, swinging his keys around his fingers. Man, he loved that era.

He walked over to me and placed his hand on my shoulder. "Did you clean up my mess yet?" He scoffed, referring to our fight the other night.

I looked straight into his eyes. "I'm working on it."

Antonio stepped in. "Vance. It's been a while." They greeted one another with an arm-to-chest hug. "What brings you to town?"

"We have some business to attend to. I've been hearing some rumors." Vance pulled his sunglasses down to meet Antonio's eyes. "I'm here to see if they're true."

Antonio looked around and straightened his shirt. "Let's step into my office."

As Vance and Antonio left the sound stage, I watched Jennifer take Vance in. Amber also looked up at him as they crossed past her. She dropped her brush. The plastic tapping the cement made Vance look over at her. He smiled mischievously. *Fuck.*

While Antonio kept Vance occupied, I texted Amber. **Keep your cool. Don't look at me.**

Amber texted back**, Is that Vance?**

Yes.

I've met him before.

What? When?

Zara asked Amber a question. She replied, "A few more minutes for the paint to dry."

Come on, Amber. When?

… The morning I met you at the Mission. He was at the cafe I went to.

I was foolish to think he wouldn't figure this out sooner than later. But how? He must have seen one of my vamps tailing him. Amber brushed foundation over Zara's face with a shaking hand, blending in the final touches while biting down on her lip. My soul alerted me to Catori's innate fear of Vance.

We've got this, I said to my anxious soul. At least I'd hoped.

CHAPTER 27

GABE

Vance strutted back into the sound stage while Antonio followed behind, head hung low. Having overheard the conversation, I'd check in on him later. The blood business is losing clients, and Vance doesn't tolerate less than perfection.

Zara got up from Amber's chair and walked toward the bar behind them. Vance grabbed her wrist, stopping her in place. "Stunning," he said, ogling her.

Zara pulled her hand from his grip. "I know."

"Of course, you do." He watched her backside as she walked away.

Amber eyed the situation as Jennifer sat down in front of her. Tuning into their conversation, Jennifer spoke, "He's hot."

Vance looked over at them.

Amber answered back, "He's alright."

I closed my eyes and took in a deep breath. That comment would guarantee more attention from Vance, especially if they've already met. He has a dangerous edge that most women fantasize about. The problem is, he doesn't follow humanity's code for life being a precious gift. He bites, kills, and wreaks havoc everywhere he goes. I'll never be able to erase the first time he took me to his hometown in England. The blood spill was a yearly ritual for him to attack newly appointed knights and their loved ones. Only the most savage of Vance's vampires went with him on these yearly treks. Little did I know, I would be expected to participate or die at the hands of Vance, dry heaving behind a dumpster after one of my first kills. I've spent so many hours coming to his aid for years. Killing for him. It became easier after a while. But I was over it.

Vance liked a chase. I had no doubt he was here on the prowl while also searching for my soul mate. Unfortunately for Zara, she caught his eye, and she'd be my pawn. I walked over to the bar where she sat reviewing her lines. Jennifer watched me through the mirror as I sat beside Zara.

"Hi," I said, leaning in knowing that Vance would be listening for any hint of a soul mate encounter. Zara looked up at me with uncertainty. I brushed her hand, and she pulled it away.

"That will be a great scene." I pointed to the line where she would have to fight Marco. My soul told me this was wrong and shoved me. I concealed the tension in my chest with an exaggerated exhale.

"It will." Zara blushed and shifted to face me. "What are you doing tonight?"

"Hmmm. That depends."

"On?" Zara asked.

"What Philip's doing tonight." I looked at Vance's reflection in the coffee carafe at the end of the bar and saw him staring straight at us. *I'm sorry, Zara.*

"Philip's out of town. He has a shoot in Mexico."

Just my luck. "Is that so?"

"Zara, you're wanted on the set," the director called out.

"We can continue this discussion later," she said as she brushed my waist while walking away with her script in hand. I smiled politely and watched her walk away to keep up the show for Vance despite my soul slamming against my gut. I knew I was in hot water with Amber as she narrowed her eyes at me while concealing Jennifer's cheeks.

Jennifer continued to watch me from the mirror and spoke to Amber. "We need to talk about Gabe."

"Girl. You're not kidding. You know what I heard?" Amber stepped back with her hand on her hip.

"What?"

"Gabe's been sleeping around with the women in Antonio's studio for years."

"Really?"

"Yes. You know. He's slick. He's a lot like Marco. A dog."

"Tell me more."

I couldn't believe the lies Amber spun while playing it cool.

"Hey. Hold still. Close your eyes." Amber applied eye shadow, and then pursed her thick lips to blow on Jennifer's face.

Damn she's hot.

The crew moved around the catwalk finishing the lighting adjustments. Antonio slid into position next to the director. The scolding he got from Vance whittled his confidence, and my bastard of a sire hovered.

"Well, I knew there was something about him. Like I told you before," Jennifer said. Amber continued to stroke the other lid with the brush. When Jennifer's eyes popped open, she threw daggers at me through the mirror. I looked down at my phone in hand.

"We haven't spoken in a while, Jenn. Did I tell you about Marco and me?" I kept my eyes pinned to my phone concealing my disgust at the sound of his name.

"No. What happened?"

"He came on to me last Thursday in his dressing room."

"He did?" Jennifer crossed her legs and propped her chin on her hand. "Do tell."

"Jennifer, we need you on the set. Let's go!" the director called from his chair.

"Damn," Jennifer said.

"Well, I guess we'll finish this conversation later. There." Amber finished with the eyeliner.

"Definitely. I want deets." Jennifer looked at herself in the mirror. "You're amazing, Amber. I look stunning."

"I know."

As Jennifer got up, I walked into a corner watching as Vance eyed Amber. He walked over to her, and I looked away toward Zara, pretending not to notice. I shifted my body to ensure I could watch all three.

"Yoga pants," Vance walked over to Amber, and she looked up at him indifferent.

Asshole.

"You again?" Amber asked.

"What a coincidence?"

"Indeed." She zipped up her bag and crossed her arms.

"Aren't you happy to see me. Amy, was it?"

Amy?

"Yep."

"We did have a connection at the cafe. Didn't we?" He leaned forward, and I watched his nostrils flare.

Her scent better be masked.

"Look. Like I said before, I have a boyfriend."

"Huh." Vance looked around casually and then leaned forward. "And is he here?"

"Does it matter?" Amber bit back sharply.

"Then what's the problem?" He brushed her arm with the back of his hand.

"I'm not interested." She took a seat in her chair, pulling her phone out, feigning disinterest. My god she's good at concealing her true emotions.

My soul chided, *Sweep in, Gabe. You can't let him ...* I tuned my soul out refocusing on Amber.

"I like a challenge," Vance said as he walked away.

Moving in next to Zara before she walked onto the set, I whispered in her ear, "Kick his ass for me," referring to the fight scene she would have with Marco.

Zara smiled and nodded.

Continuing to watch Zara, I began texting Holly. No doubt I would need extra vamps tracking Vance over the next few days. Holly would have to take the lead. She's the only one I could trust. The only other vampire existing that despised him as much as me.

Vance sat down between Antonio and the director. I stepped off to the side while Zara and Jennifer took their positions on a couch set up in a makeshift apartment. Studio folks gathered around the two of them adjusting lighting, powdering shiny spots, and perfecting positions of coffee table ensembles. I crossed my arms breathing in a whiff of Amber's scent. If I could smell it, then Vance could as well. My phone buzzed.

I'm nervous, Gabe. Shit. Was he stalking me?

I don't know. Possibly. Don't worry. Just stay put. You handled it well.

Thanks.

And who's this boyfriend you told him about?
Kissy face emoji.

I slipped the phone into my pocket as Vance looked back at me smiling. He put his hands behind his head leaning into them just as the lights began to flicker. I shifted into a defense stance. Amber looked up at the lights and back at the phone. She continued to text. My phone buzzed again in my pocket. The lights flickered some more, and Antonio turned to me. Jennifer and Zara looked up simultaneously.

"Someone check the lights. We can't have any interruptions during this scene," the director called out.

The lights flickered again. A gust of wind blew everyone's hair as if near the ocean breeze. The entrance door slammed shut, and lights flickered once more and then went completely out. Shrill screams pierced the darkness. Someone yelled out to stay put. All cell phones went dead so we couldn't access light from our devices. In the pitch-black space of this windowless sound stage, people ran into each other and equipment. Bodies slammed against the locked doors. "They won't open!" someone shouted.

A sharp slice against a rope became my focus, and I looked up spotting Vance in midair. I fled to the couch where Jennifer and Zara sat, pushing it out of the way of the falling overhead light. They both screeched. A loud thud followed by shattered glass.

Amber called out, from where she remained seated. "Jennifer!"

Antonio hollered as he was pushed backward in his chair by Vance, hitting his head on the concrete. *Fuck!*

I scanned the room trying to track down Vance. He sat perched high above on a beam watching the chaos as I ran over to Antonio to check on him. Vance's snickers echoed in my ears like a hissing snake among the panic from everyone else. As I looked up at him, he jumped down landing next to Zara and Jennifer still on the couch.

I left Antonio on the ground and charged Vance, dropping us both to the floor. We tumbled a few times, and I landed with my head in a headlock.

"Just having a little fun," he whispered in my ear.

I pulled his collar, throwing him over my body, and he landed on his feet. Still pitch dark, I ran toward him like a bull seeing a red cape.

Vance jumped up over my head and landed on top of the coffee table, crushing it to pieces.

Jennifer screamed again. Antonio moaned in agony. Someone pounded on the doors, trying to force them open.

Vance stood up tall and walked slowly toward me. Our bodies squared, fists tight, breath taunting over me, he spoke only so I could hear, "I know something's going on, Gabriel. You can't keep me in the dark. I'll find out sooner or later."

I took a step closer, inches from his face. He snapped his fingers and the lights flicked back on. The crowd around the front entrance was down on the floor. He was gone through the open door.

Jennifer and Zara hugged one another as they looked horrified at the broken light that lay all over the floor where their couch had been. My attention turned to Amber as she was down at Antonio's side asking if he could hear her. Jennifer eyed me as I stood on the set drawing an invisible line from me to the broken light. The other folks in the studio scattered. Some ran outside. Others began texting incessantly.

"What the hell happened?" Marco came out shirtless from his private dressing area followed by a petite blonde tucking her shirt into her skirt.

Amber looked over at him and then me.

"Shit," Marco said. He ran over to Zara and Jennifer, crushing glass under his sandals. "Are you two, okay?"

"Fine." Zara rubbed her arms.

"Jennifer?" Marco looked at her. "Hey, you're bleeding." A piece of glass stood erect out of her bicep.

"What?" She turned her arm to look at it. "Ow. Shit."

"Just leave it," Marco said.

Amber and I got Antonio back into the chair. Standing over him, I wiped my mouth. Piercing sirens pulled up indicating that an ambulance had arrived. Paramedics ran through the door as I walked in a full circle observing the damages.

Antonio looked at me as the medics approached him. His eyes pleaded with me.

Vance. The son of a bitch wasn't worth this much trouble. I nodded to Antonio. A silent acknowledgment that I'd take care of this issue for him.

Jennifer volunteered to go with Antonio since she was also bleeding and Amber agreed. Another fine mess Vance left behind for me to clean up, not to mention a wide-open threat this time. Convincing Amber to change had to happen sooner than expected. Her life depended on it. And I had to make sure she understood the consequences of that change.

CHAPTER 28

GABE

The air conditioning was on full blast in the car. Amber had all vents open in her direction. Watching her look out the window as we crawled onto the freeway, Vance's words reiterated in my mind. *I know something's going on, Gabriel.*

She held the phone to her ear as I listened to Jennifer on the other line say she'd been patched up, and they had to wait for Antonio's x-ray results.

"Do you think Gabe did it?" Jennifer asked.

My jaw tightened, and I stretched my arms against the steering wheel.

Out of my peripheral, I watched Amber look over at me and answer. "No. There's no way he could have. I mean, how?" She looked away out the passenger-side window, accentuating the length and vulnerability of her neck. I turned my head as my eyes churned black. The fight heightened my senses, and I needed blood.

Jennifer droned on about how creepy I was. I scoffed. *And Vance isn't the obvious villain?* I rested my hand on Amber's thigh, and she intertwined our fingers.

Traffic came to a halt, and I nodded urging her to hang up. Her cleavage spilled out of her blouse brushing my hand as she bent forward to reach for something out of her bag. She pulled out a lip gloss, moving it across her mouth, intensifying my hunger. She licked her lips, and my fangs slid into position. Sealing the cap, she threw it back into the bag.

She looked over with wide eyes and pointed to my fangs.

I mouthed to her, "Hang up." I longed to taste her.

"I'm glad you're both okay," she said to Jennifer. "Text me when you get the results of the x-ray, okay?" She paused. "Talk to you later, bye." Amber hung up. "Gabe. Jesus."

"You see what you do to me." I retracted my fangs as she sandwiched my hand in between hers.

"We've gotta talk about what happened at the studio."

"Yeah, you did a great job. Comparing me to Marco was low," I said.

She smiled. "I had to come up with something to get her off my back."

"I know."

She put her elbow on the door to prop her head up. "Are we going back to my place?"

"Yes, unless you want …"

"No, that's fine. So, let's talk about the blackout."

"Vance causes trouble. That's what he does. That's who he is. I'm actually a lot more concerned than I was before, Amber."

She shifted her body, letting go of my hand.

"Meeting you at the cafe was no coincidence."

She huffed out air. "I had no idea he was your maker, but I did have a horrible feeling when I met him. Grams had warned me of a shadow in her dream. Following me."

"I wish you would've told me that."

"Gabe, how was I supposed to know that the shadow she referred to wasn't you? It was before we united. And frankly, you are a bit of a shadow following me, right? And you're dead, which explains why I always sense death nearby."

That's one reason. Although she had a point, it wasn't how I wanted her to think of me—a crazed overprotective boyfriend. But what choice did I have?

I gripped the shifter firmly, cracked my neck, and focused on the white lines on the road. Her scent distracted me. "You know, Vance attacked today because I hit on Zara. He was testing me."

She peered out the front windshield tugging on her bottom lip.

"He will continue to find ways to attack until he uncovers the truth. I don't tell you this to scare you." I merged off the highway. "I tell you this because you need to know that you are in danger, but I'm prepared this time. I will protect you."

"How, Gabe?"

"I have a plan." Amber looked down at her hands. I pulled her fingers to my lips. "Anything else you want to know?"

Amber sighed. "Does that plan still consist of you turning me?"

"Yes. If you agree to it." *Preferably sooner than later.*

She closed her eyes resting against the headrest. Vance's voice ran through my head again, *I'll find out sooner or later.* There would certainly be consequences for my actions with Zara. I looked back over at Amber. But it's all worth it for her, and I'm better prepared this time.

CHAPTER 29

—

AMBER

The guest parking sign stared me in the face as I opened my eyes. We finally made it back to my apartment. *At least I get to sleep in my own bed tonight.* I yawned and stretched my arms on the dashboard.

Gabe's plan lingered in my mind with thoughts of what it would be like to have the agility and strength like him. I would be less likely to need him to protect me from dangerous situations like the night in Santa Monica. And flight—his graceful leaps and flips across the library reminded me of a circus act I had seen as a child with Dad, minus the sequins and leotards.

He opened my door abruptly, making me jump. I stepped out swinging my bag over my shoulder. Sweat dripped down his brow. "Are you okay?"

"Fine." Gabe rubbed the back of his neck.

"You don't look fine." I grabbed his moist hand.

"I don't, huh?" Tight lipped, I watched his tongue skim his gums. Then he closed the door behind me. Wrapping my arm through his, we walked over to the elevator, and he pushed the button.

"I still find it extremely odd that you sweat, Gabe. I mean. Come on." I dropped my voice to a whisper, "Vampires should be ice cold."

He cracked a smile through his clenched teeth. His eyes bounced between my neck and breasts. "We can take a cold shower if you'd like."

Heat rushed to my cheeks.

Gabe walked into the elevator while I stood outside looking in. "You coming?" Holding it open, his body began to shake.

"What's wrong? Seriously?"

"Nothing. I'm just hungry."

"You're shaking."

In a low growl, he answered, "I know. Let's go."

I leaned on the wall opposite of him as the doors closed. He pushed the button to my floor.

"I could eat," I said.

Gabe pinned me to the wall with his glare as he gripped the bar along the elevator. When we got to my floor, he held the door open for me to pass. He lingered behind me making me feel like his prey. The weight of his stare sent ripples down my spine. My fingers shook and fumbled with my keys. *Ugh, not now.* Gabe grabbed them out of my hands and opened the door without even using them. *That's how he does that.* He walked in and waited for me to follow. His eyes were black and he licked his lips as I passed him. He closed the door, grabbed me by the arm, and pushed me up against the door, holding me by my neck with one hand and gripping my backside with the other. His eyes pierced mine and his fangs popped out.

"Gabe," I whispered.

He enveloped my lips and his tongue entered forcefully as if he were in search of something deeper within me. I gave into his lust and placed my hands in his back pockets, pulling him closer. He groaned over my mouth. His lips hovered over my neck. The edge of his teeth slid gently along my skin. My body tightened as he parted his lips and began to suck.

"Gabe."

He moved his hands down my thighs, lifting me up. His lips found their way back to mine. As he kissed me harder, I attempted to push him away, but he held me tight in his grip. I turned my head and his tongue landed on my ear.

"Gabe, take me to the kitchen."

In a zombie-like trance he carried me into the kitchen, placing me down on the table. He began to unbutton my jeans.

"Gabe. I want you to eat."

He yanked my jeans nearly knocking me off the table.

"Gabe!" Throwing them onto the floor, he moved in between my thighs locking eyes with mine. A hazy fog drew me into his predatory hook, while his fangs hung threatening to strike. Shaking my head, I pulled him by the hair to get his attention, "Blood, Gabe. You have to eat!" I yelled.

My breath shallow, he stood over me, pulling his lips back as if in pain. He turned abruptly to the refrigerator and opened it grabbing two bags of blood. He punctured and chugged one, throwing it into the sink. Then the other. Leaning over the sink, gripping the edge, and flexing his muscles, he commanded, "Go to the bedroom, now!"

I jumped off the table at the threat in his voice, backing away slowly toward the hallway.

He attempted to soften his voice groaning as if in pain, "I need a moment."

"Okay." I walked backward out of the kitchen dragging my hand along the wall toward my bedroom. Once inside, I locked the door behind me, not that he couldn't get in if he had wanted to. Still shaken, I secured myself in the bathroom for an hour.

As I brushed my teeth, the hairs on my arms stood up. My unwelcome spirit lingered, I could feel it. As if I needed any other threat tonight.

Lying on the bed waiting for Gabe to pull himself together, I dozed off thinking that my choice—as he put it—was almost stolen from me, and I wondered how long it would be before he did strike.

CHAPTER 30

AMBER

A knock on my bedroom door woke me up. Gabe fidgeted with the knob. I looked over at the antique clock face on my nightstand. *Midnight.* Rubbing my eyes, I sat up.

"Amber?" He knocked again. "Amber? Can I come in?"

Pushing myself up off the bed, I turned on the lamp. I adjusted my cami as I walked over to the door. "That depends. Have you pulled your shit together?" I yawned, placing my hand on the knob.

Gabe chuckled. "Yes. I pulled my shit together."

Recognizing his playful tone, I unlocked the door and opened it. He leaned against the frame, standing in his jeans shirtless, his tight abs exposed. A rush of desire hit my core.

"I'm sorry."

"What the hell happened?" I pushed my craving for him back.

"Fighting makes me hungry. It depletes me. I needed to feed."

"Ah." Yawning, "Now, I see the importance of your blood delivery."

"Very funny." Gabe pushed me into the room and onto the bed. He gripped my arms pulling them over my head.

Pausing my breath, my stomach clenched heating my core. Tingles shifted down to my toes.

"You seem to like this position."

"Don't you?" He brushed his thumb across my mouth and then passed the back of his fingers down my silk top. The arch in my back exposed my belly button and his warm hand pressed softly over it. "That should've never happened."

"No, it shouldn't have. You can't lose control like that around me." I attempted to move, but Gabe looked up at his hands holding me down and kissed me softly. I teetered on the tightrope he had me on with a longing for his strength. To fulfill my own desire for immortality. Enjoying the taste of his tongue, I let out a soft moan and my stomach growled simultaneously, interrupting our kiss.

"Hungry?" He brushed his thumb under the lining of my shorts. Sending more sparking sensations around to my back.

"Yes." I pecked his lips. "Starving actually."

Gabe released my hands and pulled me off the bed. "Come on. I'll make you something." He hugged my body from behind as he guided me into the kitchen. He pulled out a chair for me and I obliged. "Let's see." Gabe opened the fridge. I noticed he'd gone through half of his blood supply. *That's a lot of blood.* He pulled out some bread and cheese. "Grilled cheese?"

I nodded. Grilled cheese is etched into my memory. My dad and I would sit together sharing a cup of milk and eating our sandwiches. We'd cover our upper lips with a milkstache and chase my mom around the living room trying to give her kisses. Dad didn't mind jumping over couches to catch her.

"What's on your mind?" Gabe asked as he flipped the sandwich over in the frying pan.

"My dad."

"Care to share?"

"He used to make me grilled cheese sandwiches actually."

Gabe smiled, setting the plate in front of me. Pulling the milk out of the fridge, he poured it into a glass and set it down between me and an empty chair beside me. He took a seat looking over at the empty chair.

"Why do you look so smug?"

"Do I look smug?" Gabe tapped the table with his knuckles as I bit into my sandwich.

"Yes," I said with my mouth full.

"No reason." He looked over at the chair next to me again and back at me as I inhaled another bite. "I'm just happy you're eating."

I swallowed a half-chewed piece and picked up the milk to help it down, cringing at the pain in my chest from eating too fast. Gabe snickered.

"What?"

"Nothing. You're just too cute with your milkstache."

I wiped my mouth and took another bite.

"Did you have a good childhood, Amber?"

"I guess. For the most part. My dad was a marine so he wasn't around much. My mom had to work a lot so she wasn't around much. She was a nurse. That left me and Grams a lot of time to play."

"Play?"

"You know. With her magic and readings."

"Do you have a similar ability as your grandmother? Besides sensing ghosts?"

"No. I didn't inherit her psychic medium powers. I've learned a lot from her though. Sal didn't surprise me the other night either. It felt kind of normal despite the circumstances." Gabe nodded as I took the last bite of my grilled cheese and got up to take my plate to the sink. He startled me as he pressed his bare chest into my back, not having heard him move. Brushing his fingers down my arms, he took the plate from my hands and began to wash it, sending tiny lemon-scented bubbles into the air. I moved under his arm and leaned down on the counter, admiring how much he liked to take care of me. "I keep thinking about my dad. He died when I was ten."

"That must've been hard on you. How did he die?"

"In Iraq. They tell me he was part of a special mission gone wrong. They were ambushed." The hairs on the back of my neck stood up. The ghost in my apartment stood near to us.

"So, both your parents are dead?"

"Yeah. Wait." I stood up straight and leaned my hip into the counter. "I never mentioned anything about my mom being dead." Gabe set the frying pan in the drying rack.

"I just assumed. You never talk about her."

I squinted my eyes at him waiting for him to reveal how he had already done his research on my family history.

"So, tell me about your mom." Gabe dried his hands on a towel, turning to face me.

"There's not much to say really. She committed suicide when I was thirteen. She just couldn't handle life without dad." I looked down at my hands and sucked in a deep breath. "Anyhow. You remind me of my dad."

"Hm." Gabe leaned his bottom against the counter, crossing his arms and awakening my desires again as he flexed. "How so?"

"Oh, I don't know. Strong, confident, protective. And there's something about your need to feed me. He was just the same."

"Well, I'll take that as a compliment. Right?" He raised his eyebrow pulling me into his arms. "Let's go to bed. You look tired."

"Yeah. It's been a long day," I yawned. We walked out of the kitchen, and I stopped in the living room to grab my purse off the floor. Pulling out my phone, I found a few texts from Jennifer and one voicemail. Gabe waited in the hallway.

"Any news?"

"Yeah. Jenn says they're fine, and we're getting the day off tomorrow."

"A day off is a good thing. Maybe you can take me to meet your Grams?"

"I have the day off and all you can say is that you want to meet my Grams." As I approached him, he took my phone out of my hand and slipped it into his back pocket.

He wrapped me into his warm chest and whispered, "We'll have time for other things in between," his lips fell into my neck.

My heart raced and my mind circled back to an eerie presence of someone else lingering in the apartment. A spirit standing close by.

Gabe tugged me down the hallway, toward my room. The presence remained against my back as if breathing down my neck, causing my hair to stand up again. Slowing my steps as he neared the door, I pulled Gabe's arm. "Do you feel that? A presence? Like a spirit?"

He turned around looking behind me, narrowing his eyes as if telling the spirit to back off. His eyes lifted ever so slightly as if following the spirit.

Hesitantly, I looked over my shoulder still holding his hand. Nothing there. My muscles relaxed as if the spirit was drifting away. "Well?"

"I didn't see anything, Amber. But if there is a spirit here, that spirit has been warned." He pulled me into the room. "And just to be certain, how about we shut this door?" His fangs popped out as he kicked the door closed, and I knew sleep wasn't much of an option anymore.

CHAPTER 31

AMBER

Traffic flowed steadily around us on I-5 south as Beethoven's "Für Elise" enchanted Gabe's Audi. His tattoo peeked through his cuff, enticing me with memories when I traced my tongue over the same stem last night. He faced me as he gripped the steering wheel. A sigh escaped my mouth drawing his attention to me, and his fingers peeled the hem of my dress up my leg. Skin on skin contact shot pangs of desire to my core. His lips curled into a smile.

Driving men away who insist on taking care of me has been my specialty, but resisting Gabe proved difficult all night. Atop my purple comforter, he had me pinned, pushed, and positioned in ways that my body craved. Like a sculptor, his hands possessed me. As a lover, his mouth discovered my most delicate places. Self-restraint kept him from filling me with his perfect form. He teased me to the point of desperation. But never took.

In most relationships, I usually wielded power. Letting him take care of me freed and scared me. With that type of domination over me, I felt myself losing my independence bit by bit. His words lingered constantly in my mind from the night our souls united.

You're mine.

I never thought I could be with a man who'd be so adamant about controlling me like Gabe. But with him, I just gave in. Maybe I was confusing possessiveness for love. He was a vampire trying to protect me after all. But still, we needed to set some ground rules for when I became vamp … if I became vamp.

Leading his hand along my thigh, I invited his fingers over my satin center parting my legs.

Buzz. Buzz.

Damn it. Perfect timing. I leaned over to pull my cell phone out of my purse in case it was Grams.

"You don't have to check that." He continued to tease.

Forcing the pause of his touch by placing my hand over his wrist, I read a text from Jenn aloud. "CU at work tomorrow." I left out the fact that she wanted to speak with me about Gabe and Marco.

The taunt of his fingers continued despite the pressure I used trying to restrain him. I squirmed as I hit the talk to text button and spoke into the phone, "Thanks for letting me know. How are you … feeling? How's Antonio? Send."

His fingers slid under the fabric.

Oh … I squeezed my seat. I've never felt like this for anyone. This unquenchable longing.

Biting down on my lip, I closed my eyes and the phone buzzed in my hand.

We're both fine. Busy tonight? Jenn wrote back.

Activating the voice function, low and breathy, I spoke, "Yes. Grams encountered a bad spirit … just keeping an eye on her. Send." The ticking of the blinker alerted me to our approach of the Carlsbad Village Drive exit. He moved his hand and pulled my dress back down. *Don't stop.*

Jenn replied, **Spooky. I'll see you at the party on Friday. Once we wrap up this film, I'm taking a long break.**

Exhaling, I tossed my phone back into my bag. *And I'll be looking for work.*

"You haven't told her anything, have you?" Gabe's brows furrowed.

"Why'd you stop?"

"I asked you first."

"No, of course not," I said.

"It's for the best." He kept his eyes on me instead of the road.

"So, I'll ask you again. Why'd you stop?"

"We're less than two miles from the exit. You need to pull yourself together." He winked.

"I need to?" I looked directly at his fangs.

"Yes. We can't have your grandmother catch you in heat."

"Hm." I turned the knob on the A/C down to the lowest level and switched the fan to high. He shot me a cunning smile. I rolled my eyes, but his desire burned through me creating an aching for more of his touch. I placed my hand on his thigh. "Can we stay at your place tonight?"

His hand landed on mine. "Why? Do you think we'll need more space?" He lifted my fingers to his mouth.

My body warmed beyond what was humanly possible. His lips. His jawline. *My God he's sexy.* He completed a puzzle in my heart that I hadn't known was wanting. I can't imagine not being with him even though I really don't know much about him.

"You said her shop's on State Street, right?"

"Mm-Hm." Muscles bulged under his tight black shirt as he changed lanes, concentrated and controlled. I squeezed my legs together.

He placed my hand down on the stick shift. With his hand over mine, I bit my lip watching as we merged into traffic off the exit. It wouldn't be long now before Gabe met my Grams. And ironically, this time, my swirling stomach and heart palpitations confirmed that it was very important that she liked the man I was bringing home with me.

CHAPTER 32

—

GABE

Grilled steak and salt water permeated the air on State Street. Her grandmother's store sat sandwiched between restaurants with outside seating where people scattered along the street enjoying the San Diego summer. We walked in as her grandmother showed a woman the selection of rose quartz, promising to open up her heart chakra. *Hm.*

She looked up from the counter and smiled at Amber briefly then glancing at me as she continued answering the woman's questions. The shop had a variety of stones, herbs, and incense burners scattered around on glass shelving, including a sample of sage burning in the corner. The white walls held dream catchers and authentic Native American artwork. Turquoise jewelry sat encased along the register counter. The turquoise reminded me of the jewelry the women would make at the mission and, more specifically, my rosary. Her customer pulled out a wallet from her oversized beach bag. *Crafty saleswoman.*

"Hey, baby." Her grandmother walked around the counter to give her a big hug as the woman with the oversized bag left. Amber hugged her, rocking back and forth. Her grandmother stepped back from Amber holding her hands. "So, this is Gabriel."

"Hello," I said.

Grams stepped closer as if approaching a statue at a museum. "Mm-hmm. Gabriel. It's a pleasure to meet you."

I tilted my lips up slightly. "It's Gabe, ma'am."

"Gabriel … Gabe. Please call me Jo."

"Certainly, Jo."

"A vampire and polite."

"Grams!" Amber looked around the empty store. "Look, can we go to the back for a little bit and talk?"

"Sure, baby. Let me close the shop. Go on back there."

Amber and I walked around the counter as Jo locked up. The back room's dim lighting and candles burning provided a perfect ambiance for readings, I suppose. Amber sat me down at a table, interlocking our hands and gripping my bicep. Even in the dark, our skin tones remained distinctly beautiful. Our combination reminded me of my father and mother—her Aztec skin shone a darker olive and my father's Spanish blood birthed him a fair tone.

Jo met us at the table. "It's so good to have you visit me twice in one week, Amber."

"Yeah. I—well—Gabe wanted to meet you."

"I see." Jo looked at me and then looked at our connected hands as she took her seat. "I'm honored to meet one of the living dead. Unless you are truly the only one."

"No. There are many more of us." I squeezed Amber's hand. Jo fidgeted with her necklace. "I wanted to discuss some things with you." I looked into Amber's eyes. "I'd like to speak to Jo alone if that's alright with you."

"Oh." Their eyes met. "If she's cool with it, then, sure."

Jo nodded.

"Thanks. I know it's important to you that I get to know your grandmother better." I smiled.

"Okay. Yeah. I'll just go out to the front of the store." Amber stood up and pushed her chair in.

Jo got up, grabbed a carbonated water out of the fridge, and passed it to Amber. "Here you go, baby."

"Thanks." Amber looked at me and then popped open the water. She walked out to the front of the store, closing the door behind her.

"So, Gabriel, what's on your mind?"

I tightened my knuckles under the table as she said my full name again. "I've heard you met Catori."

"Yes."

"So, you know how difficult it is to keep her alive when she's around me."

Grams patted the table. "Yes, Gabriel. That seems to be a problem."

"I have a plan."

"Does Amber know?"

"She does. Sort of."

Jo looked at me with narrow eyes and took a sip of her tea.

"That's not the only reason I've come today. I need your help. Amber has a presence in her apartment."

"She's mentioned it."

"I've spoken to your son."

"That's. That's incredible. How?"

"I'm a vampire. We can see souls. We hear conversations beyond the human realm."

"Oh my! Now that's something." Grams took another a sip. "And if you've spoken with him, what's he asking for?"

"He wants to find Aurora."

Jo pushed the mug back, and she clasped her hands together while leaning over the table. "No offense. I've just met you. How do I know for sure you've really spoken to him?"

"He told me about the time you took him to the races in Del Mar. He told me he chose the winning horse for you."

"That's on my website. That's no secret."

"No, but taking your husband's savings to bet on the horse isn't on your website, is it?"

Jo sat quietly eyeing me.

"He also told me that you've done a great job raising Amber. He's very grateful. He knows it was hard on you."

Tears welled up and she took a deep breath.

"He knows about the abuse and why you left Morgan. He's proud of you for leaving him."

"That's a lot to take in." She wiped the tears streaming down her cheeks. "Why did he speak to you? Why not come directly to me?"

"He doesn't just need your help. He wants mine, too."

"How so?"

"He wants to know where Aurora's body is."

"What?" Jo adjusted herself in the seat.

"Where did you bury Aurora's body?"

"We didn't. We cremated her."

Narrowing my eyes on her as her breaths increased in speed, I folded my hands on the top of the table, as sweat gathered above her lip.

She stood up, walked to the fridge, and pulled out another bottle of water. Unscrewing the cap, her hand shook. She sat back down and took a swig. "I scattered her ashes in the ocean."

"He's not convinced. He told me you'd say that."

"Gabriel, is this some sort of joke?"

"No. This is serious. I'm serious." I leaned back in the chair and tapped my fingers on the table. "What aren't you telling me?"

"Look." A creak prompted her to check the door.

I listened to Amber's fingers scooping up stones, gently clanking them together. "She's near the stones."

Jo squinted at me.

"I have super sensory abilities."

Jo nodded, "I don't know where her body is, Gabe." She brought the bottle to her mouth, water spilling out of the top as her hand shook more violently.

"What happened to Aurora?"

"I found her in the bathroom on the floor with slit wrists and blood everywhere. I held her body in my arms squealing at the sight of her, rocking her in my arms. Amber had a sleepover party, so she wasn't home. I placed Aurora's head back on the cold tile and stood up—hands covered in blood." Jo stopped and looked at the door again.

I waved her on. "Keep going."

Jo lowered her voice, "I went to the other room and grabbed the cordless phone. I picked it up and just stared at the numbers. I felt lightheaded so I sat down on the couch. I guess I was in shock. I heard a clank and felt a draft fly past me. I thought, 'shit, a ghost now of all timing.' And then I heard the backdoor slam. I jumped up and ran to the bathroom and Aurora was … she was gone."

The stories both Amber and she were telling about Aurora began to align. I kept my eyes on Jo trying to determine whether she was lying. My soul confirmed her story. Her heart raced and she had sweat along her brow. She wiped her hands on her dress, a trait Amber must have picked up from her.

"She was gone, Gabe."

"So, then what?"

"I—well—I did what I had to do. I went to one of my friends and asked for help. We held a funeral for her and told Amber she had killed herself."

"Didn't you try to find her?"

"No."

"Why not?"

"I ran out to the back and scanned the fence that night. No one could have carried a body over the fence. No human that is. We always locked our gate and the lock was still intact."

Los Angeles. Gate. Suicide. "Do you have a picture of Aurora?"

"Yep. Over here." She jumped up and walked over to her desk in the back of the room. "This is one of my favorites."

"Hm." My eyes widened as she handed me the photo in a wooden frame. I smiled at Jo doting over her beautiful daughter. I heard Amber's sigh as she approached the door. "She's coming. And look. She doesn't know that I can speak with spirits yet."

Jo looked at the door and swiftly walked to the back restroom, turning on the water. I pulled out Aurora's photo from its frame and tucked it into my pocket.

Amber knocked and then walked in. "You guys done yet?"

I smiled. "For now." I stood up and grabbed her in my arms, holding her close.

"Geez. You can't have my Grams, too, Gabe. You'll need to choose, and it better be me." I swung her around and she laughed. "Where is she?"

"Restroom." We kissed as Jo walked out of the bathroom.

"Are you two hungry?" Jo raised her hands as if to say pardon me. "Would you two lovebirds like to go to lunch?"

"Sure," I said.

"Yes, That would be great," Amber agreed.

"Then it's settled. Let's walk next door. I have another appointment coming in around three." Jo grabbed her purse from inside a drawer in her desk.

"By the way, Grams, about the presence in my apartment—would you mind stopping by this week to cleanse it?

"Yes. I can stop by but only on a weekday after rush hour traffic, baby." The two joined arms and walked in front of me.

I lingered. "I'll be right there. Just need to make a call."

In the backroom, I pulled out the photo looking into the hazels that matched Amber's eyes. *How did I not know?* This will make for an interesting conversation in the near future. I tucked the photo away, pulled out my phone, and called Sal to fill him in.

CHAPTER 33

———

GABE

A coral scarf cushioned Amber's temple pressed against the passenger side door as we crawled through LA traffic back to my place. I reached for her hand but stopped. The rise and fall of her chest along with the soothing rhythm of her heartbeat calmed me. Waking her would be selfish since she still needed sleep, unlike me.

Imagining what Amber would look like barefoot with one of my T-shirts on after finally devouring her every which way made me smile. I've gotten used to the spirit voyeurs over the centuries, but taking Amber with her father lurking would have been too much even though both of us were ready last night.

The back of her hand swept over the tip of her nose. She crinkled it. The movement brought her cheek bones to my attention. She reminded me so much of Aurora. The power of our soul mate connection goes beyond that of coincidence. Resisting the notion of a predefined path for me—for us—always seemed impossible when circumstances arose that unquestionably led us to each other every time she was reincarnated. When I grasped the picture of her mother at Jo's store, memories of the night I met Aurora flooded back. No doubt Aurora was still alive living out her free vampire life. But where? Amber would need to be told about this—eventually.

Certainly, I knew Holly would be an asset in finding Aurora. The two of them had a common interest—Eli. He was another ruthless vampire in competition with Vance's blood business. But Holly and Aurora's distaste for one another didn't start with their simultaneous affairs with Eli. It started when I first helped Aurora transition. *How am I going to break that to Amber?*

My phone buzzed. Pressed against a magnet on the dashboard, I glanced at it while pulling into the driveway.

No sign of Vance. Zara's still safe.

With the click of a remote, the gate swung open. I waved to Felix who sat in the booth. As relieved as I was that Vance hadn't yet attacked Zara, it caused me pause. Perhaps I wasn't convincing enough.

I texted back to Sal, **Stay on her tonight.** That would also keep him out of earshot.

I pulled around the side of the house and parked in the garage.

Stretched forward reaching for her toes, Amber let out a satisfying squeal that reminded me of my desire to know her. Hunger pangs shot into my gut, and I swallowed air down my dry throat. As she sat up, I swept her neck with my thumb. I would need blood before we went any further.

"You okay?" she asked.

"I'm fine."

She grabbed my arm as I tried to step out of the car. Catlike, she climbed on top of me, consuming my mouth. Her desire called me to take a bite as her soft lips commanded mine. With her body barely positioned low enough for contact, she licked my earlobe and continued down to my neck as I slid my hand under her dress, cupping her cheek.

"Let's go inside," I said.

"Okay." Her neck fell into my mouth just as my teeth lengthened and hit the edge of her skin, causing her to gasp. Muscles tensed and she paused from her clumsy attempt to unbutton my jeans.

With her face between my hands, I pulled her head back to meet my desire. In a low guttural voice, I commanded, "Inside."

The look in her eyes confirmed her want. She stepped out of the car as I followed behind her. Retracting my teeth shot another hunger pang to my stomach. She leaned against the hood with one strap hanging off her shoulder. I swept her into my arms and ran her up to her room in seconds, placing her carefully on the bed. "Get comfortable." I winked.

Amber nodded.

Leaping over the balcony railing, I landed in the center of the foyer and glided into the kitchen. The refrigerator door hit the cabinet as I swung it open. Bottles clanked together. I chugged fresh blood that Sal had ready for me. Wiping my mouth, I threw the bottle down onto the counter, and it rolled off hitting the ground as I ran back up the stairs to meet Amber.

As I breezed past her bare caramel body and into the bathroom, I clutched the sink staring into the mirror and licked my blood-stained fangs. *Damn she's hot.* I gargled, pulled my clothes off, and walked out to meet her at the edge of the bed. She narrowed her beautiful hazels as she crawled over to me. Lengthening herself upright, she traced her nail down the center of my chest. Entwining her curls through my fingers, I brought her mouth to mine with just breath between us.

"You're mine, Amber." We brushed noses.

She nodded sighing out, "Yes."

I laid her carefully onto the bed hovering over her warm skin while locked on her soulful eyes. *No voyeurs tonight.*

CHAPTER 34

AMBER

Wrapped in the comfort of tussled bedding, I woke up to Gabe lying on his side, staring at me with a sweet good morning grin. He brushed strands of hair out of my eye and tenderly stroked my arm. Remembering all the various ways our bodies fit together throughout the night, a coy smile dressed my lips.

"What's on your mind?" he asked.

"You."

Trapping me under the sheets as he penned me like a burrito, I squirmed to break free to touch him. "You're so beautiful." He held my hair out of my face and passed his lips over my chin, neck, and mouth.

"Mmmm, Gabe," I said as he pulled back looking into my eyes with intense desire. "Release me from these sheets so I can feel you."

He dropped his face into the pillow next to me. "You're going to be late." I squirmed again as he met my eyes. "I'm going to run your shower." Our lips met and he slowly lifted himself up from trapping me in place, jumped off the bed, and ran into the bathroom.

"What? No, I don't want to go to work." I stretched.

"Sal's going to take you," he called out from the bathroom.

"What?" I sat up allowing the sheet to drop. "Why?"

A faint sound of rain tapping the tiles made it harder for me to hear Gabe's answer, "I've got some business to take care of, and I know that Vance hasn't gone far." His hard body taunted me as he walked back into the room. "I need to check in on my vineyard." Positioning himself in front of me, he tapped my nose.

Instinctively, I licked my lips. "You're just going to leave me in heat." I looked him up and down while swinging my legs over the edge of the bed.

The weight of his body dented the mattress, bringing our shoulders together as he sat down. "There will be more time tonight." He brushed my back intensifying the tingling on my already sensitive skin. This tingling, unlike the one I feel when death is near, created an unmet craving only he could satisfy within me.

Jumping to his feet, he tugged my arm, forcing me out of bed.

Taking a few steps closer to him, I brushed my nipples just below his ribcage and looked up. "I don't really know that much about you, do I? How you actually spend your days." *Not much at all.* "We don't have time for learning more about you though, right, Gabe? I'm gonna be late, and you have business to attend to." I puckered my lips atop of his chest as his erection taunted me. Huffing out a sigh, I turned with my hand on my hip, and I walked away to shower.

Gabe called after me, "Amber, you have thirty minutes to get to work. I'm all yours tonight. I'll meet you downstairs." The door to my room slammed shut.

What's wrong with me? Get it together. An overwhelming need for him to want me—to be near me, to take care of me—consumed me.

I hate this.

Our conversations revolved around my life, desires, and quirks. He hadn't yet revealed much to me.

As the water trickled over my face, I closed my eyes remembering his methodical touches. *Focus.* He had really worked my heart over in such a short time. In any other relationship, I never would have let him in so easily. I'd be in control of my feelings and behaviors. I wouldn't be so jealous of others who get to be with him today. *And if I were a vampire, would we be on equal ground? Ugh.*

The closet felt smaller today despite being able to fit a studio apartment in it. I held my hand over my heart as I took in a deep breath. Dropping my towel, I knelt pressing my forehead into the feather-like carpet. *Breathe.* The pumping of my rapid heart concerned me. I closed my eyes trying to imagine away the clothing Gabe had purchased me and wished I were back in my own apartment with my own wardrobe.

My eyelids squeezed tighter. *Breathe.* Thoughts raced and a pain pierced me in the chest. Being watched over, having to conceal my feelings for him, not sharing my good news with Jenn that I found my soul mate.

One leg at a time, I stood up balancing myself with my palms on the ground and rolling my torso up as if I were a ballerina. After reaching for a simple black tank top and jeans, my go-to work combo, I got dressed and finished by clasping the amethyst around my neck. I grabbed my makeup bag and met Gabe outside in his driveway.

Sal sat in a Lexus GX, and Gabe opened the back door for me. Brushing past him, I opened the passenger side next to Sal.

"I think you'll be more comfortable in the back, Amber."

"No. This will be fine, thanks."

He closed the back door. As I attempted to shut the passenger door, he grabbed it holding it open. He looked at me and then at Sal with his locked jaw.

"I'm going to be late, Gabe. Remember?"

"Text me if you need anything today." He pushed himself into the car and pulled me down to meet his kiss. The tenderness of his intention caused me to wrap my fingers around the back of his neck. "We'll talk more later." He brushed my nose with his. I nodded and pushed him out the door. He shut it and tapped twice as Sal pulled away.

My phone taunted me. Now six-thirty. *I am officially late.* "Ugh."

"What's wrong, Ms. Amber?"

"Nothing. Just late for work, as you know."

"I'll drive fast." He pulled out onto the main road.

"It's fine. I already texted my colleague that I'd be late."

Sal adjusted the air temperature on his side dropping it a few degrees. With his forearm exposed, I caught sight of a tattoo of a voluptuous woman holding a cross. I found it difficult to consider him as a former priest. His thick black hair with streaks of silver blended into his collar at the back of his neck. I hadn't seen him in jeans and a polo before. He'd always been dressed like a mafioso around me.

"Sal. Can you do me a favor?" He looked over at me and back at the road. "Please call me Amber. Ms. Amber makes me feel so old."

Sal let out a chuckle. "Hm. You feel old, but I am old."

His strong jaw line softened as he smiled. I hadn't ever seen Sal laugh, let alone smile.

"How did you meet Gabe?"

Sal looked out his driver's side window at the clay-like mountainous curves. Then he looked back at the road.

"Well? Are you not allowed to talk to me, Sal?"

"Gabe and I served at Mission San Gabriel together. I was one of the original founders of the mission." Sal looked over at me. His eyes dropped briefly to my breasts sitting in the tank top and then he looked back out the front windshield.

The mission. A vampire, too. Made sense. Sal hid it well. "Really? That's …"

"I'm not proud of it, Amber."

I paused looking straight ahead. "So, you knew Catori?"

"Sí."

We joined the highway and headed toward Burbank. "San Gabriel. Does that mean that Gabe … was it named after him?"

"Ha," Sal chuckled again. "No, no, no. San Gabriel the archangel is who the mission was named after."

"Well, you never know."

"The Tongva people were confused by Gabe at first. They were the original inhabitants of the land. Most people lowered their heads around him because he went by Gabriel back then. The Tongva would either love or hate him. They either saw him as a saint or they saw him as the devil. Mostly devil, like all of us who came onto their land and took it from them with force."

"Oh." I sighed. Oftentimes, teachers would gloss over the truth about the history of indigenous people. Learning the truth about missions came from visiting them and reading historical records from the tribes themselves, not from textbooks.

"Looking back over centuries, I … I live with regret to this day." Sal turned onto Riverside Drive nearing the studio.

"What do you regret, Sal?"

He pressed into the steering wheel. A tear streamed down his cheek, and he looked over at me. "So much of what I preached, I didn't believe. I was forced into the priesthood. But I was no saint. Never a saint. A hypocrite actually." He wiped his eyes. "I'm sorry."

"It's fine, Sal."

"Gabe saved me from myself when Vance forced him to come back to the mission for his first vampire conversion."

"And you were his first?"

Sal nodded. "He was horrified, and I was scared to death. Quivering at the threat in his eyes as Vance hovered. But it all worked out in the end. Gabe freed me from a tormented life."

I bit down on my bottom lip as he spoke.

Sal pulled over and put the car in park close enough for me to walk to the studio. Gathering my things, I put my hand on the door, but he held my arm before I could step out.

"Stay alert today, Amber. Vance is definitely not far from Los Angeles. If you feel any threat at all, you text me right away. Hand me your phone."

After unlocking the passcode, I handed the phone to Sal. He found my contacts and began typing in his information. He handed the phone back to me. "Are you not staying?"

"I'll be around."

Whatever that means. "Is that why you feel so familiar to me, Sal?" He tilted his head. "Because we knew each other?" I rubbed my stomach.

"Es posible."

"If I let Gabe turn me, do you think Vance would still come after me?"

"I think it's best you have that conversation with Gabe."

"Oh, come on. You can't leave a girl hangin'. I really need to know. It's a big decision."

"That's why it's best to talk to him."

"Alright. You're off the hook for now." I opened the door and hopped out.

"You ask a lot of questions." He looked at me with humble eyes.

"Get used to it."

CHAPTER 35

GABE

Stale beer and sawdust masked the smell of perspiration in this remote biker bar north of Hemet. Country music played as a chorus to the chatter of leather jacket patrons. Sunlight peeked through dusty windows.

When Holly told me she had received a tip about a clan operating out of this bar led by a woman with Aurora's attributes, it made sense to me that she could be hiding out here. After her transformation, she continued to run with a rougher crowd of vampires.

The floor creaked as I walked past the early-afternoon beer-consuming customers. Their eyes followed me without interrupting their conversations. Although I had my jeans and flannel on today, I clearly looked like an outsider among the leather-wearing pierced crowd. "Hey." I placed my helmet on the bar. The balding man behind the tap looked up, acknowledged me with a nod, and continued to pour through the foamy head of the beer on tap.

"Have you seen this woman?"

The man raised his eyebrow taking the picture of Aurora into his hand. "Nah." He handed it back to me.

"Are you certain?" I sat down on a stool.

"You calling me a liar?" The bartender wiped a glass with a moist towel.

Tapping the counter with my knuckles. "Where's your boss?"

"Heh. My boss." He turned toward a couple of bikers playing pool. "You believe this guy. He wants to know where my boss is."

Muffled voices in the bar quieted. A man with a black vest and hoop in his nose dropped his pool stick on the table and walked in my direction. The silence honed my attention to the cook's fryer in the back kitchen. I surveyed the closest weapons—a bottle, a knife, and the pool stick gripped in the hand of the shorter biker approaching alongside the vested man. Attention searing into the back of my head. The observers didn't want to miss a good brawl. An increasing sense of danger ran up the back of my neck—another vampire was in the crowd.

My soul spoke, *There's a lot of confusion in this bar. A hazy fog.*

Compulsion.

I looked up at the bartender. "Well?"

"I'm the boss."

I snickered shaking my head. The two men stood on both sides of me closing in.

"Is this guy bothering you, Skins?" the short one said.

"Yeah. He is."

The pulses in the bar fired up waiting for their invitation to move in. The two men grabbed my arms, yanking me off the stool.

"This will be fun, pretty boy," the short one said as he shoved me into the larger vested man.

The vested man held my arms behind my back. His body odor akin to dirty socks. "You might want to think this over," I said.

"You believe this guy?" The short one stepped closer. As he pulled back for a punch, I jerked my legs up kicking him in the chest, throwing him across the room onto a table crushing it beneath him.

The vested man squeezed my arms tighter as a crowd of patrons moved forward. I flipped the larger man over my back, loosening his grip and tossing him into the crowd. Bottles hit tables cracking the ends as those not injured began to circle me. Both women and men approached me swinging. I flew up, landing on a beam of the ceiling just as a woman swung slicing the bottom of my pant leg with her broken bottle.

"What the …?" A man with overalls looked up.

I paused to scan the room, and then jumped down dropping my fists onto the man's back, knocking him onto the floor. Hopping over the bar, I grabbed Skins with my forearm tightly tucked under his chin. In less than a second, the knife in front of him met his cheek. "Let's try this again, Skins."

His loyal patrons dropped their weapons and helped the short one up off the floor.

"Where's your boss?" Sweat built up along his neckline. Not able to speak, he lifted his pointer finger to the corner of the room. A middle-aged woman with long flowing hair wearing black jeans and a leather jacket stood up.

"What a performance." Her slow clap echoed in the stillness of the bar. Her familiar swagger drew me in. "It's been a while, Gabriel."

"It has, Aurora." I nudged the sharp tip into Skin's cheek, drawing blood. "So, you're the boss, huh?"

Shaking, Skins stuttered, "I—I'm sorry. I—"

"Shut up," I said looking straight at Aurora. "Get your minions under control."

"Show's over. Clean this mess up!" She stood with her hand on her hip, circling her other one in the air.

Everyone hustled about straightening things up, picking up chairs off the ground, and getting back to what they were doing. A young man stepped out of the back kitchen holding his bucket and rag, and Aurora pointed to him and then the bar. "Francisco, take care of their ... observations."

He nodded and went to work without so much as a second glance.

"Now. How about you let Skins go?" Her eyes squinted as if attempting to conceal her concern for him.

I placed my mouth close to his ear. "Any wrong move, Aurora, and this one goes down first." I pushed him forward out of my grip, and he gasped for air.

"Come join me in my booth, Gabriel." My fists balled at the use of my full name. I hopped over the bar and followed her to the back corner. Muffled conversations picked back up as Francisco wandered about *talking* with each customer.

"So, you've been looking for me. Now you've found me." She leaned forward across the table, rubbing my hand. "Still jealous of my release?"

Reminding me of the fact that Vance released her from his maker bond in front of me as a punishment was her specialty. Pulling my hand back, I lingered a moment admiring the resemblance of Amber in her eyes and bone structure. "No."

"So, what do you want, Gabriel?"

"I have a message for you."

"Is that so? I don't understand why Vance always sends his kids for these grown-up conversations."

Clasping my hands on top of the table, I leaned back against the vinyl. "So how about we have a grown-up conversation, then."

"Listen. We've got lots of donors lined up." She dug under her fake French-manicured fingers. Vance had hinted at various problems with his business lately. "If Vance wants in, tell him to get a hold of me directly."

Caught off guard, I kept a stoic face and asked, "So who does Vance really need to talk to about these donors? You're not the one behind this operation, are you?"

Aurora smiled while licking her lips. "You've always been so naive, Gabriel. It doesn't take much to lead an army against Vance Hastings. Surely, even you are eager to get out from under his thumb."

Leaning forward, I asked, "Who are you working with?"

"You want in?"

"That depends. What's in it for me?"

Aurora slid closer, placing her hand on my thigh. She whispered in my ear, "We've got a cure for insanity."

Removing her hand from my thigh, I placed it on top of the table holding it firmly in place. "What are you talking about?"

"You'll be able to feed from humans the way we were made, too. No more responsibility for turning or killing them. Just pure euphoria."

"So, if I help you, you'll give me a cure." *A new possibility for being with Amber if she doesn't transition.*

Aurora smiled pulling her hand away from mine. She swept her fingers through my hair. "I still remember how you taste, Gabriel."

"Enough!" I stood up.

Cackling, "Really, Gabriel. You've always been a bit uptight. Loosen up." She looked up at me. "So, are you in?"

Not certain of what her answer would be, I took a chance and asked anyhow, "So, Eli will give me the cure if I do this deal with you."

Aurora nodded.

Eli running the operation would infuriate Vance. More so that he found a cure first. "For how long have you been working on this cure?"

"We perfected it a year ago."

"And you? Are you cured?"

Her sinister grin confirmed it as she looked past me.

I looked over my shoulder as Skins stood behind the bar with tethered eyes on Aurora. "That guy?"

"Mmm hmmm."

"To each his own."

"He's O negative." The corner of Aurora's mouth curved up.

"Hmph." I shoved the gnawing voice in my head reminding me of why I was really here. Walter asked for help. Technically, I've done my part. I found her.

"Well? Are you in?"

"I need to think about it. You haven't really given me much of a proposition."

"Euphoria isn't enough for you?"

"No. What would you need from me?"

Aurora stood up squaring her body and pressing her hands on my chest. "Lead your donors to us and we'll do the rest."

"That simple, huh?"

"And see if you can convince Holly to join in. She's hot." She licked her finger and placed it on her ass making a hissing sound.

Interesting twist.

"Don't take too long, Gabriel. This offer is time limited."

"And Vance?"

"We don't need Vance. And neither do you. Join us and we'll help you get rid of him. That is what you want after all, isn't it?"

Skins stepped in between us to hand me my helmet. I grabbed it from him, peering into his eyes. He cowered back behind Aurora.

"You've always had a way with people, Gabriel. It's sexy." She winked.

"I'll be in touch."

"I hope so."

Watching my surroundings as I exited the bar, I jumped on my bike, slipping my helmet over my head. The clear blue sky soothed me. The vineyard would help wrap my head around this situation. I revved my engine and took off. Thoughts swirled. A potential cure to our poison. Could I go behind Vance's back? Could Eli and Aurora really help me?

And the worst thought yet was of how Amber would take the news about me helping her mother transition. *She can't find out yet. If she does, she may leave me.* I couldn't risk it.

CHAPTER 36

GABE

A Spanish tile shifted under my boot as I stood on the roof waiting for Amber and Sal to return. The leaves rustled in a nearby tree as I dropped down in a crouch landing onto the driveway. I ran through the front door closing it behind me. The foyer felt cold and empty without Amber nearby. Pacing, I put my hand in my pocket to rub the cross Catori had given me for comfort, instead finding the pottery shard that I had found at my vineyard in Santa Ynez after visiting with Aurora today. *Hermosa.* Rubbing the dirt off with my shirt, I walked over to the pottery section of my collection and carefully lifted the glass to place it inside. *No doubt Chumash pottery from at least the eighteenth century.*

The Lexus's tires rolled over pavement in the direction of my home. Amber's laughter echoed off the foyer walls as if standing next to me. *Sal's getting too comfortable too fast.*

Every moment spent away from her tore a hole in my heart. The unquenched desire to be inside of her became more than an irritation and bloomed into pressing need. She's so different from the other versions of Catori, fierce and confident.

All versions of Catori had backbone. Lina was an incredibly provocative artist for the mid-1800s, painting nudes. And Marla, my God that ass. She knew how to move in those heels on the dance floor performing for hundreds of guests not always welcoming of people with varying shades of brown skin. But Amber has a fire inside that draws me to her stronger than ever before. And when we're intimate, she responded to my every touch with a quiver.

Sal can't screw this up. I can't screw this up.

The banter between Sal and Amber distracted me from thoughts of her body over mine as they pulled up. Lifting *La Historia de los Mayans* off the shelf, I tucked the picture of Aurora into the back cover. I walked into the doorway of the library awaiting their entrance. My shoulders tensed as she fell forward through the front door, holding her stomach unable to contain her laughter. Sal followed in behind her as they both said, "Ay caramba!" Guffaws followed. *Having a good laugh on my account.* I watched the man I trusted most with the woman I loved the most. But trust only goes so far. Vampires were known to turn on each other even after centuries of devotion.

"I just can't believe it. I wish I could've been there. Ahhhhh." Amber exhaled from the depths of her abdomen. She continued to snicker holding her stomach.

"Que caballeroso," I muttered to Sal behaving like a gentleman as he carried her bag in for her and put it on the bench under the new mirror we'd replaced.

His hands slid into his pockets as he looked over at me. "Hi. Uh." Sal pulled himself together, stifling his chuckles.

"You two look cozy," I said.

"Gabe, I had no idea how funny Sal was. He's been telling me the best stories about the two of you." Amber walked over leaning in for a kiss.

"Has he?" I raised an eyebrow.

"How could you punch the bartender instead of the biker?" She tried to hold in her laugh and snorted instead.

"We all make mistakes." I smiled. "Young vamps don't always know how to control their speed and reflexes. Isn't that right, Sal?"

He stood erect and rubbed the back of his neck. "Cierto."

"Anything to report?" I wrapped my arms around her waist with her back against my chest, staring at Sal.

"No, Señor. Todo bien."

"Glad to hear. Thanks for taking care of her for me today." I kissed Amber's neck while staring into Sal's eyes.

He shifted and raised his hand to us, "Good night. Amber. Señor." He walked out of the room toward the kitchen.

Amber twisted around to face me. "Why does he call you Señor?"

"It's his choice. He's always kept formalities with me in certain company."

"Huh. Seems odd based on the stories he was telling me over dinner."

"I see. And what exactly did he tell you?" I tugged her closer to me.

"Wouldn't you like to know?" She walked backward while extending our arms out and then let go. After grabbing her bag, she turned to me and asked. "How was your day at the vineyard?"

"The usual. Got my hands dirty." We moved toward each other like magnets.

"It would be great if you'd take me there someday." She lifted my hands looking at my filthy nails. "Maybe you can show me how to get my hands dirty." She winked.

I pulled her close with lust in my eyes.

"Were you really there all day? Seems you haven't even showered yet." She narrowed in on my lips.

"I just got back." Feeling like another question was coming, I cut her off with my own. "I'm wondering why Sal was holding your bag for you. Since, I've met you again in this life, you always have a death grip on your belongings."

"Sal just. I ... wait. Does that matter?" She stepped back.

"No." I stood with my arms crossed.

"Are you jealous?"

Pursing my lips, I shook my head. "I'm going to run upstairs and take a shower. Care to join me?"

"Sure. I just need to go tell Sal something." Amber pivoted on her tiptoes walking toward the kitchen.

"What?" I ran past her blocking her next step.

Her hands pressed into my chest so as not to run into me face first.

"I knew it," Amber sneered.

Cupping her face, I rubbed her cheek with my thumb and pulled her forehead to mine. "I thought I made it clear last night." Our eyes met, and I pulled her into me. "You're mine."

Breathless, she whispered over my mouth, "I am."

"Good. Then let's go upstairs, corazón!" With her body in my arms, we ascended the curved staircase unable to look away from one another—hungry for more.

CHAPTER 37

———

AMBER

The Egyptian cotton felt cold and empty next to me. I stretched my arm out further realizing Gabe wasn't in bed. "Gabe?" I sat up and looked around the moonlit room.

My cell phone buzzed on the nightstand.

What are you wearing? Marco texted.

My God if Gabe sees this he'll freak. I deleted it and another popped up right after.

I miss your body.

I deleted it again. Another buzz and text popped up.

I'm coming over.

I texted back. **I'm not home.**

Where RU?

Out.

Where? RU w/him?

Shit. I just won't answer anymore.

If u were with me, you'd be under me not on the phone.

I put the phone to sleep. Another text popped up.

CU on Friday?

Uh. Delete. Delete. Delete. Sifting through the contacts, I found Marco's number. I hit edit and scrolled down pausing over the delete button. My finger hovered over it. I shut the phone down completely and placed it on the nightstand.

A silky white robe hung in the closet so I wrapped my body in it. As I opened the door to my room, it made a creaking sound echoing throughout the quiet walls of Gabe's home. I cringed. *I'm sure he heard that ... if he's even here.* Dim night lights scattered along the walls, and I creeped toward the hallway that Gabe had never taken me to.

As I turned the corner, light from a cracked door at the end of the hall welcomed me forward along with someone playing music. *Flamenco?*

I walked closer pulling the belt tighter around my waist. The music got louder as I approached. The strings sounded like someone strumming a guitar. Suddenly the speed picked up, and I felt as if Gabe's fingers had access to my lips all over again. With faster strumming, I rubbed my body against the wall wanting to whisk the door open and straddle him.

What if it's not Gabe?

The thought swiftly escaped me, and I continued to move my hands in the air in a circular motion to the sounds of the guitar. Intermittent patting and strumming caused me to bend my elbows, bringing my hands to the back of my head as I stomped and twisted around.

I gently pushed open the door and peeked through. The size of the room before me doubled the size of *my room,* dressed in a black and white motif. I entered while snapping my fingers in the air. A lonely black couch sat in the center of the room and a very old painting of a naked woman lying on her side hung on the wall to the left of the door. I looked to the right as Gabe watched my entrance, not missing a beat on his guitar.

Continuing to stomp and circle my hands above my head, my robe slowly opened down the front revealing my form.

Gabe strummed intensely on the guitar shirtless and in his pajama pants as he drew me closer to him with his desire. I swayed my body, rolling my wrists and clapping my way around the room. My feet stomped to the rhythm. The hardwood floors allowed me to twist and turn on each beat.

He eyed me like prey as I challenged him. The twirling allowed my robe to loosen more until my breasts hung out completely, and my shoulders escaped. Holding the silk at my waist, I used it to mimic a Flamenco skirt. He slowed down his strumming. The robe fell to the floor leaving me in a steady motion twirling and swaying. Using my hands as castanets, I moved toward him with each step. He drew me in completely until I stood right before him. Our eyes connected, mingling our desires together.

The strumming stopped and he placed the guitar down. My breathing held a steady, fast pace as he placed his hands around my waist. I slid my fingers along his neck, to his shoulders, and down his biceps. His muscles tensed as he jerked me forward placing his ear against my stomach and embracing me as I ran my fingers through his hair.

He kissed my belly button, and my body quivered. Tightening my grip on his hair, I drew him up to a standing position and brought his lips to my mouth. I inserted my tongue exploring him—needing him to respond. He wrapped his arms around my waist and lifted me up backing me into the wall next to the painting. My thighs clenched around his waist as he held me in position for what I craved. Then he paused.

With a disgruntled face, he turned his head sharply to face the door. Moving my legs from his waist, he set me down and ran out into the hallway.

Not now. Oh no no no no. "Gabe!"

I faintly heard Sal's voice as I grabbed my robe and fumbled to get it on. Holding it together, I followed Gabe out to the landing. They spoke in Spanish and Antonio's name was mentioned.

"What's going on?" I leaned against the railing of the second floor looking down at a shirtless Sal, stocky but firm.

Gabe turned to me, brushed my hair behind my ears, and said, "Lo siento, corazón, but I will need to take care of something."

"Now?"

"Yes."

"Sal, are you kidding me? What's going on?"

Sal remained quiet.

"Tell me, Gabe! What the hell is going on?"

"Vance caused a problem at Antonio's tonight. I'm heading over to clean up his mess."

"What mess?"

"I'm not sure yet. I'll head over now. Antonio said it can't wait."

"I'm going with you," I said.

"You're not." Gabe pulled me toward him. "You're staying here." He looked down at Sal and back at me.

"No. Dammit. You can't keep me prisoner here."

"I'm not keeping you prisoner. I just don't know if it's a trap. I can't risk it. You're safer here with Sal."

"I just want to be a part of your world." The words flowed out without regret. I was giving in.

Gabe smiled. "I know." He pulled me by the hand into the music room closing the door behind him. Lifting me back up against the wall, his dark intensity softened my pouting lips. "You are a part of my world. You are my existence."

Mesmerized by him, clinging to him, I stopped resisting his love. "Don't go," I pleaded as I closed my eyes.

He rubbed my nose with his as he always did. "Please trust me."

My eyes popped open. "Why can't Sal go?"

"Because he can't. I need to go. Vance is my maker, and I am obligated to clean up his mess." His disgruntled eyes warned me that a vampire's life was not easy. "Trust me. You will always be my priority. But I have obligations that you might not always understand."

Our foreheads touched.

Obligations I may never understand, unless you turn me. I kept my hands interlocked behind his neck and pulled his lips to mine. In between kisses, I whispered into his ear, "I love you."

The sharp points of his fangs skimmed over my neck as my skin vibrated at the release of his guttural growl. He resisted the strike by looking into my hazels instead. I melted into his dark desire.

"Te quiero mucho. Siempre."

The warmth of his chest against mine simmered with the words Gabe spoke—of loving me always. Hugging him tight against me, in that moment I feared if I let go, I might not ever see him again.

CHAPTER 38

AMBER

A few minutes past 2:00 a.m., I sat up in bed alone. It had been an hour since Gabe left to clean up a mess. *Whatever that meant.*

Hunger pangs kept me awake, along with a tightness in my chest every time I thought about Gabe helping Vance. Kicking the covers off, I got up and walked out of my room in search of food. Blackness filled the foyer with gas lit candle sconces flickering to keep the floor's ghostly appearance.

As I descended the stairs to the kitchen, I noticed the library lights were still on. I poked my head around the corner but didn't see Sal anywhere. He had offered me something to eat when Gabe left. When I declined, he told me he'd be making preparations for another potential attack. There was something mentioned about stakes and crossbows.

The tingling sensation of death remained constant in Gabe's home. I assumed their vampire bodies were what triggered my gift. But as I walked across the cold marble floors, it felt as if someone were watching me, a similar feeling like the night at the bar when that boy-cut woman approached me from behind. I trembled, looked around, and scurried across the foyer to the kitchen. Rubbing my arms, I regretted not having wrapped myself in a robe. The silk from my cami cooled my arms with each brush against the fabric.

The lights from the overhead cabinets guided me to the fridge. I grabbed a peach yogurt and pulled the flap off leaving it on the counter. In the drawer, I found a spoon. My shoulders tensed as I got the feeling that someone was right behind me again. I turned around.

"Jesus," I placed my hand to my heart. Marco stood with his feet firmly planted and his arms at his sides. I lowered my voice to a whisper, "What are you doing here? Did Sal let you in?"

"No."

I placed the yogurt and spoon on the counter. "How did you get in?" I turned back to face him. He looked down at my chest, which was expressing the effects of the drafty air through the silk. Then he looked into my eyes, taking a step closer and backing me into the counter.

"The door was open."

"You walked in because the front door was unlocked?" I grabbed the counter's edge and gave him a don't bullshit me look.

Still whispering, "No. It was cracked open."

Open? Maybe Sal had to run out for something. His intensity and close proximity prompted me to look down at the distance between our bodies.

"Listen, Marco. You can't be here. You've got to go."

He placed his hands on my waist, and I pushed him back, but he didn't budge. The firmness of his body had changed—hardened. It reminded me of Gabe's.

"How did you know where Gabe lived anyhow?"

"I need your help. And I know you're the one who can help me."

"What are you talking about?" I placed my hands on his chest attempting to build a barrier between us, but my arms bent trapping me against him as he pinned me to the counter with his waist.

"I don't know what to do." He placed his lips on my neck. "I need to feed."

"Wait, what?" The sound of metal sharpening pierced my ears. *Fangs.* I pushed harder while dropping myself under his arm to step away.

He grabbed my arm and yanked me back into him.

Through my teeth, I said, "Let. Go. Of. Me."

He looked down at my lips squeezing my bicep and released me.

I yanked open the fridge, grabbed two bottles of blood, and handed one to him. He looked at me, fangs out, and pulled back his lips as if he were in pain.

"Drink it!"

He unscrewed the cap on what looked like a beer bottle and gulped it down. I handed him the second one. Repeating, he placed the bottle on the counter next to the other one and licked his lips. "Not what I was hoping for."

"Tough shit. How did this happen?" I stepped back a few feet.

He brushed his hand through his curls. "I met a woman last Thursday night. At Antonio's. Before I knew it, I felt my life being sucked from me. A frigid, dark, dreamy feeling. I was fading." He turned facing the counter and pressed his palms into it. "And then she told me to drink. I was so parched, weak. I shook my head no, but she forced her wrist to my mouth. And I couldn't stop myself. Like a rabid beast, I consumed her blood." He looked over at me.

"I can't help you. You really need to leave."

He spun one of the bottles around on the counter and stopped it as it landed in my direction. "She left me, and I have nowhere else to turn."

"What makes you think I could help anyhow?"

"Gabe can help, can't he? Don't deny what he is. I already know." He stood up puffing his chest out. "Where is he?"

"Marco, lower your voice."

"Is he here?" He took a step closer as I stepped back.

"Please, just go."

He took another step closer and paused looking behind me. His eyes widened with fright. "I didn't realize you had another guest."

"Guest? You mean, Sal?" I turned around looking into the den.

Nobody there. I turned back to Marco, but he was gone. *What the fuck?*

I walked out the kitchen entrance and into the foyer. "Sal?" I called out.

Nobody answered.

The front door ajar, I walked over to it and pulled it open stepping outside. Scanning the front yard. No car or vampire in sight. I put my hands on my hips.

"Where'd he go?" The cool early morning breeze had me shutter. I went back into the house and locked the door behind me.

CHAPTER 39

AMBER

As the lock clicked into place, I turned and a thick hand wrapped around my neck slamming me into the door. "Ow, fuck!" Ocean blue eyes pierced my hazels, and a familiar cedar cologne molested my nose. *Vance.*

"Amy," he whispered over my mouth. "Gabriel's been a naughty boy keeping you all to himself."

I shuddered as his hand squeezed my neck, securing me against the wall. His other hand landed on my hip, skin to skin on my waist. Breathing was getting harder. I tried to move my head but he pinned his jaw against my cheek.

"This is a pretty pendant. Did Gabe give that to you?" His thumb brushed my chest under the amethyst.

My stomach churned and heart raced.

"Your fear is turning me on." He licked my cheek.

"Let me go, asshole!"

He flipped me around pressing my chest against the door and inserting his pelvis into the center of my satin shorts. "You didn't know that Gabriel and I like to share?"

Spearmint breath tickled my neck as he pushed harder into me. I squeezed my eyes shut.

"Basta!" The lights went on. Sal's voice lingered in the air as I waited for Vance's next move. "Dejala, Vance. She's mine!"

What? Shit.

Vance squeezed my arms tighter at his words.

"She's mine. Release her or I'll shoot."

Vance let out a condescending laugh as he loosened his grip and pulled me into his chest, turning me around so his back leaned up against the door. The indentations his fingers made around my arms worried me that he'd soon break my bones not aware of his own strength.

"Go ahead. Shoot," Vance said.

A wooden stake inserted into a crossbow pointed in our direction. "She's a simple casualty in all of this. It would be a pleasure to kill you."

"Sal!" I belted out.

Vance dug his arms under my ribs as I struggled to break free lifting my knees up.

"God dammit! Let go of me! I'm his."

"Now, I find it hard to believe, Sal. That she's yours." Vance inhaled as he brushed his lips against my neck. "And that you would just let this sexy thing die."

"We all make sacrifices."

"I don't think I'd let something this stunning get away from me." Vance took a few steps pushing me closer toward the stake.

I furrowed my brows at Sal.

"If she's yours, why would she be conversing with another vampire in the dark right under your nose, huh?"

Sal's eyes narrowed, but he remained calm. "We have an understanding. She comes. I come. What she does after that is her business." His eyes shifted to mine. "Keeps things simple."

The tip of the stake aligned directly with my heart pinched my flesh as Vance loosened his grip forcing me in front of it.

"So, do it, Sal."

Sal cocked the crossbow back further, getting ready to release. I turned my head away closing my eyes and holding my breath. A tear welled up behind my closed lids as the stake taunted my heart. Vance brushed his mouth along the leather of my necklace. "Ah, Sal." He stepped back and pushed me down to the ground. I yelped as my hip hit the marble, wincing at the pain in my wrist. Vance lifted his hands up as if surrendering.

"It's time for you to get the hell out," Sal growled as he continued to point the stake at Vance's heart.

"That's too bad. I was just starting to enjoy myself."

Sal took another step closer to Vance.

"I'm leaving. Damn, priest. You're sure turning into a fine vampire badass after all these years. I wish I would've turned you myself."

Paralyzed in place, I kept my eyes on Sal.

"She's got a great ass."

I shifted my knees underneath me.

Sal commanded, "Get up. Let's go. Get up!"

Pushing myself onto my knees, another sharp pain shot up into my wrist. I got to my feet and walked over to Sal's side.

"Let Gabe know that I stopped by." Vance pulled out his keys and swung them around his finger. "And, that I left him a package at Antonio's mansion." He looked me up and down. "And keep an eye on that tight ass. Next time I'm in town, I might need to relinquish your ownership of her."

"Nobody owns me!" I squinted my death stare.

"I like 'em feisty." He nodded at me and then turned on his heels, opening the front door. "One more thing. You'll need to hire a new guard at the front gate." He walked out, and Sal followed behind him.

As Vance flew off, Sal walked back in and secured the door. He dropped the crossbow to his side, turned to look at me, and put his finger to his mouth reminding me not to speak.

"How dare you treat me like a whore?"

Sal's eyes enlarged.

"You fuck me and then try to put a claim on me."

His eyes relaxed and his mouth curled up. "You're mine and no other man or vampire will have you, understand?"

"I'm getting out of here. You vampires are nuts!"

"You're not leaving. Not tonight."

"Watch me." I walked toward the staircase as he charged me, yanking me off the first step, twisting me around to face him as he cupped the back of my neck and waist. Not having expected him to get into full character, I gasped. Sal's tight abs pressed into my stomach as my chest hit his. *Awkwardly comfortable.* I stood there in his arms searching his eyes for a playful smile, but they remained hard pressed now burning with desire. I pushed his chest with my palms and whispered. "Sal."

A piece of hair fell in front of my eye, and he brushed it back behind my ear. "He's gone." He took a step back releasing me slowly.

Our eyes kept hold of one another.

"Way to commit, Sal," I said to break the tension.

He took another step back, picked up his bow, and walked into the kitchen.

Looking up at the stairs and then at Sal walking away, I followed him into the kitchen instead. He stood at the refrigerator, opened it, and grabbed a bottle of blood. Twisting the cap off, he flipped it onto the counter and began to chug.

The bottle that Marco had spun and left on the granite was gone. *Where did it go?* I scanned the floor while leaning against the island. Sal's eyes followed mine.

To distract him, I said, "Thank you, Sal."

He took his final chug, looked at me, and wiped his mouth with his hand as he placed the bottle on the counter where Marco's should have been. "Who was he referring to when he said you had a visitor?" Sal moved up to the other side of the island directly across from me.

"No one. He was just messing with you."

"I don't think so, Amber." He rubbed his neck. "Someone broke my neck knocking me out. It wasn't Vance. If he had found me in the weapon's room, he would have used one of them against me."

Knocked you out ... Marco. I shifted. "I was in the kitchen because I was hungry and couldn't sleep. When I walked out of the kitchen, the front door was cracked open. I just assumed either Gabe or you had come in. I stepped outside and then back in. That's when Vance attacked."

His eyes acted as a lie detector as he crossed his arms at his chest. "Vance is very suspicious. He attacked the wrong girl tonight and knows it. And I think your necklace saved you once again." Sal nodded at the amethyst around my neck.

Still shirtless, my eyes fell back on Sal's chest. I walked around the island and stopped inches from him as he stood erect, staring at me. My fingers slid across the outline of his tattoo-like symbol. "So, this ..." I drew a line over the two faceless bodies intertwined. "This is Gabe's symbol as a maker?"

Sal nodded.

"It's beautiful," I said leaving my fingers over it.

"Yes," Sal whispered.

"And anyone he turns will have this tattoo?"

"It's not a tattoo. It's a brand. We are branded by our makers. Symbols contain an element of what's most important to them. Something a vampire lost while human."

"Is this Catori?" I brushed my thumb over the female shape.

"Yes." Sal grabbed my wrist and carefully put it down to my side taking heavier breaths. "I think you should go to bed."

Gabe's brand gave me goosebumps. *He really loved her. Loves me. We're bound.* "I'm worried about Gabe."

"He's fine."

"How do you know?"

Sal tapped his chest. "This always lets me know when Gabe's in danger. I will always know, and I will always be by his side if he needs me."

"Obligations," I muttered to myself.

Sal nodded having heard me. "Sí. Obligaciones."

"I need you to take me home in the morning, Sal." He shook his head. "It's not a negotiation. Grams is coming over."

He cocked his head. "The psychic medium?"

"Yes."

He nodded and grabbed another bottle of blood from the fridge. "I'll take you. Now, go on to bed. I'll be up keeping watch tonight." He walked to the den.

"Okay. Well. Thanks again." As I walked in the opposite direction, I stopped and turned around. "Are you going to tell Gabe what happened tonight?"

"Sí."

CHAPTER 40

GABE

Alcohol permeated the air in Antonio's mansion as I walked into the lounge. But a more potent scent caught my attention. I scanned the room in search of the wounded victim. Side-stepping the inebriated, dodging couples in heated conversations, and watching out for those with their nose in their phones proved taxing. For a split moment, I considered taking one of them into the cellar and feasting. *Get it together.* I bit my lip and drew blood to get my temptation under control.

Techno thumped along with laughter, yelling, and kissing. Picking out Antonio's voice over the cacophony of sound challenged even my superior sense. I opened the cellar door quickly and locked it behind me. Eight-foot-tall wine shelves lined the damp, cool cellar.

"Ahhhhhhhhhh," came out from a woman down below as I descended the steps.

"Please, Jennifer. Stop moving," Antonio said.

Handcuffed to a pipe, Jennifer's body writhed against the brick wall, scratching her naked body—blood everywhere.

Antonio kneeled next to her.

"Vance. Uhhhhh. Where is he?" She groaned.

"He's close," Antonio whispered placing his hand on her forehead. "She's burning up." He looked over at me as I knelt down next them.

"Jennifer." I placed my hand on her knee. "Look at me."

She circled her head, rolling it side to side and moaned.

"What are we going to do?" Antonio asked.

"We'll take her to the cabin." If Amber allowed me to change her, I would never bite her and leave her to suffer. Our bite confuses and torments victims creating a bond to us. And without helping them to fully transition, they go insane.

"And then?" Antonio stood up pacing in a circle.

"I don't know yet. We don't have much of a choice, do we?" I bit my lip again taming my thirst. I turned back to Jennifer as she continued to roll her neck.

"Mierda!" Antonio crouched back down watching my eyes. "She's bleeding everywhere."

My eyes must have transitioned to black.

"Go get a robe quick! And call Cali. Let her know I need her at the cabin now." I couldn't call Holly because she had other orders for tonight.

Antonio ran up the cellar stairs.

"Jennifer, I'm going to take you to see Vance, okay?" She looked up at me, her cheeks mascara lined. "I'm going to take you. We've just got to get you covered up."

"Vance?"

"Yes, I'm going to take you to him."

"I have to clean my face. He can't see me like this," Jennifer said.

"Don't worry. We'll clean you up."

"I'm in so much pain, Gabe. My head hurts."

"I know. I'm gonna get you out of here. I'm going to break your handcuffs."

"You can't!"

"I have to Jennifer."

"No! He told me to stay here."

"Who told you? Vance?"

Antonio came back down the stairs and handed me a black silk robe. I threw it over my shoulder and cupped Jennifer's chin in my hand.

"Yes. He said he'd come back to get me."

"Yes. He sent us to get you, Jennifer. He had to take care of some business." I placed my hand on the pipe above the handcuffs.

"Did you know about him?"

"Know what, Jennifer?"

"That he's a vampire? That he's a magnificent vampire!" Jennifer's eyes looked up at her handcuffs where my hands sat steadily above them. "I miss him so much."

"Do you want to see Vance?"

She nodded her head yes, biting back tears. The poison in Vance's bite was so powerful. For most vampires, a bite soliciting insanity would take days. And if he'd been feeding on her prior to tonight, it would explain her condition.

"Let's get you to him." My fingers teetered on the edges of one of the handcuffs careful not to pinch her skin, and I pulled. The silver made my skin hiss. Smoke rose from my fingertips. The handcuff snapped. I clenched my teeth and grabbed the other. It broke as well, clanking against the pipe as it slid down.

She circled her wrists. "Take me to him."

"Let's go." I put my hands out to help her up. My fingertips still blistered from the burn but healing rapidly. I steadied her. "Here, wrap this around you."

"He prefers me like this."

"I know he does. But he wouldn't like anyone else seeing your beautiful body." Her arms, back, and ass bleeding in various places from rubbing against the bricks. "Cover up!"

Jennifer pulled the robe out of my hands and wrapped herself in it.

"Let's go." I lifted her up, and she wrapped her arms around my neck. "Antonio, I need you to walk me through the crowd."

She nuzzled her head into my chest while I ascended the stairs behind Antonio. He opened the cellar door. With swift strides, I walked us down the dimly lit hallway. As I turned the corner back into the lounge, Benjamin spotted Jennifer in my arms.

He crossed the room with his hands balled up in fists. "Get your hands off her!"

"Benjamin," Jennifer whispered.

I passed her to Antonio.

"What the fuck? You and your asshole friend get your hands off her."

"She's fine." I looked into Benjamin's eyes compelling him to calm down and listen. "Jennifer went to visit her family on the East Coast. She's fine but her grandfather is very ill. We don't know when she'll be back."

"She went to visit her grandfather. He's very sick," Benjamin repeated.

"Yes. You watched her walk out of here in a hurry."

"She walked out in a hurry."

"Good boy, Benjamin." I grabbed Jennifer back into my arms. "Antonio. Take care of him for me."

"Benjamin, have I shown you my latest Van Gogh? Come. It's right over here." Antonio hooked his neck and led him away.

I carried her out the door and to the front driveway where I'd asked the valet to keep the engine warm. The kid with a red jacket opened the car door for Jennifer. As her body tucked into the seat, I turned to him and compelled him, "You didn't see me here tonight, and Jennifer left on her own in a taxi. She looked like she was in a hurry. She wore a smokin' hot gray dress."

"She was in a hurry. Smokin' hot," the kid repeated.

I placed a hundred-dollar bill in his front jacket pocket. "Thanks," I patted my hand over it.

After buckling Jennifer in, I walked around to the driver's side. Jennifer rubbed her neck where the circular scabs of her recent wounds sat. *Dammit, Vance. Another life in my hands.* I shifted into gear and took off to the cabin in the Angeles. Cali will have her work cut out for her this weekend. *What am I going to tell Amber?*

A text came in from Holly, **I lost Vance.**

Mierda. I wrote back. **Find him! This isn't a game!**

I proceeded to text Sal, and he confirmed that Amber was safe. As I merged onto the highway, I looked over at Jennifer finally resting, which wouldn't be for long. I guess there's comfort in thinking your lover was anxiously awaiting your presence. But Vance wasn't. Jennifer was another victim left behind. Instead of a welcoming lover, she was about to experience something she'd never forget. The transition. And I, once again, had to resolve this mess. A role I didn't mind, but wished the circumstances were different. *All in good time.*

CHAPTER 41

AMBER

Rotten ham and eggs assaulted me as I opened my front door. *Ugh. I forgot to take the trash out before we left last time.* Pinching my nose, I headed straight for the kitchen.

Sal walked in behind me and locked the door. "I have to take the garbage out," I called over my shoulder.

"I'll unlock it when you're ready," Sal said.

I would have to see my dentist about clenching after all of this drama blows over—if it ever did. The rational side of me knew they were just concerned for my safety. The carefree me had a hard time living under lock and key.

The smell from the garbage caused me to gag as I tied a knot. The odor lingered and touched my tongue. "Yuck."

With the bag at arm's length in front of me, I walked out to the living room. Sal unlocked the door for me, took the trash out of my hand, and walked it down the hall to the chute. Wiping my hands as I walked to my bedroom, my phone buzzed in my back pocket. I plopped down on my disheveled bed to read the incoming text.

Amber. I'm sorry I had to leave you last night. Gabe texted.

It's okay. Everything's fine.

Vance left a mess.

Tell me about it. I typed while propped up on my stomach.

What do you mean?

RU coming to the party tomorrow at Antonio's? The three dots taunted me as I waited for his reply.

Where RU? I can't connect to the cameras at the mansion. He wrote.

At my apartment.

Like a desperate teenager, I watched the phone, anticipating what he might write next. He paused texting, so I flipped through Instagram. New celebrity hair styles flooded my feed. *Nice.* I put the phone down on the nightstand and tugged at my bottom lip. My neck and lower back ached from being tossed around. Shivers ran down my spine thinking about Vance and how close I'd come to being snuffed out. I rolled my wrist. *Thankfully not broken.* The phone buzzed.

I'm here. Grams texted me. *Not Gabe.* I sighed.

Thumbs up emoji.

The tickle of hair at my back annoyed me, and I rose to the mirror atop of my dresser. Discoloring around my neck prevented any notion of clipping those annoying strands up. I left my locks down. Sal's deep voice alerted me that Grams entered the apartment. Just as I reached for the doorknob, my phone rang. *Gabe.*

"Hello," I said.

"Are you alone in your apartment? Is Sal there with you?"

"How about, 'Hi, Amber. It's so good to hear your voice. How are you?'"

"Amber, is he?"

"Yes, Gabe." I rolled my eyes. "What's the problem?"

"I asked him to keep you safe."

"And he has."

"You're supposed to be at the mansion."

"And, that's going to keep me safe?" Lifting my hair up again to observe the bruises in the mirror, I blurted out, "Vance broke in last night. Really safe."

Gabe's voice dropped, "What are you talking about?"

"Didn't Sal call you?"

A growl of fury came next. "No. What happened?"

"Vance attacked me, but I'm fine. Really. Sal protected ..."

"Puta madre," Gabe yelled. I held the phone away from my ear.

"Everything's fine. Sal told him I was 'his'."

"I'll call you back." He hung up.

The dark screen stared at me as I heard Sal say, "Bueno" from the living room. *Shit.*

Placing my phone down on my dresser, I walked to the living room and plopped down next to Grams on the couch. With deep, slow breaths, her chest rose and fell as if she were meditating, but her eyes remained locked on Sal. He stood at the window, gripping the phone tight to his ear, and spoke rapidly in Spanish. Native speakers always talked too fast to decipher. I'd learned some words in school but never pursued more than the mandatory requirement. I gripped the cushions.

"What kind of mess did you get yourself into, baby?" Grams said nudging me with her shoulder. "I sense heavy emotions in here."

"Oh. You know. Boy troubles."

"I see." Grams looked back over at Sal.

With squinted eyes as if Sal had a serious migraine, he held his hand over his mouth. Gabe's voice spewed out the phone as he yelled.

Squeezing Grams's hand comforted me. "Thanks for coming."

"Of course. Now. Along with that rotten smell in your apartment …" She tilted her head down to give me the "get your shit together, child" look. "I do feel a presence. It's strong. For some reason not yet revealing itself to me."

She sat back on the couch, sifted through her purse, and pulled out a lighter.

"Is he staying for this?" She spoke.

"Yes."

Sal turned to look at us again and nodded in agreement.

The *Glam & Fame* magazines that usually sat on the coffee table were now underneath it on the floor. Grams laid out her candles, incense, and stones one at a time across a scarf.

Holding his phone out, Sal said, "For you," his lips tight and brows furrowed. I lifted my hand up slowly, and he placed the phone in my palm.

"Hello."

"I'm glad you're alright, Amber. Next time you need to call me right away. You understand?"

"Everything was handled. Sal took—"

"That's not the point. You can't keep this type of information from me."

"You should've been there."

"That's not fair," Gabe said.

It turned into an awkward silence as I walked into the kitchen. I lowered my voice, "Look, he got into your house." *And so did Marco.* "I'm starting to think that *safe* doesn't really exist." My hand tightened around the phone, and a pain shot to my wrist. I switched ears.

"Maybe you're right." He sighed. "It was a trap but just not what I had expected. He obviously knows more about us … you, then I cared to acknowledge."

"So, what's the plan then?"

"I need to talk to him."

"That's insane. You said it yourself, you can't just rationalize with him."

"Look. I've got this. You don't need to worry about it."

"Too late. I am worried." My gut lurched. "So how much longer are you going to be? What are you doing anyhow?"

"I shouldn't be too much longer."

Is he with another woman? I closed my eyes. "Well, if you're not going to tell me. I'll just get going. I'll call you later."

"Amber, wait."

"Grams just called for me. I gotta go." I hung up and took a deep breath placing Sal's phone on the counter. "Arrrrghhh."

"Everything okay?" Sal walked in.

I shook my head, grabbed the phone, and handed it back to him.

As I brushed past Sal, he caught my bicep, and pulled me back into the kitchen. "He means well. You're everything to him."

"That's no excuse." I looked down at my arm as Sal continued to hold me then looked back up at him. "Why all the secrets with what happened last night? You were supposed to talk with him."

Sal lowered his voice, "It's complicated."

Stepping back, I forced Sal to release his grip. "Let's get to this séance already, huh?"

My upper back tensed up, and I took a deep breath as I watched Grams hovering her hands over the table swirling the incense—her apophyllite crystals placed in the shape of a figure eight. I sat down next to her and put my hand on her thigh.

"You ready?" she asked.

"Yes," I said.

Sal sat in the armchair to our right, resting his head on his fist. His presence gave me comfort.

"Let's begin then," said Grams.

CHAPTER 42

AMBER

The sacred orange candle flickered in my brightly lit living room. Sage sat burning in a clay bowl, collecting ash as the smoke traveled in front of me from the gentle breeze coming through the cracked sliding glass door off the balcony. Chanting burst into the room from the depths of Grams's throat. She hovered her hands over the crystals in a figure eight on the coffee table. She opened her eyes. Each crystal felt the caress of her fingertips as she picked one up at a time. "We know you're here. We mean no harm. Reveal yourself." She looked around the room and then steadied her gaze in the direction of the balcony. "I see you," Grams said as she squinted. "Come closer."

I saw nothing. Sal squinted as if trying to make out an image.

The tingles on the back of my neck were ever present between the vampires and the spirits themselves around me. Distinguishing between the two posed a challenge. But today, the hairs on my arms stood up.

A heaviness filled the room as Grams gasped out loud. "Walter?"

"Dad?" I spoke. "Is he really here?"

The armchair squeaked as Sal moved to the edge, resting his elbows on his knees.

"It's great to see you, too, baby. Oh, how I've missed you," Grams said.

Silence.

"She is beautiful, isn't she?" Grams's eyes focused directly in front of her as if my father stood behind the coffee table.

"Why's he here?" I asked. Grams's smile faded leaving her stoic. "Grams?"

"He's met Gabe," she said. Sal's eyes locked on Grams as she translated.

"What do you mean?" I asked.

"He likes him." *Why isn't she smiling?* "He just wanted to make sure you're alright."

"Ask him if he's okay. What's it like? Has he seen Mom? I have so many questions."

Grams wiped her palms along her thighs. "He's fine. Happy."

By the clearing of Sal's throat, doubt creeped into my mind. I watched her eyes move to the center of the coffee table as if my father stood in the middle. "He's seen her and she's fine." Grams closed her eyes.

"Grams? Are you losing him?"

"No, baby." Her eyes remained closed. "I can hear him better this way."

"Dad. I miss you. I hope you can hear me." I squeezed my hands together. *I have so many questions.*

"He misses you, too." A tear fell down her cheek, she opened her eyes, and her shoulders hunched forward.

"Dad. I don't mind you visiting but it's a bit creepy, you know?"

Sal laughed under his breath.

"Sorry. But it is. Could you somehow ... I don't know ... keep to the living room and kitchen for me?"

Sal continued to grin.

"What's he saying, Grams?"

"He's not ready for his baby to grow up. If he could, he would spook Gabe out of this apartment."

Sal cracked up.

"Sal. This is serious. What's gotten into you?" I asked.

"I'm so ... so ... sorry. Ahhhh." He continued to laugh as he stood up and walked into the kitchen.

I looked in the direction of the front door where Grams focused her eyes. "Dad. Can you bring Mom next time you come?"

Grams jerked her body and her shoulders lifted again. Still no smile. "My connection is breaking, Amber. Do you have anything else to say?"

"No. Wait. It can't. I want to know what it's like on the other side. I want to know if he can still feel and smell. I want to know if he has a home or if he wanders about. I want to know ... so much." My face fell into my hands as tears streamed out of my eyes. "I ... I ..."

Grams rubbed my back as Sal walked into the room and sat down in the chair.

"Did he answer?" I asked.

"It's complicated. He likes spending time here with you." Grams stopped rubbing my back. "Put your hand up, Amber. He's standing right in front of you." My high-five hand pressed against the air. An energy flew through me. "He's doing the same thing. And he said that he's in limbo. He's not ready to let go and allow himself to be reincarnated, yet."

"Reincarnated?" Sniffing back the liquid that lingered at the end of my nostrils. "What's holding you back, Dad?"

Grams cringed as she looked at the air in front of me. "You need to let go. He's having a hard time letting go of you. Drop your hand!" Looking at her in my peripheral, she licked her fingertips and put out the candle. "Now!"

I dropped my hand, and the pull I felt was as if a current ran through me had stopped. "No! Don't go. Not yet."

"I can't, baby." She lifted the sage and brushed the ash off the end of the clump into the clay. "Good-bye for now, son."

CHAPTER 43

———

AMBER

My childhood was spent mourning my father in silence. As Mom sat in the living room filling the air ducts with pot and Bob Marley, I sobbed into my pillow. Knowing my father was here with me yet not being able to talk to him was worse. I sat up and wiped my face with my hands. My phone had eight missed calls from Gabe and three voicemails.

I searched my contacts for Jennifer. *She'll understand.* I hit call, but it went to voicemail after the second ring. "Hi, Jenn," I let out a heavy sigh. "I could really use a girl chat right about now. Call me back." I hung up.

Where are you? I texted Jennifer. **Really need to talk.**

Tossing my phone on the bed, I walked to the bathroom and washed my face. Warm water cascaded over my skin, and I pressed into the towel to muffle my scream.

If he had met Gabe, why didn't Gabe just tell me? My swollen red eyes stared back at me in the mirror. *Go say bye to Grams before she leaves.* Adjusting my blouse, I walked out to the living room. As I neared the hallway I heard mumbling, and then I stopped frozen in place. Sal's hand caressed Grams's cheek as their lips touched. *Are you kidding me?*

"Ahem?" I stood cross-armed.

He stepped back and grabbed the doorknob.

"She can let herself out."

He backed up not taking his eyes off me.

"Baby, I'm heading out now." Grams walked over to me and hugged me as my arms stayed crossed at my chest. Her hand rubbed my back as it always did. "We'll do this again soon."

"Why do I get the feeling you didn't tell me everything I needed to know today?"

Grams pulled back and cupped my biceps in her hands. "Why would you say that?"

"You're not denying it?"

The oversized shopping bag hung at her elbow crease as she stepped away from me. "I don't have anything to hide. What do you want to know?"

"Whatever it is you didn't say." I looked over at Sal and asked him, "What did I miss? If Gabe can speak to spirits, I suppose you can, too. Right?"

Shaking his head, he waved his hands in front of him. "This is between the two of you."

"So, there is something more."

"Baby, your dad is not ready to move on. And. The truth is. He hasn't seen your mother. He's trying to find her."

"What? You lied to me. Why? What else did he say?" I clasped my hands together behind my head.

"Amber," Grams attempted to touch me, but I stepped back.

"You know what. Never mind. Just get out!"

Grams walked over to the door and stopped. "Sometimes you think you want the truth. And once you learn it, you can't unlearn it."

"I don't need to be coddled like a child for Christ's sake. I'm an adult. Jesus. Between you, Gabe, and Sal. Just get out!" I shoved Sal, and he moved out of the way as if I actually had strength to move him. The door swung open. "Get out! And you, too." I waved Sal out.

"You know I'm not leaving, Amber."

"Get out, Sal! Go!"

He stood for a minute. Grams had already stepped out the door and peered back in.

"Out. Get out!"

"I'll walk you to your car, Jo." He passed me. *First name basis?*

The door slipped out of my fingers, shutting just as Sal's ass past the threshold. I locked it behind them. "Uhhhhh- hhhhhhhh!" My fists hit the door. "Dammit, Dad! I know you're still here. Talk to me. Tell me what's going on. If you can't find mom, did she already get reincarnated?" *Or worse, was she denied that privilege because of her suicide?* I walked to my bedroom and threw myself onto the bed. Tucking the pillow under my cheek, I rolled myself into a fetal position. *They're not going to coddle me anymore. Not anymore.*

My phone buzzed, and a text popped up. *Jennifer? No.* I read the text from Marco. **Can I drive you to Antonio's tomorrow?** *Hell no.*

"Ugh. Another one who thinks he can control and cage me."

"Who's trying to cage you?" Gabe's voice came from the balcony door.

I jumped and threw myself around to face him.

"You've really got to learn to lock these doors."

I tapped the sleep button on my phone and placed it under my leg. "As if that would really stop you, or any vampire for that matter. How long have you been here?"

"Long enough." Leaning in for a kiss, his lips hit my cheek as I turned my head. He crawled onto the bed and leaned against the headboard. "Who's got you so furious?"

"You already know."

"Do I?" In swift motions, he pulled the phone out from under my leg.

"Hand me the phone." I turned my palm up waiting for him to comply.

The phone buzzed in his hand. He read it aloud, "Still waiting for my answer. From Marco." Gabe spoke between his teeth, "What answer is he waiting for?"

"Nothing. Give me the phone."

Gabe tucked it under his leg. "Come get it."

"Are you five years old? Jesus. Just give me the phone. I'm not in the mood for this bullshit."

He shook his head no and narrowed his eyes drawing them down to my pouty lips.

"Fine. Just keep the damn phone."

"What's going on, Amber? Talk to me."

"I don't feel like talking right now." I shifted away from him.

He tugged on my arm. "Come on, we need to talk."

Turning around, I crawled over and straddled him. He leaned on the headboard as his thumbs landed on the crease of my hips. My lips pulled on his as I slipped my hand under his leg. He flipped me onto my back causing the phone to fly out of my hand and onto the floor. "Dammit." Pinning me with one arm stuck to my side, he left the other free for me to grab a chunk of his hair, and I yanked it back.

He grinned and repositioned himself in between my legs while sucking on my chin. "I missed you." He held my forehead brushing my hair back. "I'm so glad you're alright."

My eyes closed. "I'm not alright." Tears streamed down the side of my face moistening my ear. "I'm not alright."

He backed himself off me, stood up against the dresser, and placed his hand in his pocket.

Wiping my face, I just lay there. "How about you tell me about your ability to speak with ghosts? Seems like you've been hiding things from me."

He nodded, pulled out an antique cross, and handed it to me. "Let's start here."

CHAPTER 44

———

GABE

The cross dangled above her as she lowered the turquoise stone to her mouth while lying on her back. Pulling it back up above her, she examined the dull stone, and then rolled onto her side wiping her tears.

My body, rigid against the dresser, yearned to hold her. Instead, I gave her space to process. "Catori made that for me. It's what's left of a rosary."

She looked at it again and placed it on the bed in front of her.

"I rub it for good luck I suppose. It became a habit that I've held onto for all these years." Even the few feet apart, my body desired to fill the void between us. I plopped down on the bed next to her, and she sat up balancing the cross on her palm. "Since we aren't fully united yet, I feel very protective over you."

"Fully united. Hmph." She shrugged. "What does this cross have to do with you and ghosts?"

"Nothing actually. But I think you need to know more about my intentions before I tell you more about my vampire gifts."

"Your intentions. To turn me?" Her face fell into her hands, and she huffed as her curls fell forward.

"Yes. We really haven't spoken much about this before, but it's time. There are two things I want more than anything else. One." I took her hand in mine. "I want a long immortal life with you." She lifted her eyes to meet mine. "And I want to be free of Vance's control over me. I need the release."

"So, I get it. You want to turn me." Amber stood up, ripping her hand from mine. "If I choose not to turn, what other choice do we have? Can we kill Vance?" She paced back and forth.

"I have tried before." I shook my head. "He's just so powerful. And there's a consequence in doing so. Vampires cannot kill their makers without killing themselves in return."

Earrings rattled in a handcrafted bowl as she leaned against her dresser holding the cross to her lips as she spoke, "So, I become a vampire to free you?"

In theory, if you choose to keep your soul.

Amber continued. "Or I don't, and he'll kill me."

"Or, I get someone else to kill him. I'll live if I don't stake him myself. No one's ever taken me up on my offer though."

She shook her head and leaned it back, opening her neck to me. I noticed the bruising. *Hijo de puta!* I clasped my hands together not wanting to ruin this moment, squeezing so hard I fractured my pinkie. I tightened my jaw as I spoke, "We … You don't have to decide anything today. I know how important life is to you. And you'd be giving up *life* so to speak."

My head leaned against her stomach, she held me, rubbing my back. "You have to turn me. I … I can't live without you. And I won't live much longer at all if you don't."

I pulled her into my lap, grabbed the back of her neck gently bringing our foreheads together. "I can't turn you, Amber."

"Why not?"

"If I do, I don't know if I'd be strong enough to release you."

"What are you talking about?"

"When we turn people, we grow stronger. It's exhilarating. If I release you, I lose power."

"Of course, you'd release me. You wouldn't let power keep you from uniting us, would you?"

"You'd be mine. Truly mine. Connected. Anything I want or say, you'd have to do."

"So, how's that different from today?" She kissed me.

I smiled. *True.* "I like control too much. We need to be equals in this."

"So how do I become a vampire then?"

"Sal."

Amber's pinched forehead seemed to be calculating her options.

Catori spoke to my soul. *She's in, Gabe. Finally.* My soul chattered on.

Amber interrupted the commotion in my head. "How do you know if he'll release me? How can you be so sure?"

A valid question. This was not something I was worried about. "He will. He has to if I command him to."

My soul spoke, *What if he doesn't? What if he uses this against you?*

What reason would he have to betray me? He's the one who refuses to accept a release. You know that. Is there something you're not telling me?

Amber closed her eyes again and spoke, distracting me from my internal conversation. "I need time to process this." She lay her head on my shoulder.

"I know. I'll give you some space. Sal just walked back in, and I need to catch him up on some business."

"Gabe, I wish you would've told me about my dad. It doesn't make sense."

"He asked me not to, and I like to honor my word. He's worried about your mom."

She nodded. "This is all too much today."

"Agreed. It is a lot to take in. Just rest. I'll check on you in a little bit." She crawled into bed turning on her side, clasping my cross against her chest. "Will it hurt?"

Excruciating. "Yes. It will be uncomfortable, but nothing you can't handle." With my hand on the doorknob, I said, "Get some rest."

CHAPTER 45

GABE

With a banana in hand, Amber walked into the room and sat down on the couch next to me. As always, everyone focused on her whenever she was near—including Sal, who watched her peel the skin back. My fangs shook within my gums. She had only slept for a couple of hours, waking around 3:00 p.m. and still looked like a sexy goddess.

While she slept, Sal and I reviewed the plan. Amber's father had stood in the corner observing the discussion. His spirit looked more transparent than normal, and he hadn't said anything to me. I figured he was just as overwhelmed as Amber as he hunched his shoulders and tucked his chin to his chest.

Distracting me from Walter, my soul spat discontent for Sal. I defended him, *He's loyal,* I told him. My soul disagreed.

A large syringe lay on top of a cheese-like sack on the coffee table. Two blue vials sat next to the syringe. Amber's eyes enlarged as she looked at it. "Whatcha doing?" She scooted to the edge of the couch.

I followed Sal's eyes as he watched her take a bite. *What the hell are you looking at?*

"Well?" she asked.

"Cleaning a syringe." I held up a microfiber cloth. The tubular needle was an inch wide in diameter, allowing for both liquid and crushed stone to be sucked up into it. Its edge was made of silver and sharply designed to penetrate the skin. "Do you want to know what it's for?"

She took another bite while watching me hold it in both hands nodding slowly.

"It's what we would need to finalize the transformation when turning someone into a vampire."

"Bloodstone," she muttered with her mouth full.

"Yes. Sal and I are ready whenever you decide … if you decide to make the change."

"It's going to burn me, isn't it?"

"Pues claro," Sal said.

Amber looked over at him as she swallowed her last bite and placed the peel down on a napkin next to her. She wiped her hands together. Her chest rose and fell as she breathed in deeply, increasing the tension in the room. Grabbing the syringe out of my hands, she moved her fingers around the circular tip. Sal's expression taunted me as he sat back eyeing her. I grabbed the syringe out of her hands and placed it on the cloth. Holly had warned me not to trust Sal, too. I figured she was just jealous.

My soul nudged again about not trusting him. *You haven't any real proof.* I said to my soul. *What have you actually learned from his soul?*

Nothing. That's why this is so suspicious, my soul said. *And why didn't he call you when Vance attacked?*

"So how will this work exactly?" Her eyes met Sal's. "Will you compel me first?"

I hadn't thought of that.

"If you'd like," Sal answered.

My soul warned me again, *You can't let him turn her.*

"Will you be with us?" Amber placed her hand on my knee, but her eyes lingered on Sal for a moment too long before looking over at me.

My teeth clenched as I drew my fingers through my hair to avoid squeezing her hand. "Yes."

Sal's attention turned to me, and we locked eyes.

He's got other plans, my soul said.

I leaped over the table and picked up Sal by his collar. His eyes widened as I shook him. "Qué diablos ves? Eh?"

"Nada!" He looked over at Amber, and I looked at her expression of horror.

She gripped the couch cushions with her slender fingers, and cried out, "What's gotten into you?"

Our faces were inches apart. "Me decepcionaste! How could I trust you?" I threw him across the room. His body slammed against the front door and then landed on the hardwood floor. His nails clawed the laminate as he scrambled to his feet.

"Gabe!" Amber yelled.

Sal held himself up against the door. "You're stretched too thin. Trying to take care of everyone else's problems. Cuando vas a aprender?"

"No necesito sermones. You had one simple task. And how can I trust you anymore? You didn't even call to tell me about Vance."

"How could I? You were," Sal looked over at Amber, "occupied."

She stood up, locked eyes with mine. The rage in her eyes consumed me. "What's that supposed to mean?"

"Nothing," I said.

She stormed out of the room to the kitchen.

"Get out!" I yelled to Sal.

"Gabe. You're …" Sal responded.

"Get … the … fuck … out!"

He grabbed the doorknob twisting slowly. He looked back at me. "Calmate hombre. No pasa nada." He walked out.

I locked the door and sped into the kitchen. Amber gripped the counter's edge as she leaned against it. Her mouth puckered and brow furrowed. I walked over to her, and she held one arm out distancing me from her.

"I can't trust him with you," I said.

"Can I trust you?"

"What? Of course!"

"Who were you occupied with?" Her nails dug into my chest.

I pushed thoughts of Amber naked on top of me out of my head. "I'm helping someone transition." *God, she's beautiful when she's angry.*

"Who?"

"I can't say." I touched her hand and she quivered.

"Why not?" she asked as I rubbed my thumb over the back of her hand, taking small steps forward causing a slight bend in her elbow.

"When people transition, it's a private matter. Just like it will be for you." I brought her hand to my cheek covering it with mine. Lowering my voice, "I just can't trust Sal around you anymore. To respect you."

She shook her head. "Why's everything so complicated?" She took a step closer placing her other hand on my face.

I wrapped my arms around her back. "I will change you. It should be me." Our lips pressed together gently, and I pulled back to allow my mouth to hover. "I can't let another man taste you." I pulled her bottom lip between mine. "You're mine." My lips enveloped hers and my tongue forced its way into her mouth reminding her that I would be the only one ever to go there again. She pressed her chest into mine and grasped the short strands of my hair.

I will need a modified plan though. Sal had a pertinent role to play.

Lifting her up, she wrapped her legs around my waist. I walked her to her room and shut the door behind us.

CHAPTER 46

GABE

1776, Mission San Gabriel

The vineyard at sunset was a magical place. A breeze played over my sombrero, and I shivered at the cooling temperature. Catori's wedding ceremony would be taking place in less than a month. I paced through the crops every evening, but grapes didn't console the constriction of my heart. There was no resolution for our forbidden love. Like being stuck at a dead end after a long journey, rage consumed me watching her with her fiancé each day. She wasn't right for him. I knew that. She knew that. We were meant to be together. Tethered souls.

I admired the glow of the sun on the grapes lined in the horizon. She had a hand in this. I kicked a stone down the perfectly planted row. I wouldn't be able to forget her. She'd always be present. I would need to leave. I couldn't possibly stay and watch her ensnared by a beastly man. She deserved me, a gentle soul with a wicked intensity for her.

The sun left a shadow of light over the earth as it fully descended out of sight. Taking in a deep breath, I pressed my thumbs between my eyes and screamed into the open air. As my lungs released into the earth's atmosphere, another yelp cried in the distance. And then another. And another. These were screams of horror, not ache. I looked at the village and fires fluttered about as if men were on horseback. My stomach dropped, and I ran toward the camp. Along the way, I grabbed a pickaxe lying against a shed and continued to run stumbling through the desert earth.

Slowing to a creep as torturous screams and fiery roars of war closed in on me. Catori. I looked toward her hut already on fire.

"No."

The torches I saw from a distance became clearer now. They weren't men on horseback but humans flying around carrying flames. I blinked shaking my head. It can't be. I circled closer to the dining quarters where Catori should have been. I crept to the window with the pickaxe at my side. I peered in and saw women on the floor. Some decapitated and others limp.

No. No, no.

Creeping around the side of the structure, I snuck into the room. I scanned the floor seeking out a sliver of hope. And then I saw a familiar embroidered skirt. Shifting my gaze up to the wrist of the body that lie limp on the floor, I recognized the bracelet she made for me that I had returned to her. I ran over, dropping the pickaxe. "Catori." I touched her neck. Blood stained my fingers as I searched for a pulse. "Catori," I whispered as I lifted her limp body into mine. Rocking, I shrieked. My dry heaving tears choked out in despair. "Catori. Mi amor. Ughhh. Mi amor."

A darkness slithered up behind me. I continued to rock her without any care of death before me.

"Look at this one. I think we touched a nerve." An obnoxious voice interrupted my despair.

"What do you want us to do, boss?" A long-bearded monster said.

"Hey. You. Stand up!" A high-pitched demand came from over my shoulder. I ignored it and continued hugging Catori close to me.

"Get up he said." A large hand lifted me into the air. My feet dangled. Blood covered my white shirt and arms. I kicked the bearded monster with black eyes in the face. He let go.

I landed on my side and scurried to my feet as a tall, blond-haired man with ocean eyes hovered above me. I stood up fearlessly swinging. He placed his hand on my head keeping me in my spot as I continued to wail. "I like this one." He looked over his shoulder at one of his hollow followers. "This one, too." The exotic one and the hollow one surrounded me.

"What? Take me. I have nothing more to live for. Hazlo ahora." I pounded my chest.

"That's exactly what I needed to hear." The blond one said as he grabbed the back of my hair drawing me to him. His blue eyes changed to purple drawing me into a swell of emotion, and his strength overwhelmed me as he jerked my head sideways opening up my neck. Fangs emerged, and my eyes grew in horror. It can't be.

He pierced my neck. I groaned, grabbing hold of his biceps with hatred knowing what he was doing. Only something we joked about as kids. Demons of the night. And here one was. Sucking on me. Draining me. Taking me. And he could have me, so long as it led to death.

CHAPTER 47

GABE

Dim lighting in the waiting room created an unusual ambiance for those in line to donate blood at Vance's largest center. Most blood banks had bare walls, bright lights, and a back room with chairs lined up only separated by cubicle partitions. This center modeled itself after a massage parlor, which was part of the allure to draw donors in. Sugar cookies shaped in hearts sat wrapped on the table at the entrance. Infused water refreshments lined the wall along with cozy couch cushions and reading material that heightened temptations. Cinnamon simmered in an incense bowl behind the empty reception desk.

A man sipping water from his reusable bottle sat cross-legged waiting for his turn. To his left, a woman with a low-cut blouse and tight jeans tipped her chin up, roamed her eyes over me and lowered her lashes attempting to harpoon my interest and reel me in. I tapped the counter, listening to Vance with a man in the back room.

My soul confirmed it prior to leaving Amber that she wanted to transition into a vampire, which meant we had a way out of this. Perhaps, we could manage without bloodshed. I had a bargaining chip to try reasoning with Vance one last time.

"Restroom?" I pointed down the hall behind the counter talking to the folks waiting. The woman nodded with a smile and the man kept his head down focused on his phone.

She's trouble, my soul said.

No doubt.

I walked toward the back, passing one vacant room and then another. In the third room, a nurse hovered over a patient with a thick, hairy forearm dangling over the side of the chair. She recognized me as I stepped into the doorframe.

"Gabe."

"Veronica. Is …?" I pointed to the man in the chair.

She shook her head. "Passed out."

"Good. I'm gonna head back to Vance then."

"Yep. Later."

I tapped the wall as I made my way to Vance's office. A door disguised as wood mocked the untrained eye as he ensured this room would be impossible to penetrate by any human. The heavy steel opened up without effort for me. He didn't think much about hiding from his own kind.

Covering the tube's end with his thumb, restricting the flow, Vance looked up.

A young college student sat on top of his intricate desk, looking straight at me. "Who's he?" The man asked Vance.

"Someone you'll respect dear friend. Maybe even give a taste to."

"Whatever. Are we done here?" The student asked.

Vance gritted his teeth and sharply turned his neck, hovering directly in front of the young man. "We're done when I say we're done." He put the tube in his mouth and sucked six deep sips. The young man's eyes drooped shut.

"You're an asshole." I crossed my arms.

"Now tell me what I need to know."

"Eli has a cure for insanity." I stepped closer to him. "He's found a way for vampires to feed from and not turn humans."

"Impossible."

"No. You're in the wrong business."

"God dammit. How did I not see this coming?" He grabbed his head as if in agony. "Too many distractions."

"Yeah, syphoning humans is quite a distraction."

He looked at me with a fierce glare.

I grabbed my stomach and hunched over. My gut twisted, and I went to one knee expecting to see my intestines come out my throat. "Vance. Shit. Don't." I grabbed my stomach and dropped to my knees.

Stay with me. My soul remained alert. *Appeal to his ego.*

"Vance." I squinted from the pain. "He's not…going…to get away…with this. We can do this. Together. I will help you, brother." His fury released me, and I stayed huddled for a moment allowing my insides to shift back into place. I stood up, one leg at a time, and took my warrior stance. "We've got this, brother." I held my hand out waiting for him to grab me in for a man hug.

He looked past me and over at the limp man on the couch. He nodded. "Yes. We've got this." He turned away from me and took a seat at his desk. "Have a seat."

Don't trust him, my soul pleaded.

It's for Catori, too. We have no other choice.

CHAPTER 48

—

AMBER

Like the first time I drove alone when I was sixteen, an exhilarating sensation of freedom and excitement vibrated through me on the way to Antonio's wrap party at the mansion. That day, I drove down to Carlsbad beach to play volleyball with some friends in Grams's gray Camry. Recognizing the liberty and power I had behind the wheel on that first drive solidified what I already knew in my core: I am an independent woman.

While driving up the mountain, I embraced my alone time and temporary newfound freedom. Driving is where I've always sought out clarity in stressful situations. It gave me a sense of isolation from the world, putting me into a trance of revolving thoughts every time despite the SoCal traffic. Since meeting Gabe, that freedom had been taken from me. And I just allowed it. I gave in.

And he claims me just as Vance taunted me about being claimed. The rapid evolution of my relationship with Gabe in less than a few weeks frightened me now that I knew what the depths of his control over me as a maker could be. Monitoring his relationship with Sal allowed me to paint a picture in my mind. Gabe's protective and commanding solutions to resolving threats had me consider that I would be isolated again as a new vampire until he could fully unite with me.

An overprotective Gabe, without his faithful Sal, just felt off. Jealousy always got the best of people. His soul claimed that Sal wasn't to be trusted. I suppose I'll learn more about soul influence when I can finally hear Catori speak to me in my vampire form. *Vampire form. Have I lost my mind?*

Sitting at a traffic light, the engine hummed quietly and a Ferrari idled next to me. The tinted windows made seeing the driver impossible. But the hairs on the back of my neck went stiff. *Vance?* Uncertain, I stepped on the gas as the light turned green and made a left turn at the next light. The Ferrari blew past me sending a release of tension through my exhale.

A deal with Vance bought us time. If Gabe could ease up on the leash he held on me for one night, then I hoped there was a chance I could walk alongside him as a partner instead of feeling like a delicate treasure locked away in his museum collection. Gabe didn't elaborate on the deal he had made before leaving me alone to take care of some business related to preparations for turning me. But he didn't truly leave me alone. A good friend of his, a trusted vampire, would be watching over me from afar. Some vamp named Holly. *Whatever.*

Film-wrap parties at Antonio's come with strobe lights, DJs along the extended driveway, pop-up tents on every piece of land surrounding the mansion, and uninvited people being rejected at the door. After handing my keys to the valet, I walked up the VIP ramp considering the power I would have as an immortal, a new VIP as a bloodthirsty, supercharged stamina kind.

Music drifted out into the foyer. A red carpet lined the floor to the back of the house. Golden ropes hung from the ceiling holding men and women acrobats, twisting, twirling, and swinging around. An ocean blue leotard grabbed my attention like Vance's eyes. Thoughts of being bound to him crossed my mind. If Gabe turned me, and we didn't unite, I'd be stuck with that crazy blond vampire. And that could never happen. *Gabe can't turn me.*

In the lounge, peopled crowded around the bar and cocktail waiters wandered about with champagne and hors d'oeuvres. A waiter stopped in front of me. The stem of the crystal flute felt like a thin twig between my fingertips.

"Hey." Zara startled me from behind and some of the champagne dribbled down my chin. "You ready to party?"

"Hell yes!" I wiped my chin. An old friend, named independence, burst out of my lungs over the music thumping in the background.

Zara pulled me by my hand across the room as she pumped her fist in the air. "Let's treat ourselves," she yelled over her shoulder as she continued to lead me through the crowd. We ended up at the VIP room where low grade pot and blow circulated freely. Zara danced by a bouncer standing at the door. I placed my glass on a cocktail table as I followed her in. Smoke stung my eyes and clouded my vision in this already dimly lit room.

Benjamin walked by, and I grabbed his arm, releasing Zara's hand. "Hey. How are you?"

"Amber. Hiiiii." Benjamin steadied himself on my shoulder.

"Have you heard from Jenn?"

"Jennifer. Yeahhhhh. Well noooo." Benjamin booped my nose. "Yeah. Jenn. She's on the East Coast. Her grandfather's ill."

"Did you say grandfather?" *That can't be right.*

"Yup." Benjamin waved at some folks who were egging him to move on from the conversation and follow them out. "Good to see you. Gotta go."

Jennifer doesn't have any living grandparents.

Zara tugged me forward and then fell down onto Philip's lap.

As I sat down beside them, Philip placed his hand on my thigh brushing it lightly as if petting a cat. "Hey, Amber." *He must have popped X.* Philip opened his palm to Zara showing her a pill. *Of course.* She grabbed it and chased it down with a water that he was drinking. He held out his hand to me.

"No, thanks."

"Are you sure?" he asked.

I nodded, and he tucked it back into his pocket.

A notification popped up on my phone from the local news station about a high-speed chase. I snuck my phone in on Gabe's request.

How much longer before you get here? I texted Gabe.

Philip and Zara started getting handsy, pushing me over. *Ugh.* I scooted to my right and someone landed on my hip. "Watch it!" I looked up and saw Marco grinning at me. *Oh.* I had wondered how he finished shooting his final scenes without satisfying his bloodlust. Surely if he could transition, I could, too.

"Hey, babe," he said.

I repositioned myself out from under his thigh. He looked at my mouth and then my neck.

"You've been ignoring my texts," he said.

"Yes." I looked down at my phone. No answer. I slipped the phone back into my mini Prada purse.

A joint dangled from his mouth, and he inhaled. He pulled it out, turned slightly, and held it out for me. As I grabbed it, he pulled my lips into his and exhaled. My chest puffed out and I coughed exhaling the remaining breath of smoke forced down my lungs. "Asshole!" I coughed some more.

Marco laughed and took another puff. "This shit doesn't affect me like it used to. Here." He shoved it in my face.

I held out my hand. "I'm good."

"No really. Here." His eyes commanded me to take it with a menacing threat of his ability to make me if he wanted to. He held it up to me again. "See, I exhaled."

I grabbed it from him and inhaled watching the crinkling paper burn up toward my nose. A long stream of smoke poured out as I released my hold on the pending high. I passed the joint back to him, "You must be feeling pretty good tonight. Star of the show and new powers."

"I do. But because I'm sitting next to you." His fingers brushed up my arm calling attention to the warmth between my legs. Him coming on to me was not unexpected, but it reminded me that I love this sort of attention.

Zara and Philip giggled into each other's mouths. *Jesus.* My eyes scanned the room at couples making out in slow motion. Some women in the corner danced for a man who sat on a stool watching their every move. Heat gathered around my cheeks. I clutched my purse and attempted to stand up, but Marco pinned me with his arm.

"Hey, come on. Where do you really have to be right now?" He dropped the joint on the floor and squished it under his shoe. Marco leaned his head back on the couch and closed his eyes.

My mind shifted to Gabe. Why hasn't he texted me back? I pulled out my phone again.

Finally, I read a text from him sent a minute ago. **An hour away.**

This was my only chance. It wouldn't be long before Gabe tightened security around me again.

Zara and Philip stood up bouncing me closer toward Marco. "We'll be back," Zara said.

"Alright." I gripped my cell phone in hand and tucked it back into my purse.

"Finally," Marco opened his eyes and angled his position to face me completely. "Their necking mixed with your heart rate has me all jacked up over here." He let out a sigh.

I shifted my body to meet his hungry eyes. "I've been thinking about transitioning."

"Of course, you have."

"Was it … did it hurt?"

"Fuck yeah, it did." He grabbed my hand. "But you can handle it."

I pulled my hand away from his and shifted further back from him. Within my gut, I knew this was the only chance I had to take matters into my own hands. It would disappoint Gabe, but I know he'd understand, eventually. "I need your help."

"A favor, huh?" He continued to bounce his eyes from my face to my neck.

"Focus. This is serious."

"I am focused." He brushed my cheek.

Ugh. "I need you to turn me." I looked over my shoulder and around the room.

"Wait, what? You're asking me to turn you?" He gaped at me.

"Yes."

"Shit. That's something. I don't think Gabe will take it well." He leaned his head back on the couch eyeing me from his peripheral vision.

"Look. I trust you. I know that you'll release me."

He looked off to the side and back at me.

"Right?"

"Amber. I don't think you really comprehend what you're asking here."

"I know what I'm asking, and I need your help." I reached back into my purse, fumbling for my phone. Pulling it out, ten minutes had passed. "Will you do it?"

"I suppose. What's in it for me?"

"My friendship."

"Hm. That's not really enough." He licked his lips.

"Would I be your first?" I leaned closer whispering over the crowd into his ear, "First vampire?" His eyes grew larger, making an internal connection to the power he wielded over me by this request. I just had to make sure I was clear that my request was for Gabe, not me.

Marco took my hand. "You really don't know what you're asking. There's no turning back."

"I know." He put my fingers to his lips.

"And Gabe?"

The vibrations of his lips on my fingertips jolted me. Pulling my hand away from his mouth, I pushed myself off the couch. "Maybe you're right. What was I thinking?"

He yanked me back down with ease. "I will help you."

My heart raced. Not like it does with Gabe but for the excitement of the possibility. That I could be in control of this transformation. An opportunity to have immortal life on my own terms. A sudden rush of doubt crossed my mind. *Gabe doesn't deserve my betrayal.* The tingles on the back of my neck intensified. *There must be more than one spirit here.*

Marco looked across the room at the boy-cut woman with the diamond face. The one I'd met before. The one who seemed to be following me. *Shit. Following me … dead.*

He waved her over. Her cheekbones perfectly molded into a classic model's pout. She sat down on his lap brushing her knees into mine. My jaw dropped ever so slightly. Her body language screamed vampire.

Her full lips spoke, "Who's this?"

"Holly. This is Amber. Amber, Holly."

Holly. "Yeah. Uh. Hi. We've met before." *And you're my personal bodyguard apparently.*

"Yes, but now it's official," she said. "I wasn't lying when I met you at the bar. Your eyes really haunt me." She grabbed my chin. "I can't stop thinking about you." Her tongue circled her lips.

"It was great to see you, Marco. I'm gonna ..." I tried to get up again, but Holly stopped me this time.

"We're looking to have some fun tonight." Her words faded into the darkness of the music.

Marco leaned in, placing his lips on her shoulder. "Do you want to join us?" she asked.

"No way, Marco."

"Why not?" he asked.

"Because. That's not happening." I clutched my purse tighter and shifted my body weight forward to stand. My head started spinning, and I squeezed the edge of the couch to balance.

Holly stood up and positioned herself in front of me. In a crouch, she placed her hands on my thighs, caressing. She gazed into my eyes. Dizzy. Foggy. Her voice seemed distant. "You'll join us."

"I'll join you." The room condensed, and the air thickened making it hard to breathe. The heaviness of my body locked me in place.

"It'll be fun."

"Yes. Fun."

"Do you like Marco?" Holly asked.

"Sometimes."

Holly sneered.

"Hey. I'm right here. But I'll take it." Marco's hand landed on Holly's and their thumbs moved in sync up my dress.

"It feels good when he touches you, right?"

"Yes."

"Good. Let's go then." She stood up and stepped to the side.

Marco followed and grabbed my hand, lifting me off the couch. I pressed my chest into Marco's arm as he held me close to him, pulling me through the crowd, following Holly.

Everyone moved in slow motion as we passed by. They led me past the bouncer and back down the hall toward the lounge. I followed willingly but there was a quiet gnawing in the back of my mind. I just couldn't place it. What was I forgetting? Marco positioned me in front of him as he continued to hold my hand, and I pressed my body into Holly as we navigated the crowd. We made it out the front door and to the valet.

"I feel like I'm forgetting something," I said to Marco.

"No, babe. I've got you. We're going to take good care of you and fulfill your favor." His car pulled up, and he walked me over to the passenger side. Shifting the front seat forward, he guided me into the backseat. Holly settled into the front with Marco in the driver's side. My mind echoed, "I'm sorry," as Marco pulled away. But I didn't know what for.

CHAPTER 49

AMBER

Sitting on cold leather, I sensed familiarity as the cushion heated under the backs of my thighs. Comfort. Loss. The oak plantation shutters in front of me were shut. This room, a den in the back of Marco's house, usually welcomed me. Trying to unscramble unsettled thoughts, I took in a deep breath. As Holly centered herself in front of me, her fiery golden eyes seared into mine. She got down on her knees and moved my face from side to side, examining me. "What does he see in you? I don't get it." A shiver ran along my body, and her touch reminded me of stepping out onto an ice-skating rink for the first time, clutching to the wall of false security.

"Release her, Holly." Marco's voice commanded.

"I'm not ready to just yet." She pinched my chin between her fingers.

"Enough!" He yanked her away from me.

Holly jerked her elbow to Marco's gut, sending him flying. "Watch your tone with me," she said.

Marco landed into the wall with a crunch. Putting a hole in wood. He pushed off the wall without injury and glided over next to Holly. Standing face-to-face, he growled, "You're going to stick to the plan, Holly." His fangs popped out startling me. "Release her now!"

"Shit. What is it with you and Gabriel?"

Gabriel. Oh. Gabe. Shit. What was I forgetting again? Think.

"Fine. But you owe me a tryst, Marco." She sucked her lips, bent over me, and grabbed my face. A piercing headache hit me behind my eyes as memories rushed back in.

"Marco?" I whispered holding my head as she walked away. "Why are we at your house?"

He took my hand and brought me to my feet. "You asked me for a favor, remember?"

"God. Did I? How much did I smoke?"

"What do you mean?"

"I have this throbbing headache. Did I? I—"

"I'm going to help you. Come on." Lifting me into his arms, he guided us to the kitchen in the middle of the first floor, passing a Picasso along the way. The disfigured person in the painting reminded me of what my brain felt like.

Marco set me down against the island, and I steadied myself. "Jesus. Do you have any pain relief?" Excessive lighting magnified the white cabinets.

He handed me a glass of water. "Come. Sit." He pulled out the stool, patting it.

I complied and took a sip of water.

"I'm sorry about Holly. She's a bit jealous." His tone rose to an irritated seven on a ten-point scale. "You'll be alright. She tried to dig around your mind a bit while you were compelled. That's why you have a headache."

"Dug around?"

"Yeah. She's been compelling for years now, and she has a technique for trying to draw out information."

"Tell her to keep the hell out of my head."

"I'm sure she heard you loud and clear."

I took another drink. "Listen. I need to get back to the party. Can you drive me back?"

"No. I'm afraid I can't." Marco leaned over the counter to my right.

Scanning the kitchen, I spotted knives behind him. "Well pass me my purse then. I need to call Gabe to pick me up."

"That's not happening either."

"Marco, you're acting like a jerk. What the fuck?" I held my head.

He stood up and paced back and forth. "You asked me to turn you, don't you remember?" His words hit me. *I did.* "So that's my plan. I will turn you."

"I did ask. But I wasn't thinking about doing that tonight. Besides, we haven't even gone over the details— made a plan."

"I don't need a plan, Amber. I know what we need to do. There's no sense in waiting." I rotated my body to face him. He walked over standing in front of me. "If you wait, you won't really do it. And I know there's a reason you asked me and not Gabe. So, let's get it over with."

"Why do you think I asked you?"

Marco grabbed my hands. "I know you love me."

Shit. "No, Marco. That's not why I asked you."

"Then why me, and not Gabe?"

Shaking my head, and hearing him ask me the question, I wondered the same thing myself. Gabe would always take care of me. But Marco, he's impulsive. Could he really lead me through the transition? Letting go of his hand, I stood up and cupped his face. "Please … just take me back to the party. I need to think this through."

Marco pushed my hand away and walked over to the kitchen sink. I darted for the knives and grabbed one just as he ran back over to me and clutched my hand, pinning me to the counter. He shook my wrist and the knife clanked onto the ground. "What the hell, Amber?"

"Stay away from me!" I lifted my knee with full force, but he caught it between his thighs and yanked me up, dropping me to the ground. I landed on my back, but his hand caught my head before it hit the ground. A pain shot down from my tailbone to my glute. His pelvis locked on my thigh and his forearm pressed against my chest holding me in place.

"That was dumb. I'm the only one here on your side."

"Are you?" I winced at the pain in my back. The distance between our mouths caused a sinking feeling in my gut.

"I love you, Amber." He kissed me as he lifted my head to meet him. I made a failed attempt to twist as he restricted my movement, and he continued to peck and tug my lips.

"No, Marco," I said as he paused over my mouth. "This isn't love. You're confused."

"I'm not confused. I know what I want."

"What about what I want?"

"It doesn't matter what you want." A voice came from above us. "Get her up!"

He pushed off me and stood up. I looked past Holly at the light above her.

"Put her in her room."

"What?" I pushed my torso up slowly and another sharp pain shot down the back of my leg. "Ow, shit." I grabbed the back of my thigh.

He lifted me up carefully into his arms.

"What's going on?" I asked.

No reply. Marco took me upstairs to his guest room that had been refurbished into a holding cell. Bars on the windows and a padlocked door. Marco lay me on the bed that sat in the middle of the barren room. A prison for people but certainly not a vampire. *Shit. No. This can't be happening. Gabe ...*

"There's water over there." He pointed to the nightstand. He put his hand on the door.

"Marco. Please don't go."

"Hmph." He looked over at me. "You had your chance." He walked out locking the door behind him.

I crawled off the bed landing on the floor, hunched over in pain around my ribs. Following the edge of the bed as I crawled, I searched left and right scanning the room for options. I pulled myself off the floor, balancing on the bed. I walked over to the bathroom. Pushing the door open, I spotted a closed window. I took a few light breaths to taper the pain as I inhaled. I pressed up on the windowpane, and it slid up stiffly and got stuck. I jerked it stretching my torso, "Ow, dammit." It budged a little more, but it had a guard on the frame and as I reached my arm through the open window, I felt the bars. *Trapped.* "Nooooo. Gabe. Sal. Please hear me."

The bedroom door swung open, and I scurried to slam the bathroom door shut. Marco blocked it with his body, forcing his way in and locking the door behind him.

"What are you doing?" He growled as he grabbed my wrists, forcing my back up against the sink. He looked over at the window and back at me. Pressing his forehead to mine, he stared down at me breathing heavily. He shook his head and looked into my eyes. "Amber."

I didn't want to be compelled again so I avoided looking at his face. Whatever it was that Holly did was done through her eyes.

"Look at me." I refused, closing my eyes tighter. "Look at me or you'll—"

"I'll what? Huh? What are you going to do?" I said keeping my eyes sealed tight as he pulled my chin up to face him.

"Look. You can either deal with me or Holly. This is your last chance." His voice was stern, then he lowered it to a whisper, "Look at me."

"I don't want to."

He let go of my wrists and pulled me in for a softer embrace. He rubbed my back as if sending me a message. *Trust him?* My anger infused with hesitant breaths, I tried to push him off me. He held my head against his chest, and I listened to a familiar ticking of his bloodstone heart as it pounded in my ear. Like Gabe's. *Gabe* ... With each breath I drew in, my ribs felt more constraint. I winced. He pulled his fingers through my hair as I pressed against him again trying to breathe. "Marco, please." I pushed again. "I can't breathe."

He pulled back gripping my biceps. As I looked up, he pulled me into a trance—foggy. "Breathe," he said.

I took a breath. "It hurts."

"Did I hurt you?"

"Yes."

"I'm sorry. You are stronger than the pain you feel, Amber. You will make it through this. In fact, you don't feel any more pain."

Clouded. "No pain," I muttered.

His fingers moved up my arms, over my shoulders, and around my neck. His thumbs brushed over the dip on my collar bone. "I'm here to comfort you."

"Mmmm. Okay." The crease in my forehead smoothed, and I relaxed my shoulders while looking into his eyes.

"We're going for a ride soon." His hands moved up to my cheeks gently stroking my face. My skin tingled. I couldn't shake this feeling of forgetting. Forgetting something. But his touch felt so good.

"I'll take care of you."

"I know."

"And we need your help."

I nodded.

He held my chin in his hand. His warm lips met mine, parting my mouth.

A bang on the door startled me. "Let's go already!"

My body began to shake.

"It's okay," he said. "She won't hurt you. Relax." My body loosened up again.

"Jesus. Let's go." Holly banged again.

I didn't move while looking up at Marco, and I wrapped one of his curls around my fingers.

"Here's your phone, Amber." He handed me my cell. "I need you to unlock it for me."

"Okay." I unlocked the phone, and he looked down at me typing.

"Great. Thank you." He took it back from me and began texting.

"What are you ...?"

"Don't worry about it. I'm adding a reminder to your calendar." Marco slipped my phone into his pocket. "I'm gonna hold this for you since your dress is without pockets." He licked his lips. He took my hand in his and unlocked the door.

Holly stood behind it with her arms crossed. She turned around and walked out of the room.

Marco followed behind her leading me to the door. He paused, turned to face me, and kissed me once more. It had a familiarity like we were ending a long-distance relationship that we couldn't make work. He pulled away embracing my face. Then he walked me downstairs to meet Holly at the car.

CHAPTER 50

GABE

Hollywood sign? It didn't make any sense. The cool air ripped at my collar as I flew over to Griffith Park searching for Amber.

I stopped at the mansion first, expecting to meet up with her. Upon my arrival, I couldn't identify Amber's voice in the crowd. She didn't respond to my texts or calls. Then I ran into Zara, and she told me she last saw Amber in the VIP room with Marco. That's when I received Amber's text. She was either teasing me, kinky as hell, or … I didn't want to think about the alternative. I sped up, tuning in all senses as I approached. Hovering over the park, my soul socked me.

She's near, he said, *Catori is calling for me.*

Squinting my eyes, I scanned the conservatory.

Marco? I asked my soul.

Yes. He's compelled her.

Shit.

I flew toward the Hollywood sign and landed at the top of Mount Lee. I scanned again—cleared of all people. Taking in a deep breath, I caught a whiff of Amber, Marco, and another familiar scent.

It can't be.

Yes, it is, my soul confirmed.

Holly.

Something splayed out on the grass at Lake Hollywood Park that I had missed on my descent caught my attention. *Amber.*

Just as I began to dive down, I looked over my shoulder. Marco's fist landed on my jaw. "Uh." I spun around to face him. "What's your plan, Marco?"

"No plan." He flew into me knocking us over the mountain. We locked arms around each other's necks hovering the park below, spinning in circles in midair.

"You thought kidnapping her would win her over?" I tightened my grip on him and flew us up higher. The miniscule Hollywood sign looked like a toy model.

He punched me in the gut trying to shake my grip.

"You've got to compel and lie to her just so she'll pay you attention."

"She came to me."

"Bullshit." I flung him into the vacant sky.

"Once you're out of the picture, I won't need to compel her anymore." His eyes darted from where Amber had lain to the Hollywood sign. He smirked.

Looking behind the sign, I watched as Holly had Amber staring at her. I dove toward them, but Marco grabbed my foot.

"Want to be a hero, do you?" He swung me around in circles throwing me toward the ground. Tucking as I tumbled, I rolled forward into a standing position. My arm was covered in blood, having shielded my fall.

"Marco. Help me please. Marco." Amber's cries of terror chilled me as Holly propped her up, sitting backward on the edge of the O in H-O-L-L-Y.

Marco charged me from the sky calling out, "You hear that, Gabe. She's calling my name."

I sidestepped his attack causing him to smash into the ground and leaving a crater big enough for a small biplane to land in.

"Marco!" Amber called out again.

Holly pushed Amber backward and cackled.

"Owwww. Shit," Amber cried out while hanging upside down over the edge of the O with her hands and ankles bound.

"Go to her!" I yelled at him as Holly landed between us.

Fear spread across his face as if watching a scary movie unfold, and he turned to Holly. "What the hell?" He bolted toward the sign as Holly laughed and charged me landing on my chest with her feet.

"I thought you were on my side." I yanked her off me, and she flipped over my head landing on her feet behind me. "No one's bitch, right?"

"You should know better. You can't hide your precious soul from Vance." She charged me again, flipping over my head and then ran around me in circles kicking out, striking me fiercely.

I blocked her kicks until one landed on my knee popping my cap. I dropped. "Arrggghhh." Dragging my knee, I pulled myself up, teetering. "For what?" I gritted through my teeth as I popped the cap back into place. "What did he promise you?"

"Why can't this just be revenge?" Holly strolled slowly around me as if circling her prey.

Marco had Amber back on solid ground, checking her for bruises.

"Revenge? It always comes back to that day, doesn't it? You know I was protecting you."

"Ahhhhhhhh." I ducked as she spun over me landing just shy of a tree. Holly stopped and looked up at Amber and Marco, while she smirked.

"What?" I didn't move, not wanting to lose sight of Holly.

"It's quite a show," she said.

With lips smacking in the distance, combined with her smile, I knew that meant Amber and Marco were busy. I balled my fist and put my hand in my pocket. Rubbing the cross, I stayed focused on Holly not looking back. I pulled out the cross and lay the cross in my open palm.

"I can't believe you still have that thing."

"I do."

"You're so desperate for your freedom you can't even see what's really going on. You've always been blind." She drew her attention back up to Amber and Marco.

Refusing to follow her eyes, I walked to her until we were twelve feet apart.

"This soul mate of yours. Hm," she said.

"You can say what you will, but I will bond with Amber, and I will be free." With hesitation, I looked over at Marco embracing Amber, the only soul I would ever love. My body tensed, but my mind cleared. I took a step closer.

Holly stood firm, locking eyes with me.

With great force, I tossed the cross like a frisbee, and the pointed bottom hit her throat. Blood began to seep out of her neck. Holly's hand reached up to grab it. It remained lodged as she tugged, gasping for air. "You always mocked me for carrying that cross around." I kicked her in the stomach and she fell back. I stepped on her chest as she desperately tried to release the cross from her throat. "You see. Catori spelled that for me long ago. To protect me from the dead, surprisingly enough. Releasing your soul was a dumb move. Bloodstone or not. This relic doesn't see your heart beating."

Holly's skin started to fade to an ashy gray. She struggled—gasped.

"Hey!" Marco flew over with Amber, setting her down before grabbing Holly. "What the …?" He reached for the cross with his fingertips and tried to pull it out, but it wouldn't budge. He stood up and hit me in the chest. "Help her!"

"I could. But she doesn't deserve it."

Marco swung at me again, and I ducked, socking him in the gut twice. He doubled over and looked at his hands. They began to shake, and his skin began to crack. He looked over at Holly as she began to convulse and her skin cracking, drying out.

"Interesting thing about makers and their vamps. The bond that is." I crossed my arms. "Oh, but don't worry, you won't die. You'll just suffer a little."

"Arrrrghhhhh. What do you want?" He gritted through his teeth.

Amber ran over toward us hovering over Marco. "Stop! Stop this! What's going on?"

"I want you to take Holly far away from here. And I want you to avoid Vance at all costs."

"Gabe! Stop this!" Amber cried as ash crumbled through her fingers trying to hold onto Marco's hand.

"You hear me, Marco?" I grabbed a chunk of his curls pulling his face to mine. "Keep her away from Vance! If I find out you betrayed me, I won't hesitate next time."

Holly's eyes closed and dust began to blow off her arms as the wind blew through the park.

"Okay," Marco said. He tried to look at Amber through the corner of his eye, but I held him by his hair at the nape. As I released him, clumps of curls fell out of my palm and into the grass.

"Jesus, Gabe." Amber covered her mouth.

I knelt over Holly and pulled the cross out of her throat. Looking at her stiff body almost completely lifeless. "Get her out of here."

Marco stood up, starting to regain some strength, his color still gray. He looked over at Amber.

"Don't even think about it." I spoke through my throat.

His eyes were bloodshot. "Give her some blood!" Marco commanded.

I pulled Amber into my arms, but she resisted until I snapped my fingers and pulled her eyes to mine. "You're no longer under his trance, Amber." Her body loosened, and she took in the scene in front of her. She looked to me, Holly, Marco, and then back to me. She collapsed, and I caught her before she fell to the ground. Wincing in my arms, she heaved breath and gasped for air holding her ribs.

A slow clap came out from a distance. *Vance.* "What a show! Man. It had all the components. Action, romance, violence. And now, let's add in a little drama."

I pushed Amber behind me, still propping her up. "We had a deal you son of a bitch."

"Ah, Gabriel. We did have a deal. Holly just didn't get the memo." Vance rubbed the back of his neck while sucking his teeth.

"So, you came here to, what? Intercede?"

He looked past me at Amber. "She gets better looking every time I meet her."

"Gabe," Amber whispered, "be careful."

"Yes. Be careful. You wouldn't want Amber to find out anything about the deal we made. I mean telling her that her mother is a vampire boss would be rather alarming."

She hobbled around to my side, my arm still holding her back.

"What the hell is he talking about?" she asked.

"Aurora. That's your mother, right? I mean the resemblance is electrifying. Your eyes." He took a few steps closer with his hand on his chin.

I looked at Amber, who stood there with clenched fists and narrow eyes, and then back at Vance. "Well. I think my job here is done. Looking forward to working with you to take down Eli, Gabriel." Vance turned around to walk away.

I pulled out my cross and threw it at him knowing the consequences. This wasn't over.

He swung around and caught it in his hand. His cunning smile transformed to anger as he charged me, lifting me up into the air. "You want to kill me, brother. In front of your soul mate? Is that it?"

Amber covered her mouth. She charged Vance, but he held out his hand stopping her motion.

He squeezed my neck, cracking bones. My feet dangling, I gripped his wrist. "Vance," I whispered. He threw me into a tree knocking a branch free and into my lap. His distant hold on Amber had her drop to her knees as she screamed out in pain.

"Noooooo." I jumped up and flew into Vance knocking him onto his back. His grip on Amber was released. I lifted the branch's sharp point up into the air and slammed it directly over his heart, but I stopped just as the point tapped his shirt.

"Do it, Gabriel. Go on." He laughed. "What are you waiting for?"

Amber called out, "Do it, Gabe."

"Fuuuuuuuccccccckkkkkk." I yelled into the night sky. I threw the branch so hard it flew over the mountain. "I can't!" I stood up over Vance, helping him up.

Amber hollered out, "What are you doing? Why are you helping him?"

Vance yelled over to Amber, "He's helping me, beautiful, because he has no choice. He's bound to me." Vance wrapped his arm around my neck pulling my ear close to his mouth. "Like she'll be bound to Marco by the look of it."

He released me with a shove. I looked over at Amber. Mouthing silently, "What the …?"

"Haaaaa. Ha. Ha. Oh man, I'm so glad I didn't miss this one." Vance bent over and slapped his knee. "Man."

I ran over to Amber and cupped her face, bringing her forehead to mine.

"Well, brother. It's been a fun night. Looking forward to," Vance swung his finger around at us, "seeing how all this pans out. Uhhh. As I predicted, drama."

Gritting through her teeth, Amber demanded, "Get me out of here."

I swept her up into my arms and took off, leaving Vance behind as his laughter slowly faded in the distance.

CHAPTER 51

AMBER

At the edge of the bed, I swayed. Like being high up on a mountain top, my ears began to clog, and I lost my sense of direction. The sound of Gabe's voice brought me back to focus as he brushed my shoulder and lifted my chin to face him, giving me a warm smile. "I'll be right back," he said as he ran into the bathroom.

A rush of water gushed out of the tub. With every breath, I cringed at the pain from the constriction of my ribs simultaneously forcing a sharp sting down my lower back. Balancing myself on the edge of the bed, I scanned my bedroom in Gabe's mansion. The room smelled like fresh paint, and the dresser seemed closer to the bed. Whatever happened to me under compulsion caused a temporary heightening of my senses. Sounds came in clearer. The fibers of the bedding pricked my fingers like splinters despite how soft they were.

My head pulsed, and Gabe caught me before I fell off the bed. "What's wrong with me?" My nails dug into his arm.

"You've been through a lot tonight, Amber."

"I don't remember much. I remember fighting with Marco at his house after the party. He locked me in a guest room. After that, I woke up next to you at Griffith Park." Gabe stood me up. I closed my eyes tight, and Marco's face popped up into my mind. I shuttered.

"I've got you," he said as he unzipped my dress. "Hold on to me." He slid it down, stretching the material causing it to tear enough to avoid additional back pain.

"Can't you just compel me so I don't feel pain?"

"You'll feel better soon." Gabe kneeled down in front of me as I stepped over the dress.

"Shouldn't you take me to the hospital?"

He stood up brushing his thumb against my cheek. "I don't do hospitals, remember?" He winked.

I tried to smile but felt a pain on my lip. Probably another cut.

"I'm going to help you to the bath. Wrap your arm around me, okay?"

I squeezed my lips together as I lifted my arm around him. Tears welled up from the pain in my ribs.

"Move slowly. This bath will help."

I doubted that.

As he walked me into the bathroom, I nuzzled into his warm bare chest. A soiled shirt lay on the floor next to the tub. Steadying me as he leaned over to feel the water, the wall color seemed a shade darker than usual. *God I'm messed up.*

"We need to get these off you." He removed my G-string, as I held on to his shoulders. Fully naked, Gabe pulled me close, and Marco's face crept into my mind again. *Shit.* My lips rested on his chest and his faint clinking heartbeat pulsed louder. I looked up at his neck. *Never noticed his vein pulsing like that before.* A deep insatiate hunger gnawed at my inner lining. He unbuttoned his pants and dropped everything to the floor. Standing present before me in all his warrior glory, I took him in. My scrambled mind with heightened senses sent emotional shifts between wanting Marco near and needing Gabe inside of me.

He stepped into the bath holding his hand out to me. "What?"

"I … I don't know. Nothing." My head throbbed.

"Come on." He gestured for me to climb in. Taking his seat first, I leaned my back into his chest. His arms embraced me so tightly that I didn't think he'd let either one of us leave the bath tonight. The pain in my ribs subsided slightly as I allowed the warm water to soak through me. I felt a surge through my body—a heightened sensitivity to the blood rushing through my own veins. The steam overwhelmed me. His arms around me began to feel like a restraint. I couldn't move. I narrowed in on the pewter faucet. *Wasn't that brass?*

"Gabe, did I hit my head?"

"Possibly." He kissed my temple.

Guilt overwhelmed me at the touch of his lips knowing that I had betrayed him. He didn't know that though. For all he knew, I was taken. But would he believe that? He constantly sacrificed to keep me safe and I betrayed him.

"I don't know what I would've done if I had lost you." His whisper met the volume of a regular conversation in my ear. A shutter went down my spine. Gabe rubbed my arms, undulating the water, our fingers interlocked.

"Gabe, I'm so sorry." A tear slid down my cheek.

"You don't owe me an apology. I owe you one." He pulled me in as far as my body would go leaving no space for water to flow in between our skin. "We need to discuss your mom."

Closing my eyes. *Alive.* "Yeah."

"First, I need to heal you." His lips vibrated against my shoulder as he spoke.

"You can do that? How?

"You'll need to drink from me."

My attempt at turning to face him caused me to wince at the sore ache in my neck. I resettled against him, keeping still. "Is that safe?"

"Yes."

Marco's dimples popped into my mind. "Gabe. I feel … I owe you an explanation."

"Maybe. But it doesn't matter right now."

"But something's not right."

"I know. You need my blood right now." Gabe bit into his wrist and blood bubbled up out of the fang marks. He placed his wrist to my mouth. "Drink."

His blood dripped into the water over me. With a keen thirst, my dry mouth salivated. I parted my lips and latched onto his wrist and took him in. The warm blood burned as it slid down my throat, providing deep gratification. Like taking a shot of tequila. But this was better. A sense of bliss mixed with an aphrodisiac. I drank him in, lifting my hands to his arm to hold him securely in place.

He tugged his arm, but I blocked his movement. "That's enough." Gabe yanked harder causing me to lose my grip.

Licking my lips. "I don't want to stop."

"I know. But for now, we'll stop." He brushed my hair back. "Just rest."

Sleepy and satiated, I reveled at the warmth in my body tingling through every part of my being. Pain began to subside from my injuries as if given a large dose of pain killers.

Enjoying the warm water and Gabe's flesh against mine, another pain crept in. Pins and needles poked along my spine down to my toes. A searing burn pressed into my chest. "God. What … is …?" I drew in a deep breath. My ribs popped back into place. "Shi … Aahhhhhh." I tried to thrash about, but Gabe pinned me to him.

"It'll be over soon."

I groaned louder and rotated my neck from side to side against him. He leaned into my neck with his chin so I couldn't move. Tears streamed down my face. "I thought you said it was safe. Ughhhhhh, God. Make it stop!"

Gabe interlocked his fingers with mine and held me firmly. "Amber, you can handle this. You're strong, beautiful. You're healing." His voice soothed me amidst the wildfire spreading through me.

My heavy breathing subsided, and my eyes began to close. Sleepy. Drifting. The weight of my body melded into his skin. Heavy. I couldn't open my eyes. Memories of the evening unraveled, and I saw myself with Marco at the park. Reliving the bite that Marco gave me. Uncertain if in a dream or reality, I whispered, "Gabe, I love …"

AUTHOR'S NOTE

Books bored me as a child. I preferred to daydream. I would find a spot in the crux of a tree and dream about "what-ifs." To fall asleep at night, I would create movies in my mind involving romance. Finding true love, or the one, has been a constant interest of mine since I can remember. When my mom would take me to the library attempting to inspire my interest in reading, I found myself choosing vampire books, mystery novels, and Archie Comics. The element of the push and pull of emotions drew me to these stories.

This book developed out of a fantasy of a man lingering in a dark corner of a billiard room, mesmerized by the essence of a woman playing pool with friends. And if you were to ask me what it was about ... I'd say control.

Control is a dynamic we all grapple with, trying to gain control or the fear of losing it entirely. This book is also about giving into desires. It's about love. It's about restraint. It's about shadows. It's about possession. It's about vulnerability. It's about surrendering. It's about determination. It's about resistance and taking matters into one's own hands. Ultimately, it's about freedom.

I began writing this story in 2010 to entertain, but recognized that through the development of my characters and plot, various themes emerged offering new perspectives to the reader around control, life after death, and sexual empowerment. This book is a work of fiction. History played a part in developing setting, characters, and plot but by no means is this book a historically accurate reflection of the Gabrielino-Tongva tribal customs and beliefs. In researching various topics while writing the book, I discovered the beauty of this indigenous group and embraced a better understanding of Spanish and Mexican influences in the United States, particularly in California.

I write and read about what intrigues me. Life and death. Eternal love and desire. Duality. Spirituality. Connections. This book is for anyone who likes getting lost in stories where characters feel relatable and powerful. It is for those who long for a new love connection, are curious about the meaning of life, or are eager to discover how each character's path has a twisted connection to the end goal.

ACKNOWLEDGMENTS

———

None of this would have been possible without:

My husband, Christian, who has encouraged me and supported my author journey for over twelve years now. When darkness dims my way, his light strengthens me.

My children, for sacrificing time with me so that I could fulfill a personal dream. To Alucio, for his voracious love for reading and his creative writing talents that inspired me to step out of my comfort zone and just write. And to my daughter, Aria, who kept me company as I wrote on my bed at night and who took many beautiful photos of me to capture this journey.

Mom and Dad, who raised me to embrace all kinds of people, believe that I am unique, and provided me with a spiritual compass of love and respect for all. To Grams who reminds me to lighten up and have fun, and to Gramps for enlightening me with his wisdom on how the world works and encouraging me to change my perspective when things look gloomy.

My Grandma Harris, rest in peace, who told stories of our family history intriguing all who listened, who I admire for her strength in a time of war, and who lived a courageous life with great love and affection for her grandchildren.

Kristie and Tom, because you know the good, bad, and the ugly and still love and accept me regardless.

My dear friend, LaNysha Adams, for your incredible ability to take risks and seize opportunities. For empowering me to do great things. If it were not for you, I would not have published this book today!

Samantha Lu, an amazing woman and friend, who drove with me across the United States to Cali. This place has no doubt been a saving grace, has emboldened me to release my entrepreneurial side, and I am eternally grateful for your generosity and friendship.

Susan Epstein, thank you for providing feedback on the book's description and cheering me on. And to Analia Mendez whose voice I hear in my head telling me to "say yes" and "do that." Coach Pam Reyes, who helped me get clear on my goals. Emilie Hersh who provided me writing tools to doodle and dream, and who continuously supports my career advancement and growth. Carleen Kreider, for jumping in without hesitation to review my author bio and support me through encouragement along the way. For the coaching session that Teresa Carpenter provided me to help me to think through the level of heat I should write into this book.

My alpha readers. Maia Farkas, for our author chats and your support as I continue on this new career path. And to Misti Cain whose conversations propelled me forward, helping me to see possibilities. You both had the hard job! Giving honest feedback on a complete rough draft. Thank you for cringing through it! I cannot thank my beta readers enough for making time to read chapter drafts here and there. Nicole Boucher, Melody Goodwin, Kathy Harris, Nubia Junco-Williams, and Kathleen Robinson, the feedback you provided helped me take the temperature of engagement, heat, and character development as well as identify gaps.

To the CSUSM College of Business Administration's senior experience team who helped me launch my website and social media platforms!

And without you, dear readers, my story would have remained a dream.

To willing experts open to sharing:

My colleague, Ron Gerevas, who gave me a robust breakdown on the stages of grape growth and drawing a vivid picture of nurturing a vineyard.

Stephanie Mazzeo, producer, makeup artist, and hair stylist, who took time out of her day to speak with me about "a day in the life of."

Doug Nelson, writer and producer, who shared his Hollywood experiences, clarified the role of a producer, and helped me identify places in Los Angeles where some of my scenes could exist.

This is a rewarding process, and I am eternally grateful:

To everyone at New Degree Press publishing who made this possible. A special thanks to my marketing and revisions editor Stephanie McKibben. You kept it real and challenged me to become a better writer, while remaining supportive.

And to the Creator Institute for doing what you do. You took me out of my comfort zone, provided me the tools I needed to accomplish my goal, and created a community of authors to support one another through this process. Your behind-the-scenes work is not lost on me. Thank you, Eric Koester for believing in imperfect strangers. And to Haley Newlin for helping me find the words to articulate themes, characteristics, and branding of my book. And I definitely could not have completed this book without my developmental editor, Ilia Epifanov. Brainstorming with you was a blast! And to Maxine Smith and Avery Lockland for being a sounding board on this wild ride.

To Mark Spencer, who critiqued my novel during the Writer's Digest Advanced Novel Writing course. My first fifty thousand words would not have been possible without the accountability and critiques you provided.

To the bookworms of my past who inspired me to give books a chance at a later stage in life: Brian Montalvo, Ciara Rivera, and Candelario Vazquez.

To my Author Community, who joined me early on in this dynamic journey and provided encouragement and publishing support: LaNysha Adams, Samantha Adams, Rick Andryc, Virginia Appleton, Anthony Arguez, Bob Bathrick, Marion Boultbee, Alesha Bryant, Barbara Campbell, KC Choi, Evelio D'Leon, Isaac de la Fuente, Desmond Dunham, Joel Duran, Ilia Epifanov, Susan Epstein, Karen Ford, Melody Goodwin, Natasha Guadalupe, Jim Hamerly, Emily Harris, Kathy and Thomas S. Harris, Fred and Marianne Hogarth, William Joering, Patrick Kennell, Jennie Kim, Sungbong and Esther Kim, Eric Koester, Carleen Kreider, Christian Laing, Dashiel Lopez Mendez, Debra Lowe, Ashley Madison, Daniel Martinez, Stephanie Mazzeo, Analia Mendez, Shelby Meredith, Lisa Neidrauer, Avril Occilien-Similien, Amber Perez, Erika Perri, Quyhn Pham, Julianne Reynolds, Kathleen Robinson, Sarah Samuels, Maxine Smith, Ashish Srivastava, Walteen Truely, Lisa Vu, Chris Woodring, Kristie and Erik Zabik.

Made in the USA
Las Vegas, NV
05 May 2022

48428299R00187